W9-BSR-309

MIND SCRAMBLER

ALSO BY CHRIS GRABENSTEIN

The John Ceepak Series

Tilt a Whirl

Mad Mouse

Whack a Mole

Hell Hole

Thrillers

Slay Ride

Hell for the Holidays

Young Readers

The Crossroads

The Hanging Hill

MIND SCRAMBLER

CHRIS GRABENSTEIN

MINOTAUR BOOKS
NEW YORK

www.minotaurbooks.com

ISBN-13: 978-0-312-38231-5
ISBN-10: 0-312-38231-6

First Edition: June 2009

10 9 8 7 6 5 4 3 2 1

For my friends since forever
Ronny and Lianne,
who helped me on the long walk home

ACKNOWLEDGMENTS

I want to thank . . .

Michael Homler, Hector DeJean, Andrew Martin, and everybody at St. Martin's Minotaur.

Bruce Springsteen for the use of his lyrics and the inspiration of his album *Magic*.

Chief Michael Bradley of the Long Beach Island police department for technical advice on police procedures down the shore.

Lesa Holstine and librarians everywhere.

All the folks whose names appear as characters in this book because they made generous donations to charities.

My über-agent, Eric Myers.

Lynn Fraser and Rhys, Kathy and Dave, and Herndon—early readers extraordinaire.

My unbelievably beautiful, not to mention talented and supportive, wife J.J.

And that wonderfully generous slot machine in Trump's Taj Mahal that paid me $150 in exchange for my dollar bill while I was doing research down in Atlantic City.

I got shackles on my wrist
Soon I'll slip 'em and be gone
Chain me in a box in the river
And I'll rise singin' this song
Trust none of what you hear
And less of what you see
This is what will be, this is what will be

—Bruce Springsteen, "Magic"

1

I bumped into my old girlfriend Katie Landry this afternoon. Six hours later, she was dead.

We met in the lobby of the Xanadu hotel and casino down in Atlantic City.

"Danny?" She had seen me first.

"Hey." I was sort of surprised. I don't think Katie had set foot inside the Garden State for more than a year, not since she took off for sunny California.

As Katie walked across the extremely carpeted lobby, I noticed she still had a slight limp—a souvenir left over from her last summer in Sea Haven, the New Jersey resort town we both used to call home.

She kissed me. On the cheek. The way cousins do—except, you know, in Arkansas.

"It's so good to see you!" she said.

"Yeah. You, too." Then I kissed her cheek and we looked French. Maybe Russian.

She stepped back and gave me the once-over. "Danny Boyle! You look great!"

"Thanks. So do you!"

She did, too. Katie had always been the most beautiful woman in the world, ever since we met in third grade. I think it's her eyes. They're emeralds—all green and sparkly. And her smile? The Mona Lisa gets jealous.

"Where's Ceepak?" she asked. "You guys still partners?"

"Yeah. He's across the street in the bus depot, dealing with the driver."

John Ceepak and I are cops with the Sea Haven PD. It's early October, the off-season down the Jersey shore, so we're on a week of what they call administrative leave, taking care of some loose ends, helping with an out-of-state homicide trial.

"We came down on the Coast City bus," I said. "The driver was doing seventy on the straightaways."

"Is that a code violation?"

"Big-time. Posted speed limit is sixty-five from milepost eighty south to milepost twenty-seven."

A former MP who served in Iraq, John Ceepak lives his life in strict compliance with the West Point honor code: He will not lie, cheat, or steal, nor tolerate those who do. Speeding on the Garden State Parkway? Definitely cheating.

"He got married, you know."

"Yeah. Olivia told me. Rita, right?"

I nodded.

Olivia Chibbs is one of our mutual friends back home. She used to work with Ceepak's wife, Rita, at Morgan's Surf and Turf, this classy restaurant where they fold the napkins to look like birds. Classy birds.

"So what're you doing in A.C?" I asked.

"New job."

"Cool."

"I was going to call," she started.

"Definitely," I said so Katie wouldn't have to further violate Ceepak's code and tell me another lie.

When last we spoke—oh, maybe fifteen months ago—Katie was working on her master's degree in elementary education at this college out in California. Before that, she had been a kindergarten teacher and worked summers at Salt Water Tammy's.

She had also been my girlfriend for most of August that last summer we spent together.

"So, what's the job?" I asked to avoid all the stuff I didn't want to talk about.

"Mary Poppins," she said, hugging a stack of books close to her chest.

I wished I were a book.

"I'm the nanny and tutor for Richard Rock's kids." She flicked her blazing red hair sideways to indicate an illuminated poster for a show called "Rock 'n Wow!" currently playing at the Xanadu's Shalimar Theater. Richard Rock, the star of the show, was a handsome dude in a tuxedo and cowboy hat.

"He's a magician," Katie explained.

"Ah-ha."

"Actually an illusionist."

"Unh-hunh."

A couple months ago, Olivia had told me Katie was dating some new guy out in California. That was fine by me. I had been doing the same thing.

With girls, not guys. Jersey girls. Nothing too serious, but then again, I'm twenty-five and there are plenty of fish in the sea. Jellyfish, stingrays, sharks, electric eels.

"They mostly do Vegas," said Katie.

"Hmm?" I said because I'd drifted off on that whole fishing expedition.

"The Rocks. This is their first gig in Atlantic City. They're based out of LA. Hired me a couple weeks ago. Hey, you should come see the show. It's very wholesome. Good, clean family fun."

Rats. I had been hoping for G-strings and feathered head-dresses.

"I'd love to," I said anyway.

"You busy tonight? I could score you guys a couple tickets."

"Cool. I need to check with Ceepak first. We're working on this thing."

"How come you're not in uniform?"

"It's an unofficial thing."

"Undercover?"

"Nah. We're actually helping out a prosecuting attorney up in Ohio. Taking a deposition from an Atlantic City drifter who's on the witness list because he once shared a jail cell with the accused."

"What's the charge?"

"Murder."

"Wow."

"Yeah."

And I left out the juiciest part: the defendant is this bitter old alkie named Joseph Ceepak—my partner's father. The guy we're deposing here in Atlantic City is a migrant con artist named Gary Burdick (aka Barry Gerduck, aka Larry Murdoch, aka various other lame aliases that all sound like his real name). Burdick once shared a drunk tank with Ceepak's old man on a night when Mr. C totally spilled the beans and bragged about how he got away with, well, murder. Burdick knows all sorts of incriminating details, enough to lock up Mr. Ceepak for life, which, trust me, would be a good thing for his son, not to mention the rest of us.

Katie took a quick glance at her wristwatch. If you want to know what time it is in Atlantic City, you need to carry a watch or a cell phone because there are no clocks on the casino walls and no windows to let you know whether the sun is up, down, or sideways.

"Katie?" a little girl hollered from behind a shimmering gold column. "Katie!" She popped out, then hid again. I think she was playing peekaboo. Either that or perfecting her obnoxiousness.

"I need to run," said Katie.

"One of yours?"

"Yep. Britney Rock."

Britney skipped-to-her-lou across the carpet. She was carrying a huge slab of peanut brittle with chomp marks in it—the kind cartoon dogs bite into people's pants. I pegged Britney to be eight or nine. Blond with a mouthful of braces.

"Hi," I said, and gave her a little finger wave.

"Who's this guy?" she asked Katie.

"Danny Boyle."

The nine-year-old made a rolling arm gesture to indicate she needed more information. "And?"

"He's an old friend."

"He was never like your boyfriend or anything, was he?"

Katie didn't answer.

" 'Cause Jake's cuter."

"Jake?" I said, as nonchalantly as possible.

Katie shook her head. "He's this guy in the show."

"He's a hottie," said Britney. "Total stud muffin."

I bent down to brat level. "Hey, you know what? Katie and I have known each other ever since we were younger than you!" I sounded so much like Mr. Rogers I should've been wearing a cardigan.

The kid crinkled her nose to let me know I had just totally grossed her out.

"Where's your brother?" Katie asked. Her eyes swept across the lobby to the Kubla Khandy Shoppe, so named, I figured, because, according to some poem an English teacher made me memorize once, Xanadu was where Kubla Khan his stately pleasure dome did decree. "Britney? Where is Richie?"

"I dunno. I'm not the nanny."

Katie did not whack the mouthy midget like I might've. She had always been good with kids. Probably why she was so good with me. No matter what, Katie Landry stayed sweeter than pancake syrup sucked out of its tub through a straw, something my buddy Jess and I did one morning at Burger King when we both ordered the French toast sticks.

"Britney?" Katie said patiently. "You promised you'd keep an eye on your brother if I let you guys go into the candy store."

"Whoops. Sorry. Forgot."

"Danny, I've gotta run."

"There he is!" the girl screeched, and pointed at a cute kid who had to be her little brother: blond mop top, blue eyes, and a supersized smile smudged with fudge.

"Hi, Katie!" the boy waved. His hands looked like he'd been soaking them in chocolate fondue pots.

"Richie!" said his sister. "You are a mess!" She stomped over to harass him.

"Hope the Rocks pay well," I said.

"More than my last teaching job."

"Cool."

"I really need to run, Danny. The kids are in the show."

"Does their father make them disappear?"

"No. They do this quick bit at the beginning."

The boy scampered across the carpet to tug on Katie's belt loops. I pegged him to be about six and already in love.

"Nanny Katie?"

"Yes, Richie?"

"Can we go for a ride in a chariot again?"

Katie clued me in: "That's what he calls the rolling chairs out on the boardwalk."

The rolling chairs are these canopied wicker love seats on wheels. Been an Atlantic City fixture since forever. You pay a sweaty person in a polo shirt to push you where you want to go. The boardwalk here is about four miles long. Wheeled chairs are a good thing.

"Please?"

"Not right now, Richie. Maybe later. After you finish your homework."

"Okay." He skipped off to join his sister, who was hunkered down near a burbling fountain contemplating a coin dive.

"What time do you guys go on?" I asked.

"Eight."

"Cool."

"Yeah."

"Yeah."

"Danny?"

"Yeah?"

"We need to talk."

"Okay."

Katie and I used to talk all the time, even before we started dating. Now, once a year, she sends me a Christmas card. I send her one of those free e-mail deals with the dogs singing "Feliz Navidad."

"They're nice people," Katie said. "The Rocks . . ."

Her words just sort of petered out.

"But?" I said.

"I don't want to say anything bad . . ."

"But?"

Her eyes were locked on Britney and Richie.

"Are you okay, Katie?"

"Yeah. Fine. It's just—families. You never know who's telling the truth. We should talk."

"Ceepak and I are heading back to Sea Haven tomorrow afternoon."

"How about breakfast?"

"Do you know a good buffet?"

Katie grinned. "Down the Boardwalk. At Bally's. All you can eat for fifteen dollars. Omelets made to order. Six kinds of sausage."

"Great. I won't wear a belt."

"How's nine?" she asked. "I have to take care of the kids' breakfast first."

"Katie?" the girl screamed. "Richie drank scum water!"

"Did not!"

Katie sighed.

I reached out, touched her arm. "Nine will be fine."

"Great. Gotta go." She dashed over to make sure the kids didn't take a bath in the fountain.

If I had known "nine will be fine" would be the last thing I ever said to Katie Landry, I probably wouldn't have rhymed it like that.

2

I stood in the hotel lobby staring at the poster of the cocky cowboy illusionist and all I could think of was this new Springsteen song called "Magic":

I got a shiny saw blade
All I needs' a volunteer
I'll cut you in half
While you're smiling ear to ear

Creepy.

Plus, Richard Rock didn't look like any magician I'd ever seen. For one thing, he was blond, even blonder than his kids. Magicians are usually dark and brooding. He was also all "aw, shucks" and "howdy" looking—not mysterious or menacing. His smile was more like a smug cowboy smirk coupled with a wide-open-spaces squint of the eyes. All in all, Richard Rock looked like a local TV weatherman from Wyoming, maybe Montana—one of the rectangle states—who thought he was the hottest thing in town. Either that or president of the I Felta Thigh fraternity up at Rutgers.

"Danny?" Ceepak had come into the hotel while I was staring at the poster. "I didn't know you were interested in magic."

"I'm not. Katie's here. Working for this Richard Rock guy."

"Katie Landry?"

"Yeah."

"Fascinating."

Ceepak, of course, knew Katie. He's the one who made sure she made it to the hospital that Labor Day weekend we'd all rather forget.

"Is Katie one of the magician's assistants?"

I shook my head. "Nanny for his kids."

"Good for her. I'm quite familiar with Richard Rock," said Ceepak. "Puts on a very wholesome, family-friendly show. His wife is his costar."

I wasn't surprised Ceepak knew more about Richard Rock than I ever cared to. My partner's interests are many, varied, and—sometimes—decidedly weird.

"You've seen his act?" I asked.

"Roger that. His Vegas TV special came on the Discovery Channel one night after *Forensic Files*. Rita and I enjoyed it immensely. Especially when he moved Mount McKinley from Alaska to the parking lot of the MGM Grand Hotel."

"How'd he do that?"

"Very convincingly. Do we have our room?"

"Yeah." I handed him a plastic card key. We were sharing a standard room. Two beds. If I got lucky with a showgirl, I could hang a tie on the doorknob to alert him. Only, I didn't pack a tie.

Ceepak, however, was wearing one. In fact, he was the only

person in the whole lobby not pushing a luggage cart or tapping computer keys who had actually dressed up to come to the Xanadu: natty blue blazer, Brooks Brothers white shirt, sensibly striped tie, and khaki dress pants with a crease so sharp it could thin-slice cheese at a deli. Ceepak thought this Atlantic City casino would be like the ones he'd seen in James Bond movies. Swanky. Sophisticated. Everybody in tuxedos and evening gowns sipping martinis.

Instead, we've got folks decked out in whatever leisure wear has the waistband that currently fits. Most of the people walking across the sea of red-and-gold carpet looked like plus-size models from the Slobs "R" Us catalog. Baggy sweatpants, sleeveless T-shirts, cargo shorts, mismatched plaids, horizontal stripes—nothing tucked in.

I looked like I belonged.

"Katie can get us tickets to the show," I said.

"Awesome. I wish I had brought Rita along."

"You want to call her?" Sea Haven was only about an hour north of Atlantic City.

Ceepak shook his head. "Negative. School night."

Right. His adopted son, T. J. Lapscynski-Ceepak (poor kid, his last name sounded like a disease), is a senior at Sea Haven High this fall. Tomorrow's Tuesday. Mom and Dad can't both be down in Atlantic City gambling away his college fund—not when there's trigonometry homework to be done.

Ceepak checked his wristwatch.

"What time is the next performance?"

"Twenty-hundred hours." I used the military-clock lingo to make it easier on Ceepak.

He kept staring at his wrist, doing the math. "That'll work. We're scheduled to meet with Mr. Burdick in the Starbucks downstairs at fifteen-thirty."

I nodded because, finally, after all this time with Ceepak, I could do the military-to-real-world clock conversions in my head: We were meeting Burdick at 3:30 PM.

"The stenographer will arrive at sixteen-hundred hours."

Four.

"We should have ample time to take his deposition and rendezvous with Miss Landry."

"I told Katie I'd do breakfast with her tomorrow at nine."

"That should not pose a problem. I have the court reporter on deck for eleven, should we or the prosecuting attorney have follow-up questions."

"Burdick's cool with sticking around town till we're all done?"

"Roger that. Apparently, Mr. Burdick is not very fond of my father."

I could relate. I met the guy once. Joe "Six-pack" Ceepak has that effect on people.

"Perhaps," said Ceepak, "Mr. Burdick would enjoy seeing the show with us."

"He might. There's a two-drink minimum."

"One can always order orange juice or seltzer, Danny."

Yeah. Seven bucks for bubble water. Viva Las Vegas.

"It's fifteen-ten now. Official check-in time was posted as three PM." Ceepak always knows all the rules. "Shall we take our bags up to the room?" he suggested.

"Sure."

We both packed pretty light for our overnight trip. I tossed together a gym bag with clean underwear, socks, and a shaving kit. I had planned on buying a fresh T-shirt for the bus ride home. Something like *I Got Lucky in AC.*

"What floor are we on?" Ceepak asked.

"Ten," I said. "The elevators are way over there."

To get to our elevator bank, we needed to hike five miles across a minefield of slot machines.

By the way—you don't have to yank down on a handle to send the cherries spinning anymore. You just sit on a stool and bop a button. The new-style machines don't pay out coins, either. They issue "credits" on a slip of paper. It's a lot like getting a gift receipt at Wal-Mart. If you miss the sound of tumbling quarters when you hit the jackpot, not to worry—hidden speakers simulate the plink and clink of cascading coins in full stereo surround sound.

"Danny?" Ceepak head-gestured up a lane between two rows of nickel-slot machines sporting a Cleopatra theme. These bad girls had five spinning reels, instead of the more traditional three, and about twenty different lines zigging and zagging across the pictograms of pythons and sphinxes and alligators and Nile river fruit that must've meant something to the cranky Italian grandmothers feeding the machines their debit cards.

"Third machine on the left," Ceepak muttered. He saw something. Something besides flashing lights and twirling hieroglyphics. He gave me a slight head bob so I'd see it, too.

Young dude. Pretending to pick up something off the floor very close to a stool where a white-haired lady—who looked a lot like George Washington on a day when his wooden teeth were giving him splinters—sat, eyes fixated on her spinning blurs and flashing lines.

"Purse," Ceepak whispered.

I nodded.

"Accomplice." He tilted his head slightly to the right.

Across from the guy rummaging around on the floor, another guy was opening up a gym bag. I figured the guy working the "oops, I dropped my nickel" scam on the carpet was supposed to snag the handbag, then toss it off to his accomplice, who'd stash it in his Adidas tote and hightail it out of the casino.

"Cover me," Ceepak said as he stepped forward.

Unfortunately, we didn't bring our sidearms with us on the bus so I knew any covering I did would have to involve fisticuffs, wrestling, or martial arts—three things I really should spend some time learning about some day.

Ceepak waited. Until the doofus on the floor made his move and grabbed hold of the shoulder straps to the lady's handbag.

"Freeze!" he shouted—almost loud enough to be heard over Georgette Washington's whoo-hoo-hooing when her lines hit a magical configuration and Cleopatra made with the *clink-plink-clink* sound effects.

"Let it go!" Ceepak demanded. Usually, when he demands like that, people listen: Ceepak's six-two, a mountain of muscle. And the military-issue haircut makes him look even stronger.

The guy on the floor, however, did not listen.

"Yo, Tony!" he yelled.

His buddy with the gym bag went for an empty stool, grabbed hold of two legs, and swung it sideways at Ceepak's head.

"Ceepak!" I shouted—half a second after Ceepak had already sensed the incoming furniture and ducked. Stool man missed by a mile. Looked like one of the Mets chasing after a clever curveball.

Now the guy on the floor popped up, ready to make a run for it.

A run right through me.

"Don't even think about it!" I yelled at him, assuming this kung fu pose I remembered seeing in *The Karate Kid.*

He didn't listen.

He thought.

He ran.

I closed my eyes, lunged forward, and crashed headfirst into his rib cage. We hit the deck and rolled around on the rug, which smelled a lot like spilled beer mixed with crushed popcorn and old shoes.

"Hey! Watch it!" yelled one of the blue-haired ladies perched on a stool above us trying to gamble in peace.

"Sorry," I said right before I flipped my guy off, rolled him over, and pinned him facedown to the floor so he could contemplate the carpet while I slapped on the cuffs—which, I remembered, I also did not pack for this trip.

In one final attempt to arch me off his back, my prisoner grunted, rocked up, and kicked out both legs. One of those legs collided with a cocktail waitress who had picked the absolutely wrong time to swing around the corner with a trayful of cocktails and beers. We got a booze bath. He finally stopped struggling.

The ladies of Cleopatra Lane were furious. I was soaked in chardonnay, Coors Light, and cosmopolitans. They, on the other hand, were thirsty.

"Police," I said so they'd stop staring at me like I was the idiot grandson they knew they should've kept locked up down in the cellar.

"Well done, Danny," I heard Ceepak say.

I had my knee in the small of the purse snatcher's back, both my hands pinning down his shoulders. I glanced over at Ceepak, who had his guy on the carpet, too. He only needed one hand to keep his suspect subdued. He was using the other one to help the cocktail waitress collect stray maraschino cherries.

"All right," boomed a big voice behind us. "We'll take it from here."

I looked up. Six security guards. A couple had Glocks strapped to their hips. One guy, a big black dude in gray slacks and a blue blazer, looked familiar, but I couldn't see his face, just a head silhouette, because he was standing right in front of a glowing purple panel at the top of a slot machine.

"These individuals were attempting to perpetrate a theft," said Ceepak.

"We know," said the big guy, who had an even bigger voice. "The eyes in the sky caught the whole show. It's all good, Ceepak."

Ceepak squinted. "Cyrus?"

"Roger that," said the big man. And then he started rumbling up a laugh. "Man, Ceepak. You and Boyle. You two always make a mess, don't you?"

3

"So what brings you boys down to sin city?" Cyrus asked as we strolled through the crowded casino.

"Deposition," said Ceepak. "Case up in Ohio."

"Your old man?"

"Roger that."

"You gonna lock him up and throw away the key?"

"Such is the plan."

"Sounds like a good one."

Cyrus is Cyrus Parker, a former Green Beret and fellow adherent to Ceepak's West Point honor code, who helped us "extricate" our way out of a hell hole back in Sea Haven last summer. Parker had served with the 101st Airborne, Ceepak's old unit, and then found a civilian job working as a bodyguard for a big shot—a job he lost when he turned against the Dark Side of the Force, to put it in *Star Wars*–ian terms, something I do on a daily basis.

"Thanks for detaining those two deadbeats," Parker said as we passed felt-topped tables surrounded by a bunch of chain-smoking Asians, tattooed bikers, and even more Italian grandmothers who, I guess, no longer stay home to bake pignoli nut cookies.

"You have that sort of trouble often?" Ceepak asked.

"Purse snatchers are the least of my worries." Parker gestured toward a dealer using a plastic wedge to shove a thick bundle of twenty-dollar bills down into a table slot. "You flash this much cash, you attract all sorts of undesirable individuals."

"How did you know we were in the process of apprehending suspects?" I asked, trying to sound like the cop I actually was.

"Saw you on TV, Boyle. Looked just like one of those Wrestle-Mania SmackDowns they run on pay-per-view. Especially that kung fu move you made." He stopped walking just long enough to re-create my *Karate Kid* pose. Not the swan. I'm not that lame. However, it did involve elbows bent at perpendicular angles.

Ceepak tried not to grin. Hey, I couldn't blame the guy. I laugh at me on a regular basis.

"Always remember, Officer Boyle," said Parker, "wherever you may roam in Xanadu, Big Brother Cyrus is watching." He pointed up at what looked like half a Plexiglas beach ball mounted in the ceiling. "This casino and hotel currently employ forty-five hundred security cameras. We can pan, tilt, and zoom underneath that opaque dome and you'd never even know we were tracking you. Got miniature cameras that can pick up the serial number on a dollar bill."

"Fascinating," said Ceepak.

"See this number here?" He pointed to a laminated plate on the edge of a blackjack table. "Tells us exactly what and where we're looking at. You boys were in slots, row forty-two."

And I had thought it was Cleopatra Lane.

"Got about fifty screens up at all times in the surveillance room, but you two were the best entertainment so far today. We figured you earned a reward." He fished into his navy blazer, pulled out a card key. "High-roller suite on the twenty-second floor in the tower. Compliments of the house."

Parker, of course, handed the card to Ceepak.

"Let Danny have it," said Ceepak. "Our original room will be fine for me."

Parker gave me a look. "Don't drink the champagne in the minibar, Boyle. Champagne isn't included." Then he winked and handed me the plastic pass to High Rollerville. "Enjoy, Grasshopper."

All of a sudden, I felt swanky. At the time, I thought I might lure Katie up to my suite after we hit the breakfast buffet. Make her forget all about Jake the "hottie." Did Jake have a ritzy room with designer shampoo in the shower stall and two terry-cloth bathrobes as I imagined I would? Doubtful.

Parker put his hands on his hips, surveying the action all around us.

So I did, too. Saw dealers raking in stacks of chips, which, being imaginary money, are much easier to part with than actual cash. They're just colorful plastic disks that resemble POGs, these juice bottle cap cardboard things I used to collect (I forget why), but are worth ten, twenty, or a thousand bucks.

Personally, I think the thousand-dollar chips should be the size of manhole covers so you really have to think about it before hoisting one onto the table in hopes of hitting twenty-one on the next flip of the cards.

"Gotta keep an eye on the players," said Parker. "Good card shark can up his bet when he has a hot hand by sliding a chip or two between his cards after the pot's good. Gotta watch the dealers, too. A bad apple might slip his accomplice an ace from the bottom of the deck 'cause he figures splitting one big score might pay better than his union wages for the year."

"That's why you can't hand chips or money directly to the dealer, Danny," said Ceepak who, I guess, studies casino security as well as Las Vegas magic acts in his spare time. "You have to place any form of remuneration on the felt to initiate a transaction."

"You're good, Ceepak," said Parker. "Need a job?"

"No thanks. I prefer Ocean Avenue in Sea Haven to Boardwalk and Park Place."

That was Ceepak making a joke. Sometimes it's hard to tell. He works in too much trivia, like the fact that all the streets in Monopoly are named after ones here in Atlantic City. If you have to hand out Cliff's Notes, the yuks are usually few and far between.

"Follow me, gentlemen," said Parker. "Mr. Boyle's suite is in the new Crystal Palace Tower back on the other side of the building."

We once again navigated the ocean of patterned carpet that was the casino floor.

"So," I asked Parker, "are you still like a trainee or whatever?"

"Negative, Officer Boyle. I am currently head of security for the Xanadu Hotel and Casino."

"Awesome," said Ceepak.

Parker shrugged. "Hey, that Green Beret thing on my résumé never hurts. Besides, I had this one absolutely incredible letter of recommendation."

"Really?" I said. "Who wrote it?"

"Who else?" said Parker, tilting his head toward Ceepak.

"I have a friend at the Casino Gaming Bureau," he said. "Another former soldier who is always on the lookout for a few honest men."

"You got that right," said Parker. "Honest men are damn few down here."

We continued our trek across the carpeted tundra, walking past this really loud lounge singer destroying some old Motown tune in a tight gown. She was lifting her knees so high while stomping to the beat she looked like a drum major who had lost her marching band.

Finally, we once again reached the registration desks and followed the signs for the Crystal Palace Tower.

"How long you guys in town?" Parker asked.

"Just tonight," said Ceepak. "We need to do Mr. Burdick's deposition this afternoon and keep tomorrow open for anything further from the prosecuting attorney's office up in Ohio."

Parker nodded. "Sounds like a plan."

We passed the poster for "Rock 'n Wow!"

"We might catch his act tonight," I said.

"You should," said Parker. "Great guy. Had a beer with him the other night. We provided technical assistance for one illusion he does."

"Cool," I said. "What'd you do?"

"If I told you, Officer Boyle, you'd have to shoot me. I signed papers. Confidentiality agreements. These magicians guard their secrets better than Dick Cheney. But you'll see. It's a nifty illusion. Lucky Numbers he calls it—like in the fortune cookies, you know? Anyhow, it's his big finish. Brings down the house."

"I understand he's quite a family man," said Ceepak.

"That he is," said Parker. "Cute kids. Britney and Richie. Met them in the Pagoda restaurant the other night. Very well-behaved young lady and gentleman."

And that, I figured, was Richard Rock's grandest illusion—fooling Cyrus Parker into thinking his daughter Britney qualified as a "cute kid."

We passed the box office and the entrance to the Shalimar Theater. According to the digital reader board zipping around underneath the chaser-light marquee, this evening's performance was *Sold Out!*

"Don't worry," said Parker. "I can get you guys in."

"So can Katie," I said.

"Who's she?"

"Friend from back home."

"Showgirl?"

I almost giggled. Katie? In some sort of nude-and-sparkles body stocking, wearing a feathered headdress? Sure, she has great curves, which we caught a glimpse of on Oak Beach on those days when she favored us with her lower-cut one-piece. But, like I said, Katie was too sweet, too much of a "good girl" to get up onstage and shake her groove thing.

"Katie takes care of the kids while Mom and Pop are onstage."

"Babysitter?"

"Nanny and tutor."

Parker nodded.

"Cyrus?" someone called out.

I turned around. The poster boy was alive! Richard Rock had magically appeared and I could tell exactly how he did it, too, because the glass doors to the theater lobby were still gliding shut behind him.

"Good afternoon, Mr. Rock," said Parker.

Rock gave Parker a head bob "howdy" like I remember President Reagan doing whenever I watched him chop wood on TV from behind the bars of my crib. Then Rock narrowed his eyes suspiciously at Ceepak and me, like a cowboy looking for Injuns up on a ridge.

"These gentlemen are friends of mine, Mr. Rock," Parker explained. "Police officers from a shore town called Sea Haven."

Rock head-bobbed some more. "Cops, hunh? That's good. Real good. Interested in moonlighting?" Rock gave us a chugging *heh-heh-heh* of a laugh. "We're gonna need us a whole mess of extra security tonight."

"Is there some problem, sir?" asked Parker.

"You betcha. *She's* coming!"

4

We followed Rock into the lobby of the Shalimar Theater. It was done up in Chinese-take-out-joint red, lacquered black, and gilded gold. A chandelier made out of ball-shaped paper shades with spindly ribs and stringy tassels hung in the center of the ceiling. The floor, where it wasn't covered with more of the casino's geometrically challenging carpet, was made out of marble or, you know, whatever tile they sell at Home Depot that shines like a polished slab of stone.

"It's safer in here," said Rock. "This is bad, boys. Real bad."

Offstage, Richard Rock looked sort of small, dressed in standard-issue frat-boy khakis and a pink polo shirt instead of a tuxedo and red satin cummerbund, which is a word I only know because I had to rent a tux for a friend's wedding and the nice lady at the mall explained, no, it wasn't an undergarment.

"I can't believe she's coming! Not tonight!"

"Who?" asked Parker.

Rock glanced around like a nervous squirrel guarding his nuts. "Lady Jasmine!"

"Who?" asked Parker.

"Lady Jasmine! No-account magician up at Trump's Taj Mahal! Plays the big room."

The Taj, of course, was one of Donald Trump's Atlantic City casinos, which, as I'm sure the Donald would tell you, is one of the most opulent, best, most extraordinary, luxurious, not to mention deluxe, casinos on the planet. I think Trump also brags about the Taj having the best buffet in the whole world: the Sultan's Feast, they call it. Where the Xanadu is all Chinese all the time, the Taj is more *I Dream of Jeannie*. Long story short, Trump's ritzy, glitzy pleasure palace, just a half mile up the boardwalk, was serious competition for the Xanadu. Therefore, Trump's resident magic act, featuring this Lady Jasmine, had to be seen as a serious threat to Richard Rock, the Xanadu's in-house illusionist.

"She canceled her show tonight!" Rock said. "Did it so she could come here. Steal my act. She's bringing her whole dadgum posse. Spies and such!"

"Have you received some sort of threat?" Parker asked.

"No, sir. She's too clever for that. A snake in the grass. Rattler. Bite you in your horse's ankle."

"Can she steal your act just by watching it from the audience?" Parker asked.

"She might could if she videos it! Sneaks in one of them digital Minicams. Hides it in her handbag. Don't want to find out when it's too late!"

"Where are you most vulnerable, sir?"

"Out in the auditorium. My security folks are all over the backstage areas like stink on a skunk. Have it sealed up tight."

"So how about I put a few more uniforms in the house tonight?"

suggested Parker. "Scatter 'em around. Let Miss Jasmine know we're watching her without ruining the show for everybody else."

"Good, good. Sounds like a plan."

"My partner and I plan on attending this evening's performance," said Ceepak. "We'll also keep an eye out for any suspicious behavior."

"Appreciate that, son." Now Rock sort of peered at Ceepak. "You like magic?"

"Indeed. I believe Jim Steinmeyer, the famed illusion designer, said it best." This was pure Ceepak: ask him a simple question, get a detailed dissertation. " 'Stage magic is an honest trickery.' I find it to be the one deception I can tolerate since I know from the onset that I am going to be deceived."

Rock cocked an eyebrow. Parker and me? We were more or less used to these Ceepakian philosophy seminars.

"You ever catch my act?" Rock asked.

"Yes, sir. On the Discovery Channel. I was quite impressed with how diligently you strive to keep your material suitable for the whole family."

"Well, you know what they say: Families are where our nation finds hope, where wings take dream."

Ceepak nodded. To do otherwise would've been rude.

"Now tell the truth, son," Rock continued, his smile set on *smug* again. "Wasn't my Vegas show *the* most amazin' collection of illusions you ever did see?"

"It was quite good."

Rock gave Ceepak the pinched eyes. "Good? Hold up, now, son. You fixin' to tell me I ain't the most amazing illusionist in the whole wide world?"

"In my opinion, sir, Franz Harary is the world's finest illusionist. I was fortunate enough to catch his act when I was stationed in Korea."

"Is that so?"

"Yes, sir. Mr. Harary transformed a woman into a python. He was also burned alive by a jet airplane engine, then rematerialized inside its flames. Quite impressive stuff. In my book, he's the best."

Sometimes Ceepak's code, the part where he never tells a lie, doesn't do much to win friends or influence people.

"Well," said Rock. "This Franz Harary fellow ain't the one coming here tonight to steal my secrets. Her name is Lady Jasmine. She's easy to spot. Long black hair. Asiatic looks. Slanty eyes. Usually travels with this midget fella. Dwarf-like. He's in the show with her. The midget-dwarf fella."

I nodded to acknowledge what Rock had left unsaid: the "midget-dwarf fella" would be easy to spot, too.

"I'll make sure my team is out front in force tonight," said Parker. "Inspecting purses, backpacks, handbags. We'll strictly adhere to the 'no recording devices' edict. Zero tolerance for digital cameras, video recorders, cell phones."

"Good. Good. Appreciate it, Cyrus. Heck, I was thinking about cutting Lucky Numbers from the show so she wouldn't have a chance to see or steal it but, well—that's what folks are paying their hard-earned money to come see."

"Richard?" This bare-chested young guy in tight black pants came into the lobby from the theater. He was ripped, jacked, and all those other words people use to describe the muscular male physique guys like Ceepak find the time to maintain while I'm home catching up on my sleep. This guy was also wearing what they call a bolo tie: the silver-tipped, braided-string-through-a-shiny-medallion deals that Texas oil tycoons wear instead of your more traditional neckties.

"What?" Rock said to chiseled chest, sounding snippy.

"We need to talk. About the costumes."

"Why?" The way he said it, I was glad Rock wasn't my boss.

"I think we've figured out the quick-change bit. It should work!"

"Well, it better, okay?" said Rock. " 'Cause I'll tell you what: in a magic show, timing's everything! You hear what I'm sayin', Jake?"

"Yes, sir."

Jake.

Aka the Hottie and Stud Muffin.

Katie's new boyfriend.

5

Having stopped to chat with Richard Rock, we were in danger of running late for our meeting with Mr. Burdick, so Parker found a bellman to take our bags up to the rooms for us.

I gave the guy pushing the luggage cart a buck. Ceepak gave him a five. I told the bellhop to hold on while I dug in my pockets, found three more crinkled singles, and a couple quarters. It's hard to keep up with Ceepak, but I try.

Then he and I headed back across the casino floor for the escalator that would take us down to the lower level where the Great Wall of Gifts shop, Grand Panda buffet, Uncle Chang's Ice Cream, and Starbucks were all located.

Of course, to get there we had to pass by several more banks of slot machines. A lot seemed to have TV themes, like *Deal or No Deal*, *Gilligan's Island*, and *The Beverly Hillbillies*, which, up top, had a plastic bust of Jed Clampett clutching two fistfuls of cash.

Another machine was called "Cops and Donuts." Made me feel right at home.

"Slot machines," said Ceepak as we rode the escalator down. "The crack cocaine of gambling."

I was still thinking about doughnuts.

"They promote the gambler's fallacy," Professor Ceepak continued.

"Hunh," I said, which is always enough for Ceepak to keep rolling.

"You continue feeding the machine money because you think past wins or losses are predictive of future wins and losses. That if you lose on one spin, you are bound to win on the next, as you might when flipping a coin. In truth, every play of the slot machine presents an equal probability of payout. Therefore you play the illusion. Ignore the reality."

Illusions. No wonder Rock's magic act was such a hit. It's why folks come to Atlantic City: they want to be lied to. Lies give them hope.

Long ago, pirates used to walk along the Atlantic City beaches holding up lanterns so merchant vessels out at sea would think they were traveling in safe waters, running parallel to the slow-moving lights they assumed to be other ships on the horizon. The real ships would eventually run aground or crash against the shoals. The pirates on the beach would yell, "Yo-ho-ho," drop their lanterns and bottles of rum, and head out in rowboats to pillage and plunder the shipwrecks they created.

I guess people are still losing their treasures down the Jersey shore, making shipwrecks out of their lives. The lights are just a little brighter now, the illusions slicker.

We reached the lower lobby. More slot machines. A bunch based on those *Pirates of the Caribbean* movies. Good choice.

"Would you gentlemen care for a beverage?" Ceepak asked the three men seated around the small café table in Starbucks. One was Gary Burdick. I recognized him from his mug shots. The man to his right was an old guy, about eighty-nine, wearing a three-piece polyester suit from the 1977 JCPenney catalog: plaid with fresh dandruff chunks sprinkled atop the shoulders. The oldster looked like he could really use a double shot of espresso because his chin kept bouncing against his Windsor knot every time he nodded off for a quick two-second nap.

The third man at the table was the oddest: a black guy with a powdered-sugar mini-Afro and a neatly trimmed goatee. He was wearing a red silk tunic underneath his black satin cape, which, by the way, was decorated with embroidered flowers.

"You buying these beverages?" asked Burdick. His hair was thin, wispy, and parted half an inch above his left ear. A good wind gust and he'd be bald. His eyes were droopy; so was his mustache. He also had very little noticeable chin—just a long neck that sloped up from his collarbone to his lower lip.

"Yes," said Ceepak. "I'm buying."

"Your old man wouldn't. He wouldn't do nothing for nobody."

Ceepak blinked a little. "What would you like to drink, Mr. Burdick?"

"A beer and a shot of Jack black."

"No you don't," said the man in the cape.

"Meet the Great Mandini," said Burdick. "My AA sponsor."

Ceepak nodded at Mandini, who nodded back.

"How come you don't look like your old man?" asked Burdick.

"Actually, many people say my father and I share several physical characteristics."

"Really? That's funny. You don't look like a drunk old asshole to me!" Burdick wheezed up a chuckle.

"Gary?" said Mandini.

"What?"

"Take the cotton out of your ears and put it in your mouth."

"That's an AA slogan," said Burdick, I guess to prove he'd been to at least one meeting. "Mandini here's the one who encouraged me to come forward. Testify. Make some amends. Work my ninth step."

"Commendable," said Ceepak.

"Yeah. I guess," said Burdick with a shrug. "Besides, your old man? He's a prick."

That's when the geezer woke up. "Are we assembled? Very good." He started patting his pockets, which, when you're wearing a three-piece suit, there are a lot of. "Have you seen my pen?"

I had no idea who he was asking.

"I brought my own pen," he said. "Prefer the blue ink to the black. I know it plays havoc on the mimeo machines, makes extra work for the gals in the secretarial pool, but it certainly helps identify the original signature from the copy, don't you agree?"

Burdick nodded toward the pocket-patter. "Meet my lawyer." The old guy stretched out a liver-spotted hand in Ceepak's general direction. I don't think he could see so good.

"Rodney P. Squires," he said. "Attorney-at-law. I will be advising Mr. Burdick during the forthcoming deposition process. Perhaps you'd like one of my cards?"

Now he was back to the pocket search, looking inside his coat, tugging at his lapels, pulling a tissue wad out of the pocket-watch slot in the vest.

"His rates are pretty cheap," said Burdick. "Mandini recommended him."

"Mr. Squires has represented me a time or two when I have had disagreements with our local municipal authorities," said Mandini, who sounded like a king or something.

"So," said Burdick, gesturing toward the antique lawyer, who was still frisking himself, "don't think you can, you know, trick me into saying stuff I don't need to be saying. I got me a lawyer."

"We only need to talk to you about what my father, Joseph Ceepak, told you on the evening of February thirteenth when you two shared a jail cell in Cuyahoga County."

"Was it the drunk tank?" asked Mandini.

"Yeah," said Burdick.

Disappointed, Mandini shook his head. "You need to lay off the liquid courage, Gary."

"This was years ago."

"Makes your hands shake too much," said Mandini, holding up one hand, sideways—thumb flat against his index finger. Then he flipped the hand back and forth and plucked the ace of hearts out of the air and handed it to me.

"Oh!" said the lawyer. "Have you found my pen?"

"No," I answered so somebody would. Then I looked at Mandini, hoping maybe he could pluck a pen out of the air, too.

"Sorry," he said with a wink. "The Great Mandini only does card tricks. Learned everything I know from the mystics in Tay Ninh, a few kilometers northwest of Saigon, or, as it is known today, Ho Chi Minh City."

"He does tricks with a bunny, too," added Burdick. "On the boardwalk. He's good. You rub the bunny's fur, the bunny will pick your card out of the deck with his nose. I'm thinking about doing an act with a magic cat. There's all sorts of strays living under the boardwalk. Thought I could trap one, dress it up like a wizard. Maybe put the cat in a pointy cap."

"It's a very special pen," said the lawyer, jolting awake from another one of his chin-dip mini-naps. "Tremendous sentimental value. A beloved client presented it to me upon the completion of a very complicated divorce settlement. He was from one of this city's most prominent families. This, of course, was before the casinos came in. Changed everything and not for the better, if I might be permitted to editorialize momentarily."

"So," said Ceepak, trying to wrap things up, "would any of you gentlemen care for a beverage before we proceed upstairs to the conference room we have reserved for—"

The lawyer held up his hand. It shimmied in the air like the tail of a kite. "Not for me. My doctor says caffeine is unhealthy. Of course, I'm certain he meant to say it is 'unhealthful,' as the coffee beans, per se, are most likely quite healthy and robust."

I tried to help: "They have decaffeinated stuff, too."

"Ah! Here it is!" He fished a cheap plastic pen out of the back of his pants. "Wasn't in the coat after all." He rolled the pen around between his thumb and index finger. I noticed that there was something printed on the side of its barrel. "You know, there's a very interesting story behind this pen."

The Great Mandini raised a hand. A quick flame flared off the tip of his finger when he did. "I'll have a grande soy latte, extra foam," he said to Ceepak.

"What's that?" asked Burdick. "What's a latte?"

"Very similar to a cappuccino."

"What's a cappuccino?"

"As you can see," said the lawyer, rolling the pen around so I could read what was written on the side, which I couldn't because it was chipped and faded, "my client was in the vending machine business. That's why this pen says, *Change Is Good.*" The old guy chuckled and I smelled fish mixed with cigar. I wondered how many billable hours this tale would take. "I said to my client, a very important man, by the way, I said, 'Well, let's hope your wife only wants her alimony in nickels and dimes.' " Another chuckle, and I knew for certain he had had pickled herring and a White Owl sometime in the last twenty-four hours. "However, what was most fascinating about this particular case, as I'm sure you'll agree—"

That's when Ceepak's cell phone rang.

The prosecuting attorney's office in Ohio.

Mr. Ceepak had just changed his plea.

Admitted he was guilty.

6

There would be no deposition.

We bought everybody their coffee drinks, caffeinated and otherwise, and asked them to stick around town because the folks in Ohio wanted to make sure Mr. Joseph Ceepak didn't change his mind before they saw the judge the next morning and officially entered his guilty plea.

"I don't trust my father to keep his word," Ceepak confided to me. "We may, indeed, be reconvening with Mr. Burdick and his entourage tomorrow morning or early afternoon." That meant Ceepak and I would still be spending the night in A.C. "There is nothing more for us to do today besides hurry up and wait."

We stood in Starbucks and watched our three new amigos go their separate ways out the revolving doors to the boardwalk and the white-hot sunshine.

Class was officially dismissed.

"I'm thinking about hitting the Absecon Lighthouse," said

Ceepak. "It's one of the oldest in the country and New Jersey's tallest. You have to climb two hundred and twenty-eight steps to reach the top."

"Really?"

"Yes, but it sounds well worth the effort. I'm told the views are breathtaking. They also have the lamp, which was first lit in 1857, equipped with its original Fresnel lens."

Ceepak. Some guys come to A.C. to get lucky. Some to hike up a spiral staircase and look at a giant lightbulb.

"Care to join me, Danny?"

Sure. And then maybe we could stick knitting needles in our eyes. "No thanks. I mean, it sounds like fun, but I—you know, promised Sam I'd buy her a souvenir."

Sam is Samantha Starky, a part-time summer cop up in Sea Haven who's back at community college for the fall semester. We've dated a couple times. Probably will again. We're at the souvenir T-shirt stage of our relationship; haven't advanced to snow globes or teddy bears wearing destination-specific clothing. Not yet.

"You still want to catch the magic show later on?" I asked.

"Roger that. I'll ask Cyrus to arrange for our tickets."

"Cool."

He flicked up his wrist, consulted the Casio. "Let's reconvene in the theater lobby at nineteen-hundred hours. That way, Cyrus can use us as needed in his heightened security plan."

"You really think this Lady Jasmine wants to steal Rock's secrets?"

"Doubtful. However, Cyrus needs to appear proactive at this juncture. Remember—he's only been on the job a few months."

That, too, is Ceepak in spades. If you're his friend, he's always got your back. Trust me—I know. He's had mine on several different occasions.

Ceepak shoved off for his lighthouse adventure and I headed

back up the escalator to the main casino floor so I could find a T-shirt shop and head over to the Crystal Palace Tower to finally check out my swanky high-roller suite. To reach my new room, of course, I had to pass more slot machines. Lots and lots of slots.

So, with a little time on my hands, and one crisp $10 bill in my pocket, I decided to sit down and play. Just to, you know, see what all the fuss was about. I picked the machine I had seen earlier, the one called "Cops and Donuts." In the next row over, they had these "Wheel of Fortune" machines with a big wheel up top that spun around if you hit some magical combination of letters. It also had sound effects of a crowd chanting like on the TV show: *"Wheel! Of! For-tune!"* Then the musical bird chirps. I figured this was the Xanadu's take on Chinese water torture.

I slid my ten spot into the "Cops and Donuts" bill muncher.

The illuminated front panel showed a couple of cheery cartoon cops with beer bellies riding in a patrol car and chasing after a burglar who was on foot. In the background, you could see Dunky's Donuts, apparently the officers' favorite drive-in dining destination and why they were too obese to climb out of their car and chase the fleeing bank robber on foot.

This was what they called a 5-reel-and-20-payline machine, because there were five reels depicting stuff like doughnuts, coffee cups, handcuffs, and police badges, and you could play up to twenty lines at a time. All those lines made the video screen look like a blinking EKG. There was also a Donut Eating bonus game that was triggered when three or more "Fresh Donuts" icons appeared on the first, second, and third reels. Having fun in Atlantic City was almost as complicated as calculus.

I slapped the spin button to play five credits. Stuff spun. Lines zigged. I slapped the button again. Doughnuts whirred by. Lines zagged. A few spin cycles later, my credit balance had hit zero.

Game over.

It was like I had fed my money into a soda pop machine, hoping that all the cans in the hopper would tumble out the first time I hit the select button and when, instead, I got nothing for my money, I just shrugged, put in more money, pushed the button again and hoped I'd get lucky. I could have more fun making change at the Laundromat.

Having gambled my $10 limit, I followed the signs and arrows for the Crystal Palace Tower and walked through an arcade of high-end gift shops. Brooks Brothers. Chico's. White House/Black Market. I guess if I had hit the jackpot, I was supposed to dress better.

I ducked into a T-shirt shop. Thought about getting Samantha this "snake eyes" shirt until I realized the single dots of the two tumbling dice were located in the lewdest possible position on the chest. I went with one that said *A.C.* and hoped that wasn't supposed to be lewd, too.

I exited the store and strolled through this indoor piazza that reminded me of Disney World—a bunch of restaurants and nightclubs, all built into a three-story-tall movie set meant to appear like a Chinese village square at sunset. There were golden clouds painted on the domed ceiling and I was surrounded by fine dining options: Panda Pete's Potstickers, the Pagoda Place, General Tsao's Chicken Xpress, and Hooters.

Upstairs, on the second level of the fake village square, I could see a couple nightclubs: Yuk-Yuk-Ho-Ho's Comedy Club, Pandamonium, and the Forbidden City. Oh, and a karaoke bar. Lip Sync Lee's.

I try to avoid karaoke bars.

Finally, I reached the Crystal Palace elevator bank. Doors slid open on one of the cars and Richard Rock stepped out. He was wearing sunglasses and a baseball cap pulled down tight. He carried a plastic shopping bag.

"Hey," I said. "How you doing, Mr. Rock?"

"Sorry. No autographs."

Not that I had asked for one.

Then he was gone.

I shrugged and stepped into the elevator, which was like that one from *Charlie and the Chocolate Factory*: all glass!

I checked out the floor buttons and realized that I would be staying in the penthouse: my floor, number 22, was all the way at the top. I took my time depressing the button so everybody else in the elevator would have ample time to realize just how high of a roller I was.

My room was pretty awesome.

A better-than-a-lighthouse view of the boardwalk and beach. I wished I had brought some binoculars. There was a swimming pool about nineteen stories down at this other hotel and even though it was October and no scantily-clad women were lounging in the chairs, let alone tossing off their tops, you just never know when a girl might go wild. My friend Jess has the videos.

I could see the other high-rise casinos: Bally's, the Tropicana, Resorts International, Caesars, and Trump's Taj Mahal. I could also see the foam-rippled Atlantic Ocean, stretching off to the east. The sand down on the beach was clean and white and dotted with a few bright blue umbrellas and cabana tents, not as many as you'd see in the summer, but enough to let me know somebody was out there, breathing in the fresh, salty air instead of the recirculated casino stuff.

I left the window so I could check out what was in the cabinets surrounding the TV set.

As Parker predicted, I found chilled champagne in the tastefully hidden fridge. I pulled out a drawer and discovered a basketful of really expensive snack food items in sealed jars. Stuff like spicy cheese stix, gourmet popcorn, teeny cookies, and Toblerone candy bars—all of which cost like fifteen bucks, each.

On the bed, I counted twelve pillows propped against the headboard. All different shapes, sizes. I couldn't figure out what I was supposed to do with so many. Maybe elevate my feet. I slid open the closet and, as predicted, there were two bathrobes. Plush. Swanky. His and Hers. Or, in my case, His and His Other One. There was also a small safe where I could store my valuables. If I had any, I might've used it, too.

Then I made the mistake of looking out the other window. The one that faced to the west, away from the golden shoreline.

The one that gave you a bird's-eye view of Atlantic City's urban blight.

Two blocks away from the boardwalk, everything looked like a ghetto circa 1975. It's where the Xanadu's bus depot was located, so Ceepak and I had seen it up close and personal when we pulled into town. Shabby homes. Garbage blowing up crackled streets where nobody seemed to live. Liquor and cigarette stores with placards out front proclaiming CASH FOR GOLD, which meant somebody was inside hocking their wedding ring, hoping their luck would change. If it didn't, there was always a quart of Colt 45 and a pack of Marlboros to ease the pain.

From my lofty perch in the high-roller suite, I could see this sign on top of what looked like a church or a castle: CHRIST DIED FOR OUR SINS. In Atlantic City, I guess that meant He died so everybody else could sell their gold for cash and hit the slots.

A cloud blocked out the sun and every drab thing twenty-two stories down looked even drabber. I turned away and, now that the room was a little darker, I could see a red light flashing on the phone on the bedside table.

Meant I had a message. Probably Ceepak. Reporting in on that view from the lighthouse.

But he would have called my cell.

I scanned the icons over the top rows of buttons on the phone. It was almost as complicated as playing "Cops and Donuts." Housekeeping. Spa. Room service. Parking. Golf. Golf? Messages!

I depressed the messages button, put the phone to my ear, and awaited further instructions.

"You have—one—new message," said the friendly recorded lady. "To hear your new messages, press two."

I did as pleasantly commanded.

"First new message. Received today at—four—thirty—five—PM."

I checked the high-tech digital alarm clock on the bedside table. Ten minutes ago.

"Hey, Danny."

Katie. Meant she had forgotten my cell phone number. Erased it from her memory—literally. When they do that, it's definitely over.

"Hope I'm not bothering you."

Katie didn't sound like Katie.

"I was just wondering . . . if maybe you could come see me tonight. After the show. When the kids are asleep. I need to talk to you. About Jake."

Great. It was the Call.

I heard someone yell, "Katie?" in the background. Female.

"I found something."

"Katie?" The woman again.

"I gotta go," Katie whispered. "Oh, we're in room AA-four."

I jotted down the number on the little Xanadu notepad near the phone.

"Thanks, Danny."

And those were the last words Katie Landry ever said to me.

7

"Relax, guys. Enjoy the show."

So said Cyrus Parker when Ceepak and I reported for duty at 1900 hours—better known as 7:00 PM. or "an hour before the show actually starts."

I, however, was having a hard time obeying Parker's orders. I couldn't relax.

Not when Katie wanted to see me after the show so we could talk.

About Jake.

"You sure you're covered?" asked Ceepak.

"Roger that," said Parker. "Called in my whole crew. We'll have twenty security guards positioned throughout the theater. We've also organized a dedicated TPZ camera to be locked on box three-oh-one in emperor's row, right where Lady Jasmine and her posse will be seated."

"TPZ?" I asked, because somebody had to.

"Tilt, pan, zoom. Here you go, guys." He handed us our tickets. "You boys are in three-oh-two. Right next to our person of interest."

"Mr. Parker?" A very officious guy clutching a hardcase clipboard strutted across the lobby.

"Yes, Mr. Zuckerman?"

Zuckerman was probably thirty-five. Had that cue ball sheen of scalp showing though his shaver-shorn hair, the kind of 'do that looks like it's spray-painted on your skull skin.

"You're certain we're secure?"

"Absolutely."

"What about dogs?"

"Excuse me?"

"Have you swept the theater with bomb-sniffing dogs?"

I tried not to grin. Was Rock's magic show really that bad? A bomb?

"Mr. Zuckerman," said Parker, "I was given to understand that the perceived threat was theft of intellectual property, not an improvised explosive device."

"Wouldn't you rather be prepared than sorry?" Zuckerman sniped.

Ceepak stepped forward. "Sir?"

"What?"

"Rest assured that Mr. Parker has taken every conceivable precaution to insure the security of Mr. Rock's illusions."

"Who are you?"

"John Ceepak. Sea Haven police department."

"Who?"

"Friend of mine," said Parker. "Former soldier. Another set of eyes that will be glued on Lady Jasmine this evening."

Zuckerman grunted.

"Mr. Zuckerman is Richard Rock's manager," explained Parker. "Runs a tight ship."

"I try."

"We're good to go, sir," said Parker.

"I certainly hope so," said Zuckerman. "Hey, you!" And he was off to nag an usher who must've been unpacking souvenir programs the wrong way.

While Zuckerman showed the guy how to do his job, I eyeballed some of the other souvenirs for sale. Sparkly kid-sized cowboy hats. A whole rack of those stringy bolo ties like the one Jake had been wearing when he forgot to put on his shirt this afternoon. A mountain of cuddly stuffed tigers and equally cuddly Richard Rock dolls caged in a glass display case, not to mention autographed portraits of his whole wholesome family. His wife was a very buxom blonde, all cleavage, golden hair, and white teeth. The kids were frying the camera lens with their bright teeth, too. I wondered if they bought tooth bleach in bulk-sized barrels at Costco.

Soon, the lobby started filling up. Hundreds of pumped people, all jazzed about seeing Richard Rock pretend to make stuff appear and disappear. A lot of kids were in the crowd. One boy, about eight, already wore his bolo tie and spangled cowboy hat. They clashed with his New York Yankees Jeter jersey, but what the hey.

Around 7:40, this scrawny beanpole of a guy came tramping into the lobby. He had greasy black hair with two stringy strands dangling down to make a parenthesis on his forehead. Under his bugged-out eyeballs were bags so huge they resembled half-moon water balloons.

"Martini," he snarled at one of the bartenders serving $10 bottles of Bud and $15 cocktails.

"One second, sir," said the bartender.

But the guy couldn't wait. "Where the fuck is David Zuckerman?"

"Who?"

"David fucking Zuckerman."

The bartender poured Bug Eyes a double shot of vodka in a plastic cup, tossed in a lemon peel and an olive skewered on a pink plastic sword. "I'm sorry, sir, I don't know Mr. Zuckerman."

"He's Rock's manager. He's expecting me. Kenny Krabitz. Tell him I'm fucking here!"

Ceepak, who's basically a thirty-five-year-old Eagle Scout, went over to talk to the loudmouth in the loud jacket.

"Mr. Krabitz?"

"What?" The guy was sucking on the pink plastic sword. Chomping the olive.

"There are children present."

"So?"

"Please watch your language."

"What?"

"Kindly refrain from utilizing foul language."

"Jesus! Fuck you, you fucking fuck."

Ah, yes: the New Jersey state motto.

Ceepak moved closer. Let the undernourished weedling take note of just how huge and in shape he was.

"I'll ask you one more time to refrain from using profanity in the presence of minors."

"And who the fuck are you?"

"John Ceepak. Sea Haven PD."

"Sea Haven? Fuck that noise. Get out of my face, meathead. I'm drinking here."

"Mr. Krabitz?" Zuckerman returned to the lobby.

The weasely guy slammed back his cocktail. Crunched an ice cube. "So, David—what's the big fucking problem? I thought everybody was happy as a clam over here."

"Let's take this outside," said Zuckerman. He put a hand on Krabitz's shoulder, ushered him toward the door.

Ceepak shook his head as he watched them leave the lobby.

"What an asshole," I muttered.

"Danny?"

"Sorry."

"Come on, we should go find our seats. The show will start in approximately ten minutes."

We followed the crowd into the fifteen-hundred-seat theater, which was set up Vegas-style. Ten raked tiers angling down toward the stage. About two dozen tables on every level—some round, some the shape of cafeteria tables for families and big parties. The place reminded me of Medieval Times, this castle up in Lyndhurst, New Jersey, where you sit at long banquet tables, chomp on turkey legs, swill grog, and watch knights on horseback joust each other down in the arena. In here, they were pushing magical elixirs (most made with vodka or rum) instead of grog. The kids got soda pop in Big Gulp–sized tubs and a magical squiggly straw. I think they glowed in the dark. The straws, not the kids. Unless they ordered Mountain Dew.

Our box seats down in the emperor's row were the poshest in the house. They were banquettes, actually. Padded seats. Fancy fabric. Our table was covered with a cloth. We were three tiers up from the edge of the stage and had our own bar and waitstaff, too. I don't think ordinary people were even allowed to traipse across our quadrant of the carpet without a work visa. Very VIP. Very high roller.

"Drinks, gentlemen?" asked an impossibly well-endowed young cocktail waitress in a red silk minidress and black China-doll wig.

"Do you have grapefruit juice?" asked Ceepak.

The waitress batted her mascara-thickened lashes several

times to ponder his request. It looked like two tarantulas clapping. "I think so. Maybe."

"If not, cranberry juice will be fine."

"There's a two-drink minimum."

"Then make it one of each!" said Ceepak, just to show how wild and crazy he could be.

"Okay." She looked at me with high hopes that I might redeem our table by ordering something more interesting. Beer. Wine. Sangria.

"I'll have the same thing," I said.

Hey, when Ceepak's on a "let's-keep-our-heads-clear-so-we-can-do-our-job" jag, I usually play along.

We settled into our plush bench seat. I nibbled the free Chinese snack mix: shiny crackers, sesame sticks, and green wasabi peas. The stage was draped with a fifty-foot-tall red velvet curtain, made even redder by all the red-gelled stage lights aimed at it.

"Curious," said Ceepak, examining the empty box next to ours. "Five minutes till showtime. No Lady Jasmine."

The waitress returned. Ceepak and I took our two Juicy Juice glasses each. I saw a bunch of security guys stationed around the perimeter of the auditorium. Two or three on every level. A couple were talking into their sleeves, probably trying to figure out where the heck their prime target for the evening was. I noticed that Parker himself was stationed near the emperor's row bar, rubbing the top of his bald head, staring at the empty box next to ours, worrying about it.

I swiveled around, expecting to see Lady Jasmine come waltzing into the auditorium at the very last second. Instead, way off in the distance, over the crest of the tables rising like a terraced cake behind us, through the open doors to the lobby, I caught the briefest glimpse of Katie, standing near the souvenir shop.

I waved but she didn't see me. Maybe because I was half a mile away. So I stood up and waved more frantically—like the guy with the orange flashlights who shows the jumbo jets where to park at Newark.

That was when I saw who she was talking to.

8

Jake.

I couldn't see much.

Only that Mr. Muscle Chest still hadn't found a shirt. Up top, he was bare-skinned and bolo-tied. Even from this distance his shiny black pants looked tighter than the casing on an Italian sausage, which was an image I really didn't want in my brain right then, but there it was.

Katie took both of Jake's hands into hers.

He pushed her away. Were they having a spat? Interesting.

"Danny?" This from Ceepak.

"Hmm?"

"The house lights are dimming," he whispered. "Perhaps you should take your seat. Otherwise the people behind us may not be able to scc the stage."

"Right. Sorry." I sat.

"You okay, partner?"

"Yeah."

"What's wrong?" he asked because he could tell something was.

I gestured backward with my head. "Katie."

Ceepak turned around, straining to see what I had just seen.

"Where?"

"In the lobby."

"Sorry. The ushers just closed the doors. The view is currently obscured."

"She was with Jake," I said. "That dancer we met."

"We met a dancer?"

"He came out to the lobby when we were talking to Rock."

"Ah, yes. The muscular young man. I suppose being a professional performer forces one to stay in peak physical condition."

Yeah. I noticed that, too.

"I'm gonna go see her," I said. "Katie. Right after the show."

"Awesome," said Ceepak.

"Yeah. She said I should swing by."

"Then it's all good."

No. Not really. But, of course, I left out the part where she said she wanted to "talk to me about Jake."

The auditorium lights went dark. The audience applauded.

"Welcome to the Xanadu's Shalimar Theater," boomed a disembodied voice. "As a reminder, the taking of photographs and the use of recording devices is strictly prohibited during this evening's performance."

Spotlights started swinging around the curtain. Drums rolled.

"Ladies and gentlemen, boys and girls, are you ready to be amazed?"

"Yes!" said the audience.

"Are you ready to be astounded?"

"Yes!" The second response thundered even louder.

"Are you ready to be astonished?"

"Yes!" Now the rafters rang with it, which was good, because I think the announcer was just about to run out of *A* words that all meant the same thing.

"Are you ready to Rock?"

One more "Yes!" and music started blaring. Disco music. Throbbing, synthetic, steady four-on-the-floor beat. Think "It's Raining Men" only different. Not better, just different. Seven dancers hit the stage: four girls in thigh-high cowgirl skirts and spangled tops, three guys in bolo ties sans shirts. It looked lopsided.

Four girls. Three guys. Guess Jake missed his entrance. He was too busy having a romantic tiff out in the lobby with my old girlfriend.

The seven dancers who had shown up for work did some sort of yee-haw, side-to-side, leg-lifting dance—the kind of hoedown stuff they teach you in kindergarten square-dancing class when you're too young to realize how stupid you look.

I almost recognized the tune. "Could This Be Magic?" Barry Manilow, maybe. Definitely not Springsteen.

More leg kicking, cowboy hat lifts.

I think they called this "choreography." Hyper-peppy boys and girls stomping and clomping in a line, grinning and smiling and tipping their sparkling cowboy hats at one another.

Yippy-ki-yi-yo.

The girl without a dance partner did her best to pretend she had an invisible friend who knew all the moves.

At the end of their hootenanny, all seven dancers pointed up toward the ceiling and shouted, "Let's! Rock!"

That seemed to be the cue for a smoke ball to explode in front of the curtain—about thirty feet above center stage. When the cloud cleared, there he was—Richard Rock. Floating. He swung out his arms to feel the love and started drifting down toward the stage.

"There is obviously a crane apparatus of some sort concealed behind the curtain," whispered Ceepak, eager to explain how the trick was done. "Perhaps a jib."

Then there were these other explosions. Three new smoke bombs: One over our heads in the middle of the auditorium, one on either side of the stage. Mrs. Rock and the two kids magically materialized and started drifting down toward the stage as gracefully and effortlessly as magic carpets. I saw no wires. No crane apparatuses. Smoke but no mirrors, except for two billion tiny sequin ones on Mom's dress.

"Fascinating," said Ceepak.

Yeah. I had to admit: it was pretty impressive. Amazing, astounding, and astonishing, even.

Richard Rock descended to center stage and stood in front of the curtain. He put his hands on his hips and pretended to be perturbed as his children floated toward him. Richie and Britney were wearing pajamas. The fleecy kind with feet.

"What? Are you kids still *up*?" Rock said to his airborne offspring, earning his first family-friendly chuckle of the night.

Mrs. Rock and the kids made soft landings on the stage and walked over to join Richard. Again, I couldn't see any wires being unhooked from harnesses, no jetpacks being slipped off. Maybe the kids were friends of Peter Pan and he had taught them how to fly by thinking happy thoughts. Christmas. Puppy dogs. Beer.

"Where's your nanny, children?" said Rock, playing the put-upon poppa to perfection. "It's past your bedtime!"

"Yes," said the boy. "Time *flies* when you're having fun!" The kid nailed his line and knew it. Soaked up his laughs. Beamed.

Mrs. Rock propped a hand beside her mouth so she looked like an elegant hog caller. "Nanny Katie?" she cried out. When she moved her left hand up to her mouth, she blinded us with the laser beams shooting out from her gigantic diamond ring. It was so huge, it looked like one of those gumball-machine-sized ones six-year-old girls give out as birthday party favors.

"Nanny Katie?" she called out again

"Yes, Mrs. Rock?" said Katie from the back of the theater. Her voice sounded shaky. I figured she was nervous about going onstage. Katie was always kind of shy. Modest. She marched down the side aisle toward the stage.

Jake wasn't with her.

He hadn't made it onstage to join his bare-skinned brethren yet, either.

"Take the children up to their rooms, if you please!" Rock said to Katie with a dramatic flourish.

The boy tugged on the tails of his father's tuxedo.

"Yes, Richie?" said Rock, rolling his eyes.

"Can we fly up to our rooms, Daddy?"

"No," said Mrs. Rock, stiffly shaking her head back and forth long after she'd already said her line. Guess she never studied acting. "You're both *grounded* for the night!"

Another chuckle.

I checked out Ceepak.

Yep. He was grinning.

Me? I was trying not to groan. The Rocks' banter reminded me of the cornball jokes you hear on the Jungle Boat ride at Disney World: "Keep your hands in the boat, folks—the alligators are always looking for a free handout."

"Ladies and gentlemen," said Rock, pointing toward his kids as Katie climbed up a set of steps and took the two children by their hands and led them offstage into the wings. "How about a nice hand for Richie and Britney?"

The audience cheered.

"And Nanny Katie!"

I would have whistled. Chanted *"Kay-tee, Kay-tee, Kay-tee!"*

But I was too busy thinking about Jake. Wondered where he was. It was something Ceepak and a whole bunch of other cops would be wondering in a couple hours, too.

9

Richard Rock's family-friendly show was pretty awesome.

Over the next forty minutes, he turned a tabby into a tiger, cut his wife—whose name we learned was Jessica—in half, rearranged her body parts and put her back together in this Rubik's Cube–type deal, caught a bullet fired at him from a pistol with his teeth, walked through a solid brick wall, transported his wife from one side of the stage to the other in under a second, escaped from silk ropes tied around his wrists, ankles, legs, and torso, and made a flock of seagulls appear out of torn-up newspaper.

He even shot an arrow with a ribbon attached to its tail through his wife's tiny stomach. She had so much cleavage tumbling out of her low-cut gown it was a good thing Rock hadn't aimed higher. Could've caused a serious silicone spill.

Ceepak was impressed but reminded me in a whisper that, "Magic is the art of misdirection."

And I had thought it was real. You just had to go to Hogwarts and study hard.

"Ladies and gentlemen, boys and girls, I wouldn't deceive you for the world," Rock proclaimed from center stage.

"Actually, just by saying that, he's doing so now," said Ceepak, who really enjoyed being able to relax knowing everything he saw or heard in this theater was a lie. Lady Jasmine missed it all. Box 301 was still unoccupied. Even Parker was relaxing. I saw him leaning up against the emperor's row bar, laughing at the corn popping out of Rock's mouth.

Around 8:40, Rock moved into the mentalist portion of his show. He read the minds of two volunteers from the audience: a woman named Jo Karpen and her son Rich. Poor kid. He was so totally busted when Rock revealed the real grade (to the decimal point) on his most recent American History pop quiz.

I wondered if Rock could've also predicted that's when Lady Jasmine would finally show up?

While Rock read the Karpens' minds, Lady Jasmine, a guy who looked a lot like Mini-Me in the Austin Powers movies, another Asian-looking lady, and a knockwurst-necked guy in a black leather jacket, slipped into box 301.

I was going to tap Ceepak on the shoulder but he was already looking over at the latecomers. He gave me the knowing nod. We were on it. Lady Jasmine was officially being surveiled.

"Ladies and gentlemen," said Rock as the Karpens climbed down the steps from the stage, "I hope you and your families are enjoying your time here in Xanadu, a palace more incredible than the stately pleasure-dome the mighty Kubla Khan did decree."

Guess Rock and I had the same eighth-grade English textbook.

"As you know, when Marco Polo first journeyed into the mystical lands we now call China, he returned with many wondrous treasures. Fireworks!"

A flick of his wrist, and indoor fireworks exploded.

"Spaghetti!"

Another flick of his wrist and a wad of wet noodles fell from the sky, smacking one of the dancers on the top of his head, making him look like he was wearing a mop.

"Sorry about that, Blaine," Rock quipped.

He then tugged at his sleeve, setting up another wrist flick. The three dancers onstage—all guys—covered their heads, not knowing what might come tumbling down or exploding out next. The crowd chuckled.

"And, of course," said Rock, milking the moment for all it was worth. "The greatest treasure of them all: fortune cookies!"

He plucked one out of the air.

I could feel the crowd heave a collective *"Hunh?"*

Now the giant TV screen behind Rock showed a slow-motion shower of cash.

"You will win a great deal of money," said Rock, reading the tiny slip of paper from inside the cookie.

Then he turned it over.

Several times.

"But wait—where are my lucky numbers? Wise sages through the ages have told us, the fortune inside a fortune cookie will only come true if the reader plays his lucky numbers in a game of chance! Where are they? Where are my lucky numbers?"

Ceepak leaned over. "This must be his famous Lucky Numbers illusion," he said.

I was sort of thinking the same thing, but Ceepak said it first, so he was still, officially, the smartest boy in the class.

Out of the corner of my eye, I sensed Lady Jasmine leaning forward in her seat. I glanced over and saw her gesturing for everybody else in her box to settle down and pay attention.

Rock stared at the cascading cash on the JumboTron at center stage.

"I'll bet I could win a whole heap of money if I played my lucky numbers out on the casino floor! But I don't have any lucky numbers in my fortune cookie."

He turned to the audience. The house lights brightened.

"Do any of you folks have a lucky number?"

Hands shot up. People started shouting.

"Hold your horses. I need another volunteer. You there. Yes, you."

A woman sitting about six rows back with her husband and kids stood up.

"Do you have a lucky number, ma'am?"

"Yes, sir. I sure do."

"Have you ever attempted to use it to win money?"

"One time. The lottery."

"And you won?"

"No."

Rock did a comic frown. "You lost?"

"Yes," the woman giggled it out.

"Dang—and it's still your lucky number?"

"I hope so."

"Me, too." He flicked his wrist again. Produced a purple-striped poker chip. Moved it artfully across and through his fingers. In the close-up on the TV screen, I could read the center of the chip: *Fifty dollars.*

Rock gestured for the woman to join him onstage.

She giggled the whole way up the steps.

"What is your name, ma'am?"

"Cassie. Cassie Hannington."

"Cassie, have we ever met before?"

"No," she said. "Unfortunately!" Then Mrs. Hannington grabbed hold of Rock's tux and nailed him on the cheek with a quick but noisy kiss.

"Please," said Rock. "Not in front of my wife!"

Jessica Rock—now dressed in a different low-cut gown more dazzling than all the rhinestones in Nashville—strolled across the stage like Vanna White heading over to the big board to flip a few vowels.

"Sorry," said the audience volunteer. "You're just too handsome."

"Ain't it the dadgum truth?" said Rock. Then he gave her a grin and a wink to let her know he was just joshing her.

Their whole little scene was playing up on the giant TV screen behind them, which is where my eye always goes in any kind of arena-type situation. Even if I'm at Madison Square Garden and Bruce Springsteen and the E Street Band are live onstage, I'm focused on the JumboTron, watching TV Bruce instead of Live Bruce.

"Very well, Cassie Hannington. You say you have a lucky number?"

"Yes."

"Is it between one and thirty-six?"

"Yes."

Mrs. Rock disappeared into the wings and returned with a rolling easel that had a white marker board propped up in its tray. Then she smiled and pointed and posed some more.

"Excellent," said Rock. "You know, numbers can be dadgum powerful. Now, I know what you're thinkin': my cow died so I don't need your bull anymore. So, I'm gonna prove it to you. Cassie, I want you to think about your lucky number."

"Now?"

"Might be a good idea. We only have this theater until nine-thirty. Then the Rotary Club comes in."

The audience laughed. So did Cassie. Then she closed her eyes, scrunched up her face. Thought hard.

"Are you seeing your number? Visualizing it?"

"Yes."

"Good. Concentrate on it."

"I am." She squeezed her face tighter.

"Cassie, I want you to stay here in the theater with my wife."

"Okay."

"Meanwhile, I'm going out into the casino to make us some money! Jim Bob?" he called to one of the dancers. "To the high-rollers' room!" He took a step forward. Stopped. "Hold up. Let's make this even harder. Where's my blindfold?"

Jessica Rock whipped out a black hood—the kind executioners wear, only without the eyeholes.

"Thank you, dear," said Rock as he slipped the black sack over his head and stumbled around the stage like a blind version of Frankenstein's monster.

The dancer took Rock by the elbow, led him toward the steps.

"Wait a second, Jim Bob! If I'm going to play with the high rollers, I need to look like one."

He magically plucked a few items out of the air: A glitzy pinky ring sporting a horseshoe of diamonds. A white rose for his lapel. He slid the ring on his finger. Jim Bob pinned the boutonniere to his tux.

"All righty. Let's go win us some money!" Rock followed Jim Bob's lead and descended the staircase.

"Can you folks still hear me?" he asked.

"Yes!" we all said.

"Good. Means my radio microphone is actually working! And, can y'all see me?"

The TV screen now showed a handheld shot of Richard Rock moving through the auditorium. I glanced over at real life and saw a camera guy with a cordless portable unit walking backward about six feet in front of Rock. It reminded me of the Letterman show, when Dave leaves the stage to go out into the street to do something wacky with taxi drivers or water balloons.

"We can see you, Mr. Rock!" shouted one of the kids in the auditorium.

"All righty then." He started smacking his lips. "Shoo-wee. My mouth is drier than a tumbleweed outside Amarillo. I need me a drink, Jim Bob."

The dancer led Rock out of the side aisle and up emperor's row. When they passed table 301, Rock froze. Just for a second. Then he strolled past our table and headed over to the VIP bar.

"I'll have a Shirley Temple!"

"You sure you wouldn't like something with a little more kick?" the bartender asked.

"No, ma'am," said Rock. "This here is a family show."

While the audience tittered at that, the bartender handed Rock a tall pink glass with two shiny cherries sticking out on top.

Rock put the glass up to his hood. Couldn't drink it through the cloth.

"Reckon I need a straw," he said.

The waitress plunked one into his glass.

"Thank you kindly." Rock maneuvered the tube under the front of his hood, took a loud sip. "Ahh! Dee-licious. Now then, it will take a few minutes for Jim Bob and me to make our way over to the Ming Dynasty High Roller Room where the stakes are higher, the winnings bigger. You folks can watch our progress up on the TV screen. To prove that we are not doing this with trick photography, we will be utilizing the casino's very own, high-tech, tilt-pan-zoom security cameras to track my progress in real time."

The giant TV screen turned into a quadrant of grainy black-and-white video images—live, overhead shots from four different cameras positioned above the casino floor and in the corridors just outside the Shalimar Theater. There was a rolling digital time stamp in the lower right corner of each frame. 8:50 P.M.

"Cassie?" Rock called out to the volunteer onstage.

"Yes, sir?"

"Keep thinking about your number. Girls?"

The chorus girls came bounding back onstage like gazelles to join the male dancers already out there, elbows cocked, eagerly anticipating their next hoedown.

"A little traveling music, if you please!"

The six remaining dancers launched into a huge production number, lip-synching to a prerecorded track about Lucky Numbers.

I don't think anybody was listening to the stupid song or watching the dancers kick and pump, even though two of the girls were more or less dancing with each other since Jake still hadn't shown up and Jim Bob was escorting Rock out of the theater. All eyes were glued on the TV screen and Richard Rock as he sipped his Shirley Temple, went out the swinging doors, and strolled through the theater lobby.

I wished I could've gone with him.

The Lucky Numbers song sucked. Totally.

10

On the giant TV screen, we could see Rock and Jim Bob in the wide corridor outside the Shalimar Theater.

They were standing underneath the blinking marquee as all sorts of people straggled past—many of them staring at the strange dude in the tuxedo with a black bag over his head who was being led around by a topless seeing-eye dancer.

"Show Cassie and the other folks where we are, Fred."

The camera whipped around to take in the wide carpeted hall leading off to the slot machines and blackjack tables. Then it zipped back to frame up Rock again as he and his escort walked past all the shops and restaurants Ceepak and I had walked past earlier.

"All right, Fred. You can go back inside with that thing. Switch to the hotel security cameras, fellas!"

The TV screen cut to a shot from the ceiling surveillance camera closest to where Rock was walking. When he left its coverage area, the scene switched to the next camera down the line. The whole time he walked, Rock chattered away. I think magicians call it patter.

"Ladies and gentlemen, boys and girls, it was the ancient mathematician Pythagoras who once declared, 'The world is built upon the power of numbers.' Tonight, we will put his words to the ultimate test. We will witness just how powerful one number can be!"

The camera angle switched and he was entering the main casino floor, walking past some blinking slot machines, of course. With that black hood over his head and white rose in his lapel, he looked a little like the Grim Reaper on his way to the senior prom, but nobody seemed to notice. They were all too busy staring at their spinning Sheriff Roscos, General Lees, Daisy Dukes, and whatever else spun on the *Dukes of Hazzard* slot machines.

Another camera. Another left turn. This time past the electronic poker machines.

"Do you believe one number can change your luck, change your life?"

Onstage, a spotlight swung over to make Cassie the volunteer look like a Bambi caught in the searchlights during a prison break.

She giggled. Mrs. Rock gestured for her to answer. "I don't know," she said, sounding nervous. "Maybe. I guess so."

Rock and Jim Bob hung another Louie, the camera switched, and we watched them pass that cocktail lounge where the athletic woman in the too-tight gown was stomping through another Motown hit.

Thankfully, we couldn't hear her. Just Rock's voice over.

"We're almost there, ladies and gentlemen. The Ming Dynasty Room! Where the highest of the high rollers win and lose millions of dollars, all on a single turn of the cards or a solitary spin of the roulette wheel. And you know what?"

"What?" said the volunteer.

We could see Rock and Jim Bob walk down a carpeted corridor toward an ornately decorated door right underneath a pagoda-shaped arch.

But Rock didn't answer his volunteer.

So Cassie leaned in closer to her microphone. "Yes, Mr. Rock?"

Mrs. Rock turned toward the wings. Daintily tapped at her ear. It looked like she was signaling to a technician. Audio problems. Where's the Best Buy Geek Squad when you need them? Probably chatting on their cell phones and drinking Snapple, which is what the clerks do behind the cash register every time I stand in line for thirty minutes, trying to buy a game for my Sony PlayStation.

A *Please Stand By* title flickered on the TV screen as Rock and Jim Bob walked toward the golden door. I was assuming it was golden. The security cameras only broadcast in black-and-white.

The camera angle switched to a view from behind the two guys and we could read what was scrolled above the door: Ming Dynasty Room. A security guard stationed outside signaled that it was okay for Rock and his helper to enter.

I heard this *thump-thump-thump*.

Onstage, the volunteer from the audience was tapping on the microphone. "Hello? Mr. Rock?"

Next we heard a crackle of static. "I'm sorry. I believe I was in a dead zone there for a second. Can you hear me now?"

"We can hear you fine," said Cassie.

"All righty. We are now in the Xanadu's world-famous Ming Dynasty Room." He walked past a bearded man in robes who I figured had to be an oil sheik.

"Admission to this exclusive gaming den is by invitation only," said Rock. "However, tonight I have arranged for us to play one fifty-dollar chip on the high rollers' roulette wheel. The house rules are simple. I can play one number and one number only. I can only play one spin. I cannot play the odd or even, nor the black or red. Just your lucky number. And, for this one spin, no one else in the room is permitted to play with or against me. It's just us. You. Me. And your lucky number!"

The camera view shifted to an overhead shot, angled down at the roulette wheel's green felt betting board. Actually, given the black-and-white camera, the board looked gray. But you could tell by the different shades which numbers were red and which ones were black.

Rock stepped into the picture: we could see the top of his hooded head.

"Now then, you said your lucky number was between one and thirty-six . . ."

"Yes. It is."

"As you can see, those numbers are all available here on the roulette table. Please—write your number on the marker board so the audience can see it. I, of course, won't be able to read what you write because I'm in another room with no video monitors and I have a big ol' black bag over my head! But, to eliminate any lingering doubts, kindly write your number large enough so the whole audience can read it without the aid of the TV screen. Turn off all the cameras in the theater, gentlemen! Do it now!"

The camera operators in the Shalimar made a big show of twisting knobs, powering down. On-screen, we were still looking down at the roulette wheel.

"Now," said Rock, "please show everyone your lucky number!"

Mrs. Rock handed Cassie a thick Magic Marker and pointed at the white board.

"You want me to write it down now?" asked Cassie.

Mrs. Rock nodded. Pointed at the marker board.

Cassie, her hand shaking slightly, scrawled a giant *22* on the board.

"Can everybody in the audience see your lucky number?" asked Rock from his remote location.

"Yes," said Cassie. "I wrote it real big."

"Very well. Let's see how lucky your number really is!"

Rock set down the stupid Shirley Temple he'd been carrying. Without the drinky-poo, both of the magician's hands were free to dramatically hover over the felt. You could see the horseshoe-shaped pinky ring sparkling as he moved across the numbers, hunting down the lucky one.

"Legend has it," Rock said as his hands moved across the first twelve numerals, "the man who invented the roulette wheel bargained with the devil to obtain its secrets." His hands moved down to the second cluster of twelve numbers. "This, of course, is based on the fact that if you were to add up all these numbers, add one and two and all the numbers through thirty-six . . ."

His hands passed right over the row with 22, 23, and 24. Moved into the final third of the board.

". . . if you were to add 'em all up, they'd equal six hundred and sixty-six. Six-six-six. The so-called Number of the Beast for those of you who ever watched that devil movie *The Omen*. But I don't believe in all that hooey. No, sir. I only believe in my Lord and Savior, Jesus Christ and—your lucky number!"

His hands hesitated. Reversed direction. Moved back up the board. Rock manipulated his fingers and magically produced the $50 chip, which he plunked down in the middle of the square numbered 22.

The audience applauded!

"Is twenty-two your lucky number?" Rock asked.

"Yes!" Cassie was squealing.

"Hold your horses, folks," said Rock. "We're just gettin' started. Croupier? If you please?"

The TV screen switched to another overhead shot—looking

down directly at the roulette wheel as a pair of dainty female hands gave the wheel a good spin in one direction and sent a silver ball sliding in the other. The ball, which looked like it had escaped from a pinball machine, glided along on the tilted surface running around the outside of the spinning wheel. We watched the ball whiz. The wheel whirl.

"No more bets," the croupier announced.

The ball and wheel lost momentum.

The big silver marble bounced down into the rolling number slots. It bounded in and out of a couple boxes. The wheel slowed down some more. The ball leapt up over the ridged edge of a box. Then another. Bounced again. Landed.

It ended up in the pocket numbered 22.

"Twenty-two wins," announced the croupier.

Inside the theater, the audience went wild! We had a winner.

"What's the payout?" asked Rock.

"Thirty-five to one," said the croupier.

"Congratulations, Cassie! You have just won one thousand, seven hundred and fifty dollars!"

The screen cut back to a wide-angle view of the whole high-roller room. The pit boss slid a stack of chips over to Rock. He pulled off the hood. Grinned at the camera. Scooped up his winnings.

"Come on, Jim Bob! Let's go take Cassie her jackpot! And this time, we'll take the shortcut!"

They made their way over to this pair of ceramic dragons on pedestals in front of a paneled wall. Rock bopped one of the dragons on the head, and the wall swung open! It was pretty cool. Like Batman and Robin opening that secret closet where they hid the bat poles in Wayne Manor.

The audience was still cheering when a dozen spotlights swung across the stage and came to rest as a blazing circle at the bottom of the JumboTron TV screen. A hidden door swung open and, from inside the TV set, or so it seemed, out stepped Richard Rock and Jim Bob!

Apparently, after all those left turns, the Ming Dynasty high-roller room was located somewhere behind the Shalimar's stage.

"Yes, we could've gone out that way, too," said Rock, "but what kind of fun would that've been? Thank you, Cassie!" He handed his volunteer the stack of chips. She nearly fainted. Dancers escorted her over to the steps. Mrs. Rock swung out an arm, kicked up a heel, and rolled the easel offstage.

"Ladies and gentlemen," said Rock, "luck is what you have left over after you've already given one hundred and ten percent. Truth be told, we all make our own luck! So, boys and girls: study hard, listen to your teachers, just say no to drugs, and go be the winners I know you were meant to be! Jessica? Where are you, honey?"

Mrs. Rock came running out onstage, her spangled dress working like a disco ball as she jiggled into place beside her handsome husband.

She took Rock's hand. He smiled. She smiled. I thought I might need an insulin shot.

"Good night, everybody!" said Rock "And—Go! Get! Lucky!"

The Rocks dipped into a big bow, then skipped off into the wings while the audience rose to give them a standing ovation. The seven dancers scurried into a line and took their bows.

"Fascinating," said Ceepak and I could tell: he was having a hard time figuring out how Rock did the Lucky Numbers trick.

Me, too.

Then I glanced over at Lady Jasmine.

She was shaking her head and laughing.

11

The houselights came up. The audience was still buzzing, keyed up by Rock's performance.

"I'm gonna go see Katie," I told Ceepak.

"Roger that."

We slowly made our way up emperor's row and into an aisle where we got stuck behind a wall of people moving even slower than we'd been moving. Fifteen hundred humans. Four exits. This was worse than the Lincoln Tunnel at 5:00 on a Friday.

"I'll catch up with you later," I said to Ceepak, even though neither one of us was going anywhere anytime soon.

"Give Katie my regards."

"Yeah. I will." I shuffled forward. A whole foot. "Geeze-o man. What's the holdup?"

"I am given to understand that Mr. and Mrs. Rock typically visit the lobby after every performance to meet and greet their fans."

And to bump up trinket sales.

Finally, some ushers opened a couple side exits and the crowd started to part and thin.

"That'll work," said Ceepak.

We reached the lobby.

"Mr. and Mrs. Rock will be right out!" announced one of the souvenir vendors from behind her chirping cash register. "Form a single line to my right and have your items ready to be signed."

"I'm going to purchase a stuffed tiger for Rita," said Ceepak, dutifully taking his place in line, falling in behind a couple kids studying a booklet so they could learn how to pull quarters out of each other's ears.

"Catch up with you in the AM," I said.

I crossed the lobby and came out into the wide-open plaza in front of the Shalimar Theater, realizing I had no idea where room AA-4 was. The Crystal Palace Tower? The Shanghai wing? Some other part of China?

Fortunately, I saw a security guard stationed in front of what looked like a service entrance—double metal doors painted the same color as the walls so nobody could see them.

"Excuse me," I asked. "Which way to Room AA-four?"

"The performers' suites?"

Made sense. Katie was working for the Rocks. The Rocks were performers.

"Yeah," I said.

"Someone expecting you?"

"Yeah. The Rocks' nanny. Katie Landry. She's an old friend from Sea Haven."

The guard sized me up some. "You live there? Sea Haven?"

"Yeah. I'm on the job."

"Cop?"

"Yeah."

"They still got that miniature golf course? King Putt Putt?"

"Yeah. King Putt."

"They still have that crocodile where you shoot your ball up the snout and it rolls out the butt?"

"Yeah." It's actually the tail.

"We used to spend a couple weeks up in Sea Haven every summer. When the kids were younger. Now, they're all grown up. Don't want to know from putt-putt and Boogie boards."

"Room AA-four?"

"Yeah. Use this door." As he worked the thumb latch, I read the tiny sign that said AUTHORIZED PERSONNEL ONLY.

"Thanks," I said.

"No problem. Hey—they still got that pancake place?"

"Yeah." Sea Haven has about six pancake places. I figured one of them had to be the one this guy was remembering.

"They still make that thing they make?"

"Yeah."

"Good times."

"Yeah." I gave him a little two-finger salute and headed up the hall.

The corridor on the other side of the door was drab compared to the rest of the Xanadu. Back here, instead of Chinese red and gold wallpaper, the walls were cinder blocks painted a wet gray. The floor was scuffed linoleum illuminated by sporadic can lights up in the dropped-tile ceiling. I noticed one of Parker's TPZ cameras on a naked metal arm. In the bowels of the building, they don't hide the spy cam under a smoky gray dome to keep it discreet.

I passed a door that looked like it opened into a janitor closet or one of those rooms with nothing in it but a billion jumbled telephone wires, all different colors, screwed to metal posts on a switching plate. I heard humming and thrumming—like a gigantic refrigerator gurgling through a cycle.

I saw another guard stationed near another dull door just like the dull door I had already passed. He looked Samoan. Some kind of Polynesian. As big as a refrigerator crate with a Fu Manchu mustache and curly hair pulled back tight into a ponytail. EVENT STAFF was printed on the breast of his windbreaker.

"Yo, bro—can I help you?" the guy asked.

"I'm here to see Katie Landry. Room AA-four."

He nodded and tilted his head to the left to indicate that I should head up this corridor to where it dead-ended into another hallway. "Take the right, bro. AA-four's the second suite down."

"Cool," I said. "Thanks."

"Mahalo."

I think that's Hawaiian for "later, dude."

I headed up the hallway and wondered if Jake, Mr. Chippendales Dancer, would lose his job since it was pretty clear he had bailed on tonight's performance. I figured he might be forced to find gainful employment some place where shirts were required. Then Katie would leave him like she left me.

Okay. Katie never really left me. She left Sea Haven. I just happened to be living there at the time and had no desire to move out to California with her. I'm allergic to avocados.

I hit the *T* where the two hallways intersected, took a right, and kept thinking about Katie and me. How we used to lie on our backs in the sand on Oak Beach late at night every August so we could stare up at the sky and watch the meteor showers. How we used to save each other seats on the school bus because we liked sitting next to each other and shooting the bull. How we used to race each other on our bikes to Skipper Dipper, our favorite ice cream place.

When we were kids, Katie and I lived that whole Jersey Shore life Springsteen sings about: screen doors slamming, breezes blowing up the beach, rubber balls smacking off walls, baseball cards stuck in bicycle spokes, the girls in their summer clothes.

I reached room AA-4.

The door was ajar.

"Katie?" I called out.

No answer.

I pushed the door open. Stepped into the room. It was pitch dark.

I stepped on something hard and plastic. Probably a toy.

The kids. Were they going to be here, listening to everything Katie and I said?

"Katie?"

Nothing.

"Richie? Britney?"

Still nothing.

Only the distant sound of a woman moaning.

I made out the silhouette of a lamp on an end table next to a couch. I crunched across something that crumbled, maybe a cookie. I made it to the lamp. Flipped it on.

I wished I hadn't.

Katie was naked except for a black garter belt made out of studded leather. She'd been trussed up to a wooden chair, hands tied behind her back. Silky white rope coiled around her body, pinching into the flesh above and below her freckled breasts.

I felt cold. Felt like I might collapse.

The woman in the other room kept moaning.

I wanted to see Katie's face, her emerald eyes. I couldn't. She was wearing a blindfold and some sort of muzzle that forced a red ball gag into her mouth.

Around her neck, she wore a silver-tipped bolo tie.

The lanyard had been pulled up tight.

Too tight.

Tight enough to kill her.

A letter come blowin' in on an ill wind
Somethin' 'bout me and you
Never seein' one another again

Don't worry Darlin', now baby don't you fret
We're livin' in the future and none of this has happened yet

—Bruce Springsteen, "Livin' in the Future"

12

Maybe I don't know Katie Landry as well as I thought I did.

Our relationship a couple summers ago only went so far before it was rudely interrupted by a bullet. I guess I had crowned her with a halo, put her on a pedestal.

What I saw in room AA-4 did not jibe with the Katie I thought I knew.

They say everybody has a secret life. A dark side they keep hidden. Guess that includes Katie Landry.

Was she really a dominatrix or submissive or whatever they call it when you get your kicks being tied up while wearing leather harnesses, black masks, and ball gags?

And where were the two kids?

Did Katie send them away so she could play rough with Jake?

Was Jake the one who taught her about erotic asphyxiation?

They explained "breath control play" to us at the police

academy, told us to look for it when analyzing a strangulation crime scene. Seems some folks intentionally reduce the amount of oxygen to the brain during sexual stimulation in order to heighten the pleasure received from orgasm.

For real.

But Katie Landry? It doesn't make sense.

I'm sitting on the cold floor in the cinder block hallway backstage, trying to make sense out of all that has happened today, thinking about this ride back home in Sea Haven called the mind scrambler.

It's a spin-and-puke sort of amusement on the boardwalk with three steel arms radiating out from a central pylon. Each arm has four cars rotating under it while the whole three-legged rig twirls around that central pillar. It spins and whirls like a three-beater Mixmaster.

Crank the mind scrambler up to full speed and you go soaring in then out and round and round until you feel like the slimy blob of oil being whipped into Aunt Jemima's pancake mix. You spin, you slide, you sail toward the other cars, then slip away. You feel sick, quick.

To mess with your head even more, the whole contraption reels around inside a dark dome painted black and decorated with Day-Glo paint. They strobe lasers against the walls, then pump in mist, ultraviolet light, and extremely loud music.

When the ride comes to a stop, you raise the safety bar and wobble out of your seat, but the world keeps spinning round and round.

The late Katie Landry?

It appears her mind-scrambling abilities are even better.

"How are you doing, Danny?" Ceepak comes out of AA-4.

"Okay."

"You need anything?"

Yeah. For Katie Landry not to be dead.

"No," I say.

"Parker and I have secured the crime scene."

"What was that moaning?"

"Come again?"

"I heard a woman. In the other room."

Ceepak nods. "Pay-per-view pornography. We'll want to dust the television remote for fingerprints. Check hotel records to determine when the movie was activated. The Atlantic City police are on the way."

"They need to find Jake."

"The dancer?"

"Katie's new boyfriend. Maybe this is why he missed tonight's performance."

"It's a possibility, Danny."

"He's probably the one she was with."

How do I know there was someone else in the room with Katie? Easy—you can't tie yourself to a chair like that. It takes two to do that particular tango.

"I guess he pulled too tight on the bolo tie because he was, you know, busy. Doing other stuff."

Ceepak grimaces. "Perhaps you should return home to Sea Haven, Danny."

"Yeah. Maybe."

"Do you have your cell phone handy?"

"Hunh?"

"You might want to call Becca. Olivia. Some of Katie's closest friends. Karen Decosimo. Madeline and Julie Delianides."

Ceepak. He pays attention. Remembers more of Katie's pals than I do right now.

"I know Miss Landry has no surviving family members," he says. "However, the friends we choose in life often become our true family, more so than blood relations."

I slump down another inch because he's right. We were the only family Katie really had.

"Hang here, partner," says Ceepak. "We will continue to safeguard the integrity of the evidence until the ACPD arrives." Ceepak has swung into full Ceepak mode. Gone is the goofus who gets his kicks marveling at Las Vegas illusions. Back is the gung-ho MP.

"Where are my children?" At the far end of the corridor, I can see Richard Rock. He's sort of lurching and careening down the hall. Mrs. Rock and their business manager, David Zuckerman, lurch and reel behind him.

Guess the Rocks had been in the lobby signing autographs when I came out of room AA-4 with enough functioning mental faculties to call Ceepak, who called Parker. After the two ex-military men made their preliminary assessment of the situation, Parker radioed one of his security guys, told him to alert the ACPD, then find the Rocks and bring them back to the family's living quarters.

I stand up.

"Where are Richie and Britney?" asks Mr. Rock. He looks worse than I feel.

"Where are my babies?" Mrs. Rock looks ready to faint.

"You're a cop, right?" snaps Zuckerman.

Ceepak nods. "John Ceepak. Sea Haven police department."

"Do something!"

"We have contacted the local authorities."

"Where are my children?" Rock asks again, his voice shaky.

"They are not in their room," replies Ceepak. "Hotel security has initiated a search and is currently screening surveillance footage in an effort to ascertain their present location."

"What about Jake Pratt?" Rock asks. "He cut the show tonight! Did that boy have anything to do with this?"

"What did Jake and that slutty little whore do?" asks Zuckerman.

I am so ready to belt the prissy bastard. Then Ceepak gives me the slightest shake of his head to let me know Zuckerman isn't worth it.

"My babies," Mrs. Rock stammers. "How could they—Jake and Katie—in front of Richie and Britney?" she asks the world swimming around her as she churns along on her own mind scrambler.

Zuckerman braces her under an arm. "I'll take care of it, Jessica."

Now Cyrus Parker comes out of room AA-4, pulls the door tight behind him.

"Where are my children?" Rock asks again.

"We've initiated a search."

"I can't believe this." I sense Rock's climbed on the mental spin-and-puke ride with his wife. "You hire a girl. Check out her references. Entrust her with your children, your most precious possessions."

"Was Nanny Katie a sexual deviant?" Mrs. Rock asks the ozone.

Zuckerman tightens his grip on her arm. She covers her eyes with a trembling hand. For whatever reason, I notice Mrs. Rock is wearing a wig. Maybe because it just slipped forward half an inch.

"The children could be inside!" blurts Rock. "Hiding under their beds." He steps toward the door.

Parker holds up a hand to block him. "You can't go in there, sir. It's a crime scene."

"My children need me!"

"We checked all the beds and closets, sir," says Ceepak.

"Mr. Parker?" A new voice is heard from: a guy hustling up the long hall in a white helmet and bicycle shorts. He's also wearing a blue shirt, police badge, and, if I'm not mistaken, a Sig Sauer P226 automatic in his holster. So is his partner, hustling right behind him.

"Yeah. I'm Parker."

"Vic Tinsley. ACPD. Detective Flynn, our homicide guy, is on his way. We were on patrol, caught the call. We need to keep this room locked down until Flynn arrives."

"Roger that," says Parker. "You might want to call the major crimes unit."

Tinsley takes off his bicycle helmet. "That bad, hunh?"

"Yeah."

Rock turns to the cops. "What about our children? They're missing!"

"We know, sir," says Officer Tinsley. "Mr. Parker gave us full descriptions."

"Why don't you folks head back to your rooms?" Parker suggests. "Wait there. That way, we'll know where to find you as soon as we locate Richie and Britney."

Rock sighs. Nods. "All right. I don't like it none, but all right. Come on, Jessie. David."

The three of them enter AA-6. The Rocks' room is right next door to Katie's. No wonder she and Jake could only have their rough sex while their employers were busy onstage.

The two A.C. cops take up guard positions on either side of the entrance to Katie's room. I hear their radios cackle with all sorts of chatter. A shooting. A stabbing. A drunk-and-disorderly.

"Busy night," says Tinsley as he dials the volume knob down.

Ceepak turns to Parker. "Can we help you search for the children, Cyrus?"

"Definitely. I'll take all the help I can get."

"Did your people see anything of interest on the casino's surveillance cameras?"

"Yeah. They sure did."

"Do you know where they went? Richie and Britney?"

"We don't have that," says Parker. "Not yet."

Then he looks at me.

"Boyle?"

"Yeah?"

"Stick close to Ceepak, okay?"

"Is there some problem?" asks Ceepak, because he heard the same tone in Parker's voice that I just did.

"Maybe."

Now Parker nods up the long hall. Toward the lone surveillance camera.

"Mr. Boyle was the first and only person seen coming down this corridor tonight after the show started."

13

Now my mind is scrambled worse than that scorched egg in the old "this is your brain on drugs" commercial.

Parker thinks I killed Katie Landry?

"Danny was inside the theater for the entire performance," says Ceepak. "He was with me. You saw him, Cyrus."

The big man nods. "They also saw him on the videotape. First person to come backstage after they sealed off the area at seven-fifty-five PM."

"What about the guy guarding the stage door?" I ask. "Samoan-looking dude with a ponytail."

Parker shakes his head. "You were the only one they saw, Boyle."

"Impossible. I talked to this guy. He was one of Rock's security people. Had on a jacket. Said *Event Staff*. He was guarding the stage door."

"Camera didn't see him. Just you."

"At what time?" asks Ceepak.

"Twenty-one twenty-five."

Nine twenty-five PM.

"Look," says Parker, "the medical examiner shows up, pegs the time of death at sometime prior to nine twenty-five, Boyle is in the clear. For the time being, however, he has to be considered a suspect."

Ceepak nods. "Agreed." He turns to face me. "Don't worry, Danny. You will be exonerated. Soon."

Well, duh. I know I didn't do it. Unless I'm one of those psycho serial killers with an alter ego who takes over my body at night and makes me do all the dirty deeds I only dream of doing. Maybe I'm Dr. Danny and Mr. Hyde.

"Hey," I say, "I couldn't have done it. I don't own a bolo tie."

"That may be," says Parker. "But they're readily available at the souvenir shop in the theater lobby."

Oops. I didn't inspect the string tie around Katie's neck. I was too busy freaking out.

"It was one of Rock's?"

Ceepak nods. "The silver medallion at the center was embossed with the 'Rock 'n Wow!' show logo."

Just like the five billion ties they sell wherever Rock takes his show on the road. Like the one Jake and the other dancers wear instead of shirts.

"Come on, Officer Boyle," says Parker. "You need to stick close to Ceepak and Ceepak needs to help me go find those two kids."

We enter another restricted area.

Casino surveillance.

"Welcome to the eye that never blinks," says Parker as we step into a cramped room that reminds me of the Starship *Enterprise*. I see a whole wall filled with flat-screen TVs; at least fifty. Another wall is made up of digital video recorders stacked on top of one another inside steel racks. Two guys and one girl sit in swivel chairs at a console with built-in keyboards and computer screens. All of them are chewing gum like crazy, staring at the images flashing up at them. They click their mice, crack their gum, clack their number pads, make different camera angles pop up.

"We got anything, guys?" asks Parker.

"Maybe," says the woman, who is working her gum the hardest, occasionally pausing to blow out a bubble when she sees something of interest, then popping it when she decides it's time to move on. She never takes her eyes off the screen as it shifts through a rapid-fire series of frame grabs. "They're what? Six and ten?"

"Right," says Parker. "Boy and girl. Blond."

"Great. All we get in here is black-and-white."

"They're in the show."

She nods. "They float in wearing pajamas, right?"

"Yeah."

"One of 'em digs tigers?"

"Come again?"

She taps her screen with a pen. "Got a boy here. Seems to be with his sister. She's holding his hand, dragging him along, almost yanking it out of his shoulder socket. Twenty twenty they were outside the Shalimar Theater."

The kids were both onstage at eight. Katie and her S and M buddy must've torn off the kids' costumes, shoved them into jeans and hoodies, and kicked them out of room AA-4 as soon as they got back there.

"Twenty twenty-two, they're near the shops. Twenty twenty-five they're waltzing across the casino floor. The boy has what looks like a plush tiger strapped to his back. Could be a backpack."

"My nephew has one of those," says the guy sitting next to her. He's clicking through a series of shots from another camera: the one in the long hallway backstage. The one where I'm the star; I can see my back walking down the corridor. "They make a monkey, too."

"Is that Officer Boyle?" Ceepak asks.

"Who?"

I step forward. "Me."

All three computer jockeys look up at me with bleary eyes. They chew their gum in perfect sync. It's like I'm standing in a lineup in front of a barn full of cows.

"Yeah," says the guy. "That's him. First person backstage."

"Why is there no one else in that hallway?" asks Ceepak. "Surely during the show it's a highly trafficked area."

"Not really. There's never anybody back there. Rock's people won't allow it."

"He has his own security guy back there," I say. "Big man. Polynesian. Wears a navy blue windbreaker. Stands near the stage door."

"You mean right here?" He taps on his computer screen at an empty space near the door. "Must be invisible 'cause I've never seen him."

"What about Katie and the kids?" I ask.

"Hunh?"

"If they go backstage after they do that opening bit, why don't you see them in the hallway?"

"Maybe they used a different exit or something."

"Wouldn't matter. You'd see them back there. Crossing the *T* where the two corridors intersect."

"Hey, I don't know," says the guy, who's used to staring at pictures, not listening to them talk back. "Maybe they didn't go to their rooms."

"Yes they did! That's where I found her body."

"Boyle?" says Parker. "First things first. We gotta find the children."

"But . . ."

"Parker's right," says Ceepak.

Fine. But I can tell: he and Parker know I'm right. How the hell could Katie end up dead in her room if the camera didn't even see her walking backstage?

"Put your best shot up on the screen," Parker says to the woman. "Frontal if you've got it. I've met the kids. Know what they look like."

"Hang on. Here we go. This is a head-on shot. Twenty thirty. They're riding escalator E-three."

"That's them," says Parker. "Richie and Britney. Where did they end up?"

"Can't say for certain. I thought they were headed for the ice cream place downstairs. Twenty thirty-two, however, they leave the building."

"Which exit?"

"Boardwalk."

"For a chariot ride," I mumble.

"Come again?" says Parker.

"The boy. He likes the rolling chairs. Calls them chariots."

"This way."

Parker leads us out a side exit—another *Authorized Personnel Only* door. It's faster than trudging across the casino floor.

We come out on a sidewalk running along what must be the service-entrance side of the Xanadu. No flashy lights. No dazzling neon. Just plaster white walls and fluorescent fixtures filled with dead bugs. I see a cluster of uniformed pit people in black vests, white shirts, and red bow ties taking a smoke break near a bench. Across the street is a very seedy, triple-decker motel: the Royal Lode. I think it used to be the Royal Lodge but the *G* is burned out so the sign reads like a bad toilet joke.

To our right, of course, are the ocean and the bustling boardwalk. Under the streetlights, I can see guys in baggy pants and polo shirts pushing those canopied chairs on wheels. The chariot races are underway.

"Let's go," says Parker.

The three of us jog up the sidewalk, hit the boardwalk, slow down as the crowd swarms around us.

"Evening, officers," a voice calls out. "Over here." It's the Great Mandini—the street magician we met in Starbucks, Gary Burdick's AA sponsor. He's wearing his bright red Chinese tunic and a black cape, shuffling cards behind a table with collapsible legs that's covered with a shimmering blue cloth. A shaggy bunny rabbit sits in a frayed top hat, nibbling on a carrot.

"Looking for someone?" he asks.

Guess we look like we're looking for someone, what with the running-up-the-sidewalk-in-a-bunch bit.

"Two children," says Ceepak. "Six-year-old boy. Ten-year-old girl."

The Great Mandini nods. Points. "They went thataway." He grins. "Always wanted to say that."

"Blond hair?" says Parker.

Another wise nod. "Very much so. Just like their father, Mr. Richard Rock."

"You recognized them?"

"Of course. Richie and Britney. I saw their show when it was in previews and the tickets were somewhat less expensive. I was surprised to see the children out this late unsupervised. So I kept one eye on them, the other on my cards."

"Where did they go?"

"Not far. About three hundred yards due north. The girl said she wanted candy apples. The boy wanted a rolling chair ride. They eventually compromised. Hired Royal rolling chair number three-oh-five and proceeded up the boardwalk to my friend Andy's candy-apple stand. You can't miss it. Blinking lights. Smells of hot buttered popcorn and melted caramel."

"Thank you," says Parker.

"Semper Fi, gentlemen. Semper Fi."

What do you know—Mandini's another soldier. Actually a marine. *Semper Fi* is short for "Semper Fidelis," the Marine Corps motto. "Always faithful." It's why some people call their dogs Fido. Short for Fidelis. Ceepak taught me that, back when he named his dog Barkley. I don't know what Barkley's short for.

Anyway, Ceepak and Parker, both former military men, shoot Mandini a quick salute. I sort of wave buh-bye. Mandini rubs the fur behind his bunny's ears.

"Godspeed, gentlemen!"

We run up the boardwalk, bobbing and weaving through the strolling crowds, dodging the rolling chairs. We pass about six psychics and tarot card readers, a couple open-air T-shirt shops, and maybe a dozen Chinese full body massage parlors. Who knew the Chinese were so tense?

"There they are!" I see them first.

"Richie?" yells Parker. "Britney?"

Britney smiles and waves—the queen riding in the back of the homecoming convertible. Her lips are a bright red ring. She looks like my grandmother when she tries to put on lipstick before putting on her glasses. Guess Britney went with the cinnamon-flavored apple.

"Hello, Mr. Parker," she says. "Did they send you to tell us we can go back now?"

"Who?"

"Jake and Nanny Katie. Jake gave us fifty dollars. Told us to go have some fun. Guess they wanted to have some fun, too, hunh?"

14

"You really can't buy all that much with fifty dollars, can you?"

Britney. What a chatterbox.

"When Jake told us to get lost, he gave us a brand new Ulysses S. Grant—that's the president who's on the fifty-dollar bill, in case you've never seen one—I figured I could score like a billion candy apples but, nooooo. They cost like five dollars each and big baby Richie wanted to ride in one of those stupid push chairs that cost like ten dollars. The man who pushed us? He was from Bosnia. Smelled like ass because he had BO. That means body odor."

I just sort of nod. We're in this tight little knot, walking down the boardwalk, making our way back to the Xanadu. Parker is up front, talking into his handheld radio, letting the parents know that we found their two adorable children. Ceepak is behind me, covering our "rear flank" as he called it. I glance over my shoulder and see him scoping out the crowds, searching for a murderer mingling among the mob. Who knew you could do military maneuvers on the boardwalk in Atlantic City?

"Katie made Richie take his homework when they kicked us out," says Britney. "That's what's in his backpack. She made him take it because she's supposed to be our teacher and Richie is a slow learner. I think he might be dyslexic or retarded or something."

I am so glad I never had an older sister. Well, I had Katie. She was a couple months older than me, definitely more mature. But Katie was the cool kind of sister, the type who'd clue you in to what girls really think and tell you all sorts of secret stuff about what was hidden inside the girls' bathroom. Kotex machines. Who knew?

"Richie has to take remedial reading. He's doing *Hop on Pop* while I'm reading *Ella Enchanted* and stuff because I can already read at a seventh-grade level even though I just turned ten and would only be in the fifth grade if we went to regular school."

Richie hasn't said a word since we found him and his sister at the candy-apple stand. Maybe his big sister never lets him talk. Maybe she's right and he has some sort of learning disability.

"You okay, Richie?" I ask.

He nods a *yes*.

"You eat a candy apple?"

He shakes his head *no*.

And that is the extent of our conversation.

"So, did Jake and Katie hook up and get busy?" says Britney. "Did they beat cheeks? That's slang, you know. For 'having sex,' but doing it in a different kind of way. Some ways are pretty gross and look stupid, too. I've seen a book."

"You're ten?"

"Yes. But I'm very mature for my age. Precocious. That's a word I memorized. Means I'm more developed, especially mentally, even though I'm already getting my boobies, too."

The kid talks faster than those TV commercials for prescription drugs listing side effects that may include death and anal leakage.

"Richie, on the other hand, still eats his boogers and blows snot rockets when he isn't busy floating air biscuits. *Air biscuit* means fart."

"Here we go, kids," says Parker. Holding open a door into the casino. "Your parents would like to talk to you."

"Why?" asks Britney.

"I guess because you took off like that."

Britney freezes. Plants both hands on her hips. "We only did what our stupid nanny told us to do!"

"We know," Parker says, leaning down and grinning like he's the friendly ol' bear in a picture book. "I think they want to talk to you about, you know, something else, too. Something pretty serious. Kind of grown-up."

"Oh. Like Jake and Katie doing the nasty?"

Somehow, Parker keeps smiling. "Your mom and dad are downstairs. Uncle Chang's Ice Cream Parlor. Do you like ice cream, Britney?"

She blows Parker the lip-noise equivalent of one of those air biscuits. "Well, duh." She marches into the casino shaking her head and muttering, "Do you like ice cream? Jesus!" like the big man is retarded, too.

We happily drop the kids off with their parents and head back to room AA-4.

The Atlantic City homicide detective has arrived and wants to talk to us. More specifically, he wants to speak to me—the guy who discovered the body and, if the digital video in the surveillance control room is to be believed, the only human being to set foot backstage after "Rock 'n Wow!" started.

"Brady Flynn's a good guy," says Parker as we make our way past two of his casino security guys stationed outside that *Authorized Personnel Only* door near the Shalimar Theater. "Ex-boxer. Former Golden Gloves champ."

We head down the hall.

"He also used to work with Sandy McDaniels. State major crime unit. You know her, right?"

"Roger that," says Ceepak. "I've studied her forensics field guide extensively. Danny and I also had the privilege of working with her on one or two occasions."

"Well, Detective Flynn is almost as good. Helped McDaniels update the fifth edition of her book. Wrote the chapter on computer fraud."

We pass the stage door. I'm looking for Mr. Event Staff. Of course he isn't there. But the door is propped open and I can see some of the set pieces from the show: the archery target, the human-sized Rubik's Cube, and the two glass booths that they used to transport Mrs. Rock from one side of the stage to the other in under a second.

"There he is," says Parker as we hit the *T* and take the right. "Detective Flynn?"

"Yo?"

There's this stocky guy in a suit that looks too small for all his muscles standing outside room AA-4. I figure he's in his late thirties or early forties. Caesar-style haircut. Crooked nose where he took a punch or two from someone else's golden gloves. He's twitching his shoulders a lot.

"I'm Cyrus Parker. Head of hotel security. We've met before."

"Sure, sure. How you doin'?" His head jerks sideways like he has a crick in his neck he can't crack out.

"Been better," says Parker. "This is Danny Boyle. He's the one who found the body. He's also a cop, up in Sea Haven."

"Boyle." Flynn shoots out a hand the size and texture of an antique catcher's mitt. "How you doin'?"

Parker continues with the introductions. "His partner, John Ceepak."

The mitt moves right. "How you doin'?"

"Pleased to make your acquaintance," says Ceepak, who doesn't realize "How you doin'?" is the official manly-man greeting of the Garden State and has been long before Joey showed up on *Friends*.

"Excusemeyouseguys." Flynn mumbles worse than my dad, who always sounds like he's talking to himself even when he's talking to you. The detective turns around. Looks up the hall, toward Mr. and Mrs. Rock's rooms and whatever else is up that way. Leans back. Examines the ceiling tiles.

"Wheresdacameras?"

"Excuse me?" says Parker.

Flynn points up. "How come there ain't no cameras back this way?"

I think that's what he said.

"No need," says Parker. "Security department always considered this hallway an area of minimal interest."

"Yeah. Untiltonight."

"Say again?"

"Until tonight. Major interest tonight, am I right?"

Flynn turns around to gaze in our general direction again. Scrunches up his nose. Doesn't mumble anything so Ceepak jumps in: "I can vouch for Mr. Boyle from nineteen hundred hours through twenty-one twenty."

"Unh-hunh. And that'd be like from seven to like what?"

"Nine-twenty PM," I say since I do the time-clock conversions quicker than Ceepak. "I found the body around nine-thirty."

"Hunh."

Oh-kay. If this guy helped Dr. McDaniels rewrite her book, why do I think the forthcoming fifth edition will be totally incomprehensible?

"You two busy?" Flynn suddenly asks, with another triple twitch of the neck.

"Sir?" says Ceepak.

"Busy?"

"We are at your disposal."

"Good. Good." He nods, tugs at his suit coat, sniffs. "Iheardaboutyousetwo."

Ceepak gives him a quizzical look. Me, too.

"Sandy. McDaniels? Says you're sharp. You guys watch cowboy movies?"

Ceepak looks totally confused. I'm right there with him.

Flynn is unfazed. Guess he's used to nobody understanding what the hell he's talking about.

"Westerns. *The Searchers*? John Wayne?"

Ceepak nods slowly, the way you do when somebody tells you the CIA has implanted GPS transponders in your teeth.

"Too many crimes in this town. Drunks. Disorderlies. Shootingstabbings. Fugghetaboutit." He shakes his head, twitches twice, tugs three times at his lapels. "As youse two undoubtedly know, all New Jersey officers have the authority and, I might add, the duty to enforce all state laws within the confines of New Jersey twenty-fourseven, regardless of your current geographical location. So, I'm hereby deputizin' youse two until we figure out what the hell is goin' on here. And don't ask about the pay. There isn't any. Cyrus?"

"Yeah?"

"I need to see that tape."

"Which one?"

He jabs his thick thumb in my general direction. "Boyle here. Walking down the hall." He scissors two stiff fingers back and forth to, I guess, illustrate a person walking.

"You got it," says Parker.

"Have you established the time of death?" asks Ceepak.

"Hmm?"

"The time of death." Ceepak is accenting every syllable, the way you might if you were talking to a deaf person in a noisy airplane hanger.

"Yeah. Sure. I got a good guesstimate."

"And?" Ceepak waits.

"Hmmm?"

"Is Danny in the clear?"

Flynn nods, which sets off another spasm of sideways head jerks and some more neck-cracking.

"Detective Flynn?" Ceepak wants an answer. "What do you postulate as the time of death for Ms. Landry?"

"Nine. Maybe nine-fifteen. Definitely before the show was over."

"You're certain?"

"Absolutely. Used the Glaister equation. Ninety-eight point four minus measured rectal temperature divided by one point five."

Great. He took Katie's temperature. That way.

"Extremely reliable in this instance what with, you know, the temperature inside being thermostatically controlled since the room is windowless and all. So, like I said, I like Glaister in this particular instance."

Yeah. Me, too. Except for the rectal thermometer bit. Nine or nine-fifteen means I didn't do it.

"That tape?" Flynn says to Parker.

"Yeah. I'll go grab it."

Ceepak raises a finger as if he has a question, which, I guess, he does.

"Hmmm?" says Flynn.

"If we have established that Danny was in the theater at the time of death, why do you still need to see the tape?"

"I'm looking for her."

"Ms. Landry?"

"Yeah. How come, if you see Mr. Boyle walking down the hall, you don't see her?"

Oh, yeah. I love this guy.

We ask the same kind of questions.

15

Around 11:00 PM Parker heads back to his office to deal with the impending PR crisis.

I think the general manager of the Xanadu is coming in for a meeting with his security chief. Probably bringing lawyers and spin doctors. Kinky sex, celebrities, backstage romance, murder, death. This is the stuff *Access Hollywood* and *ET* live for. The Xanadu will try to keep a lid on it.

The Rocks have sent their children upstairs to a regular hotel room. One of their wardrobe supervisors from the show has agreed to be the kids' nanny for the night. Little Richie was still clutching his tiger backpack to his chest. Britney? She wanted her special synthetic down pillow because she's allergic to feathers and threw a temper tantrum when the Atlantic City cops guarding her old room told her she couldn't go in and get it. Kid wailed all the way up the hall. Sounded worse than that singer destroying the Motown oldies out in the lounge.

I follow Ceepak and Detective Flynn into AA-4. When I walk past the two bicycle cops still stationed outside the door, they both nod grimly, glad, for the moment, that they're riding bike patrols instead of being me.

Yeah, I wish I wasn't me, too, because it's time to examine the crime scene. Again.

Detachment.

This was one of the first tricks Ceepak taught me back when we first started working together. He advised an otherworldly separation between your personal feelings and the demands of the job. A cold, analytical approach to stuff that would otherwise tear your guts out. I guess it's how he survived over in Iraq. Yes, your buddies are getting blown to bits by improvised explosive devices but if you freak out about it, you won't be able to save your own ass or help your buddies who are still alive stay that way.

You forget that the body you're examining for clues is the same body you used to admire in a tight white one-piece on Oak Beach when you were both fifteen and that body held all the secrets to everything you ever wanted to know.

"Danny?" says Ceepak. "Is this how you found the crime scene?"

"Yeah." I find just enough voice to push out the one syllable.

"We know the victim," Ceepak says to Detective Flynn.

He nods. Gestures toward Katie's naked, trussed-up body, her grisly S and M death pose. "This sadomasochism situation consistent with what you know of her history?"

"Negative," says Ceepak.

I just shake my head.

"Hunh." Flynn squats into a crouch, rubs his chin, stares at Katie.

So, I look again, too.

We're in what I'll call the sitting room of the two-bedroom suite because there's a couch, two chairs, a small dining table, and four wooden chairs. Lots of places to sit. One door leads into the master bedroom. Another into a smaller bedroom, which, judging from the trail of toys spilling across its threshold, is where Richie and Britney sleep. A third door is open a crack, revealing a tiled wall and floor. Bathroom.

In the center of the sitting room, Katie is pinioned in a spread-eagle seated position on a wooden chair situated directly in front of the armoire storing the TV set. Her hands are cuffed behind her back. Her ankles are lashed to the rear legs of the chair.

"I found a couple pubic hairs, here on the floor," says Flynn. "Black. A whole clump of them."

Katie is—was—a redhead.

"Running the DNA?" asks Ceepak.

"We will," says Flynn. "But the test takes five days. So first, we'll eyeball 'em under the microscope. Match 'em against samples taken from any potential suspects. Dance belts."

"Come again?" says Ceepak.

"This dancer. Jake Pratt. The one what missed the show tonight. Can't nobody find him."

Yep. Jake is definitely a suspect.

"We tagged and bagged his dance belt out of the dressing room. It's like a jockstrap, only for ballerinas. Anyway, we examined this guy Pratt's dance thong. Harvested a couple short curly ones. Black."

Ah, the glamorous life of *CSI: Atlantic City*. Combing through jockstraps.

Detective Flynn goes back to staring at Katie, so I do, too.

I see it all again, in better light this time. The blindfold. The ball gag. The black leather garter belt studded with steel rivets. The silky rope wrapped above and below her breasts.

The bolo tie cinched tight into her neck.

Now Flynn stands up. Shakes his head.

"Not hers," he says.

Ceepak nods. "Agreed."

"What?" I ask.

Flynn nods at Ceepak, encourages him to go ahead and field my question. "The S and M costume," he says. "Ms. Landry did not purchase it."

"We don't know that," I say. "She might've, you know, been into this kind of stuff and kept it secret."

"In which case," says Flynn, his diction crystal clear, the way it must be when he goes to court, "we can safely assume Ms. Landry would have purchased a garter belt that fit. This one is loose—even though the waist strap is buckled through the last slot available. It's two inches too big. A medium when she needed a small. This here was staged to misguide us."

My turn to mumble: " 'Trust none of what you hear and less of what you see.' "

"Hunh?" This from Flynn.

"Springsteen," says Ceepak. "Song lyrics."

"Oh. Right. I'm more a Bon Jovi man, myself. Keep the faith."

I know it's a Bon Jovi song title. Might also be good advice because Detective Flynn just confirmed what I hoped was true: Katie Landry was not a skanky sex kitten. True, she may not have been the Saint Katie I imagined her to be, but the loose-fitting garter belt means she wasn't filling out applications at Larry Flynt's Hustler Club, either. Somebody was trying to trash her reputation, make us believe a lie.

"Could be fingerprints on that silver tie ornament," says Flynn, now eyeing the murder weapon.

"Unless, of course, the perpetrator was wearing gloves," says Ceepak.

"Which he probably was," says Flynn. "He came in here prepared. Had a limited window of opportunity. Time constraints."

Ceepak nods his agreement. "He wanted to commit this murder while Rock's show was still in progress."

Now Flynn nods. "While the backstage security camera was disabled."

"Do we know that?" asks Ceepak.

"Had to be." He does the finger-walking bit again. "Otherwise we would've seen her with the kids, seen the kids leaving. Payperviewporno?" Flynn's mumbling again, nodding toward the master bedroom.

"Roger that," says Ceepak. "Mr. Parker has already requested information on when the movie was ordered from the front desk."

"Uhm-hmmm. More window dressing. Misdirection. Make us think Ms. Landry was some kind of sex addict. Swiftboat her."

"Still," says Ceepak, "the time of the video activation coupled with your time-of-death analysis should help us pinpoint more precisely when the killer was in these rooms."

"Yes, indeed, it should," says Flynn, with the faint hint of a grin. "Sandy was right. Youse guys are good."

Now the two of them shift their attention to a stack of books sitting on the small table. I see a couple marble-covered Mead composition books, *Hop on Pop*, and a world history textbook. There are also a couple more Meads scattered on the floor—near the table legs.

Ceepak bends down beside one of the notebooks and extracts a small leather case from his right rear pocket. Unzips it. Removes stainless-steel tweezers.

Usually, my partner packs all sorts of evidence-gathering gear into the pockets of his cargo pants. When he attends the theater, however, he dresses up. Banana Republic khakis. No spare pants pockets. I figure this little cordovan wallet must be the tool kit he packs for a night out on the town.

He uses the pincers to open one notebook with a childish scrawl on the front: *Math.*

"Multiplication tables." Ceepak opens a few others. "English compositions. History reports."

"Ms. Landry their teacher?"

"And nanny."

"I want to take a sample of the rope," says Flynn. "Odd color. Silk, you think?"

"Definite possibility," says Ceepak. "It looks very similar to the ropes used in Mr. Rock's magic act."

"Okay," says Flynn. "MCU is on the way. Dr. McD's people will comb the carpet. Fibers. More hairs. Dust for prints. Call the coroner."

My detachment disintegrates.

The coroner.

They're coming to take Katie away. Put her in a body bag, take her to the morgue. Put her in a coffin. Put her in the ground.

Ceepak places a hand on my shoulder. "Danny?"

"Yeah?"

"Perhaps you should reexamine the bathroom for us."

"Yeah."

In other words, "get outta here, partner." No need to remain in the living room with the dead body. No need to watch the somber men come in and zip Katie inside a black vinyl bag, tote her out the door looking like lumpy ski luggage.

"That's the kids' bathroom," says Flynn. "Dora the Explorer toothbrush. Cherry-flavored Crest. Footstool. Tub is full. Up to the drain latch. Must've been bathtime for one of them. Probably the boy."

Guess the detective has already checked it out.

"That would suggest," says Ceepak, "if she had been drawing a bath for one of the children, Ms. Landry had not been expecting her assailant's arrival."

"That it would," says Flynn. "That it would."

Wow. This guy's good, too.

Flynn head-gestures toward Katie. "I still want to . . . before the coroner . . ."

"I assumed as much," says Ceepak.

Why do I think they want to examine Katie for evidence of what they call *entry*?

"I'll be in here." I head into the bathroom. Seems appropriate: I'm off to the kids' table so the grown-ups can discuss adult stuff.

I use a fingertip to close the door, steer clear of the doorknob. Don't want to contaminate any potential fingerprint fields.

There's a brightly colored toy tugboat floating in the placid ocean filling the tub. Guess that's how Flynn figured it was the boy who was getting ready for a bath when Jake came in and handed the kids fifty bucks to go get lost. I wonder if he even gave Richie time to dry off.

I stare at myself in the bathroom mirror.

I look worn out. Older than I remember being this morning. Yes, I'm still twenty-five, but I feel like I'm seventy-five or whatever age it is when you start going to more funerals every year than weddings.

I use one finger to lever open the sink taps and let water rush into the bowl. Hot. Nearly scalding.

I just let it run.

The sound is reassuring. A faint mist rises. When I was a kid with a cement head, all stuffy and congested from a cold, my mom would spoon Vicks VapoRub into the little medicine cup that came with our humidifier and make me breathe in big clouds of eucalyptus-scented steam.

Guess the Xanadu's hot-water heater works better than my mom and dad's because the mirror is already starting to fog up. Fast. I adjust the knobs to cool it off. Cup some lukewarm water into my hands. Splash it against my face. Taste the sweat and some of the fear as it washes away. I turn off the hot, put my hands under the spigot, bowl up a load of cold and splash it into my eyes.

When I blink them open again, I'm staring at the mirror.

Reading what somebody had finger-written there the last time the mirror fogged up:

J Luvs U.

A loopy, Valentine's Day heart frames the letters.

J.

Jake.

16

Who needs a pubic-hair match when the killer basically smears his confession on the bathroom mirror?

Jake.

He killed Katie in a fit of rage. Maybe because she wouldn't spice up their sex life and go buy her own S and M outfit. So he bought one for her. Kicked out the kids. Forced Katie to put the stuff on, hoping she'd warm up to the idea of dressing like a bondage freak. Maybe he tried to turn her on to the whole erotic asphyxiation game.

And when he tugged too hard, he killed the woman he loved.

Guilt-ridden, he ran in here, took a shower.

No. Wait. He would've had to drain the bathtub first.

So, maybe he finger-painted the message this afternoon. Maybe they had a quickie on Katie's lunch break and Jake scribbled his fifth-grade mash note after *that* shower.

Whatever. This definitely implicates him. Jake.

I'm all set to call out to Ceepak and Detective Flynn—show them our newfound evidence—when I hear voices.

They're muffled. This bathroom has two doors: one opening up into the room where Ceepak and Flynn are still examining Katie. The other?

Guess it connects to Mr. and Mrs. Rock's suite because I recognize his voice.

"You're a big stupid fuck!"

"Yes, sir."

"How could you let this happen?"

"I don't know. . . ."

"What the fuck *do* you know, you fucking moron?"

Richard Rock, Mr. Family Values, has quite a temper offstage, not to mention a severely limited vocabulary. Most of his words come out of the *F* file.

"Fuck, fuck, fuck . . ."

"Yo, sir—I'm sorry. Chill."

Now I recognize the other voice, too. It's the big Samoan bruiser who told me, "Take the right. AA-four's the second suite down." Mr. Event Staff. The invisible man.

I shove open the door.

"Hey!" Rock says when he sees me. "You can't come in here. This is a private room!"

"Ceepak?" I'm shouting. "Detective Flynn!"

The Samoan, still in his navy blue windbreaker, takes a step forward.

"Don't move," I shout at him. "I'm with the police."

The Hawaiian whale throws up both his hands to let me know he isn't looking for trouble. "I'm cool, bro. We're cool."

"Get him the fuck out of here!" screams Rock.

"Freeze!" Ceepak. Behind me.

"That's him!" I flail my arm and point. Highly unprofessional, sure, but I'm excited. "That's the security guy who was backstage when I came down the hall after the show."

"What's the problem?" Detective Flynn squeezes past me.

"Nothing," says Rock.

"Somebody stole Mr. Rock's secret notebooks!" says the Samoan, pointing at a small trunk tucked underneath the table in Mr. and Mrs. Rock's sitting room.

"You were burglarized this evening?" asks Flynn.

"Maybe," says Rock. "We don't know for sure."

"It's nothing," says Mrs. Rock as she breezes into the living room, trailed by Zuckerman. "No need to involve the police. David can take care of it."

"Of course I can, Richard."

"Don't you fucking fucks tell me—"

"Mr. Rock?" Ceepak's booming voice. The one he probably used to clear traffic jams when he was an MP. Tank traffic jams.

"What?" Rock's frat-boy face is burning red with rage.

Ceepak remains calm. "Please sit down, sir." He indicates that the nearby couch would be a good place for him to do that.

"Who the hell are you again?"

"John Ceepak. Atlantic City PD."

"What?"

Detective Flynn nods. "He's one of my new deputies." It's his turn to point at the couch. "Sit. Stay. All of youse."

It's a good thing we're in a hotel.

Lots of rooms to send people to while we try to sort a few things out.

The message scrawled on the bathroom mirror.

The miraculous reappearance of Mr. Event Staff.

The possible theft of Mr. Rock's secret notebooks.

We'll talk to Richard and Jessica Rock first. One of the uniformed cops escorts the ponytailed security dude to a small room up the hall where he'll wait to be questioned. Meanwhile, the state's major crimes unit has arrived—a trio of highly skilled crime-scene investigators dressed in sterile white Tyvek coveralls so they look like a walking subdivision before the vinyl siding goes up. They just added the bathroom mirror to their to-do list.

Detective Flynn is with the CSI crew in AA-4, helping them comb the carpet. This leaves the interrogation duties in AA-6 to his two newest deputies: Ceepak and me.

The Rocks sit side by side on the couch. David Zuckerman, their manager, sits in one of the cushioned chairs with matching fabric. Gray with color sprinkles. Mr. Rock sips a warm glass of milk. His wife nuked it for him.

"Reckon I owe you boys an apology," he says, giving us his best head bob and aw-shucks grin. "Didn't mean to bust loose like that."

"Richard is usually very calm," says his wife. "And he would never, ever use that kind of language onstage, not in front of children."

" 'Course not. Feel bad enough I used it in front of you folks."

"Understandable reaction," adds Zuckerman. "There's been a murder here tonight. The children went missing. And now, this?" He flaps a hand at the footlocker. Snicks his tongue.

I check out my partner's reaction. Ceepak's jaw is set. Eyes locked. None of the apologizing means diddly-squat to him right now. He's in the Zone.

"What was stolen?" he asks.

"Couple notebooks," says Rock.

"That's all?"

Rock nods.

"Estimated value?" asks Ceepak.

I'm guessing $3.50 at Staples.

"Priceless," says Zuckerman.

"I take it these notebooks contain the secrets to your illusions?"

"That's right," says Rock. "See, I do me up one notebook per trick. Helps me keep organized. If I get a new idea, I open a new notebook. Mix 'n match 'em when puttin' together a new show. I never let nobody else look at 'em. Top secret."

"They took Lucky Numbers," says Zuckerman. "No wonder the sneaky bitch was so late!"

"Lady Jasmine?" says Ceepak.

Zuckerman nods. "She took her seat two seconds before Lucky Numbers went up because she was back here burgling us. The goddamn slant-eyed—"

I think Ceepak's heard enough family-unfriendly tirades for one night. He cuts Zuckerman off. "Where was your security man stationed?"

"Tupula?"

So. Event Staff has a name.

"Where was he during tonight's performance?"

"Outside the stage door," says Zuckerman. "Same place he's always positioned."

And yet he never appears on camera? Interesting.

"Did Tupula see Lady Jasmine or any member of her entourage in the backstage area?"

"If he did, he ain't telling us about it," says Rock. "But, come to think of it, ol' two-ton Tupula could be on the take, you know? Workin' both sides against the middle. You're either workin' for me, or against me. Tupula Tuiasopo? Boy's slicker than fried lard." Mr. Rock appears to be winding himself up again. F-bomb alert now in effect for the entire tristate region.

"Why is he unseen on the surveillance tapes?" asks Ceepak.

"Confidential," says Zuckerman.

"Come again?"

"That information is classified."

Ceepak's eyebrows rise in what I'd call extreme puzzlement. These guys run a magic show, not the CIA.

Zuckerman reads his expressions and tries to explain: "We need to maintain a veil of secrecy over our illusions or we'll disappoint the loyal fans who flock to Richard's shows. Look, here's how I propose we handle the situation." He flips open his clipboard case. "We will hire, at our own expense, a private investigator. In fact, we already have a PI on retainer, a private contractor who helps us handle ongoing security issues. This gentleman will be charged with locating the missing notebooks and keeping their highly confidential contents under wraps. We see no reason to sidetrack you gentlemen with a second investigation. You do the murder. We'll handle the burglary."

"Sir?" says Ceepak.

Zuckerman blinks like someone just blew soot in his eyes. "Yes?"

"The two incidents are most likely linked. The time for secrecy and prevarication is over."

In other words, Ceepak's all done tolerating lies and liars, something he will only do within the confines of a casino theater and only for the short duration of an abracadabra cowboy's blatantly bogus hocus-pocus. After that, the code kicks in, baby, big-time.

"Why was the security guard unseen by the camera mounted in the hallway?"

"As I stated previously, we are not going to answer that," says Zuckerman. "Not now. Not until you get a court order and, even then, we will need to talk to our own legal representation regarding the privacy and copyright protection issues such an answer might entail."

"Who is Jake?" Ceepak zigs to Jake when Rock and Company expect him to keep zagging on about the camera.

The magician puts down his milk glass. "Jake Pratt? He's one of my chorus boys. A very talented but very troubled young man."

"Why did he miss this evening's performance?"

Rock shrugs. "I wish I knew. Boy's nineteen. Loose as ashes in the wind. But, I tell you what, I'm gonna give ol' Jake a good tongue-lashing next time I do see him. Might even hand him his walkin' papers, too."

"Do you know where Mr. Pratt is currently located?"

"Probably in a bar somewhere getting soused," says Zuckerman.

Rock gives his manager a head shuck. "Now, David."

"The boy's nothing but trouble, Richard. Always has been. Juvenile delinquent." Zuckerman turns to Ceepak. "You'll see. The kid's got a record. Done time. Big-time."

"He was in a home for wayward boys," says Rock. "But that don't mean he's beyond redemption. He's very talented, David. Don't misunderestimate him."

"Where is Mr. Pratt staying while you're performing in Atlantic City?" asks Ceepak.

"I can't recall," says Zuckerman. "When we're on the road, we give the cast and crew a housing allowance. Some of the kids room together. Find a place, split the rent. Mostly motels. Not the Xanadu or any of the other major casinos. We're generous with our per diems. Not crazy. Most find more affordable accommodations at the local Holiday Inn, Econo Lodge, Super Eight. Places like that."

"Do you have a list of the cast members' current residences?"

Zuckerman nods. "Sure. Our stage manager Christina Crites has it. Addresses. Phone numbers, too."

"We need a copy. ASAP."

"Consider it done."

Finally. Stubble head cooperates. He actually pulls out his cell, walks into the other room, makes a call.

"Were Jake Pratt and Katie Landry romantically involved?" Ceepak asks Mr. and Mrs. Rock.

"I don't know," says Rock. "Don't pay much attention to backstage hooey like that. Although I personally disapprove of premarital sexual relationships, I figure it's none of my business if folks are eatin' supper before they say grace."

"They were," says Mrs. Rock.

"Really?" Her husband seems surprised.

She smiles at us. "Men. So oblivious."

"Were they dating?" asks Ceepak.

Now she gives my partner a coy little grin as she smoothes out her lap a little.

"Well, Officer Ceepak, I don't think they were sipping ice cream sodas down at the corner drugstore, if that's what you mean. However, Nanny Katie, like many women, was not immune to the allure of a younger man, especially one as attractive as Jake Pratt. Many of the gals in the show felt the same way."

Now her mischievous blue eyes tell me something else: Mrs. Rock was one of those "gals."

17

"Mr. Richard Rock is a great, great man," says Tupula Tuiasopo. "I'd cut off my right arm for him."

Of course he'd need a chainsaw: the arm in question is as wide around as one of those redwood stumps out in California, where, we learned, Mr. Tuiasopo grew up after moving to the mainland from Hawaii. He played football for UCLA, graduated, went into the Hollywood bodyguard business, and has been wearing Event Staff windbreakers for close to fifteen years, ten of them with Richard Rock.

Such were the preliminaries gleaned when we sat down with Mr. Tuiasopo. We're in another backstage room. The sign on the door said WARDROBE. The clothes in here could blind you: Mrs. Rock's glitzy gowns, the dancers' spangled cowboy hats.

"I love Richard Rock. Love what he's doing for the kids, you know?" Tuiasopo tugs at his corded hair rope. "He tells the kids to stay away from drugs. Just say no, you know?"

"Commendable," says Ceepak. "Mr. Tuiasopo, where were you at eight PM this evening?"

"Where I always be."

We wait. Tuiasopo rocks in his chair. Guess that's all he's got on that one.

So Ceepak helps him out: "And where are you typically positioned at eight PM?"

"At the stage door. Eight PM is when the show starts so I need to be backstage, keep that area secure. Can't let nobody back that way."

"Why?"

"You know."

"No. I don't."

"Security concerns."

"What kind of security concerns?"

"Secrets."

"How do you subvert the video feed?"

"Hunh?"

I translate: "How come we didn't see you on the surveillance camera? We saw the door, but not you."

"For real?"

"For real."

"That's wild, man." I'm starting to wonder if Tupula Tuiasopo might've "just said yes" when somebody offered him a spliff of Maui wowie, primo bud imported from back home.

Ceepak tries again: "Mr. Tuiasopo?"

"Yo. Dude. Call me Toohey."

"Do you disable the video camera on a nightly basis?"

"Can't say what I do or what I don't do, except to say I do my job, you know?"

"Does your job include disabling surveillance equipment?"

"Can't say."

"Can't or won't?"

"Can't, dude. I signed the papers. Stack this thick." He spreads open his thumb and index finger to indicate the phone book or a nice T-bone. "Richard Rock Enterprises confidentiality agreement. Signed it when they hired me so if I told you what I know, somebody would have to kill me."

"Like somebody killed Katie Landry?" I say because the big macadamia nut's aloha spirit is starting to drive this Jersey boy up the freaking wall.

"Yeah. I heard about that. Bummed me out bad, man. Nanny Katie was a sweet kid. Cute, too. Didn't know she was into the kinky costume action. Guess we can never know another person's soul if they choose to keep it, you know, unknowable."

"All we want to know," I say, "is how the hell you screwed with the goddamn camera!"

"Danny?" This from Ceepak. With a head shake.

Toohey holds up both his paws. "Yo, little brother—listen to what the big man says. Chill. Hang loose." He makes a fist, extends his thumb and pinky, and jiggles his hand. The surfer's salute.

"So, tell me," says Ceepak, "how did you compromise the camera's integrity?"

Okay. Fine. Ceepak used his grown-up words to ask the same thing I just asked.

"Like I said, dude—I can't say. I took an oath of office."

"Did you see Miss Landry this evening?" Ceepak asks.

"Sure, sure. Said, 'Hey, Katie' when she and the kids came out the stage door like they always do."

"What time?"

"Usual time."

Ceepak finger-drums a solo on his kneecap to let Toohey know we're waiting for a better answer.

"Five or six after eight," he says. "Right after they do the floating pajamas bit with their pops onstage."

"Did you see anybody else in the backstage area? In the corridor?"

"Nobody who wasn't supposed to be there."

"Who did you see?"

"Somebody from the show."

"Who?"

"Dancer."

Ceepak's neck tendons stretch taut. "Who, Mr. Tuiasopo?"

"Just this dude."

"Who?"

"Jake. Jake Pratt."

"When?" asks Ceepak.

"A little later."

"How much later?"

"I don't know. Minute or two. I thought it was kind of weird, you know, cause Jake was supposed to be onstage. Like I said, he's one of the dancers. He's also supposed to help slide props around and stuff. He's totally important for the tiger bit."

"Where the tiger is turned into a tabby cat?"

"You seen the show, hunh?"

"Yes. What are Mr. Pratt's duties during the tiger trick?"

"Dance around. Push the mirrors away when nobody's looking because Mr. Rock has those sparks coming out of his fingertips and Mrs. Rock is wearing that gown over there." He points at the rack. "It, like, totally shows off her hooters, so nobody's gonna be lookin' at what cowboy Jake's doin' in the background, not while Mrs. Rock is shaking her bazoombas, am I right, dude?"

Ceepak nods. Grudgingly.

"I wonder who Jake's understudy is." Toohey kneads his chin thoughtfully. "Somebody else probably had to fill in for him, you know? I mean, if he was coming offstage, he couldn't be onstage at the same time sliding mirrors. Oh, shit."

"What?"

"I don't think I'm allowed to, you know, say that. About the mirrors. Shit, dude. I am so totally screwed."

"Don't worry," says Ceepak. "The use of mirrors to mask illusions is not news to anyone who has studied the practice of magic."

"For real?"

"The simple manipulation of reflected space is how Houdini made a giant elephant named Jennie disappear at the Hippodrome in 1918. Angled mirrors in a large box." He pauses. "Or a small one. Danny?"

"Yeah?"

"How far up the hallway is the surveillance camera?"

"About halfway down, between the stage door and the exit to the casino corridor."

"Did you pass any other doors before you reached the camera?"

"Yeah. One."

"What did it look like?"

"The same, I guess. Gray. Steel. Nothing special."

Now Ceepak smiles at Toohey. "So, tell me, Mr. Tuiasopo—who flips the mirror in front of the camera lens prior to curtain time? You or Mr. Rock?"

"Hah! Neither one! Mr. Zuckerman does it! Heh-heh-heh. Man, dude—for a cop, you are one lousy detective!"

18

We abandon Tupula Tuiasopo and head out to the hall, down to where that solitary surveillance camera is mounted.

We stare up at the eye in the sky. As I noticed earlier, it's not covered with a dome: just a boxy camera jutting out from the wall on an angled metal arm.

"See it, Danny?"

"Yeah. I think. Maybe." I don't see a thing.

Ceepak, however, does. He reaches up, in front of the camera's lens, and pinches what looks to me to be empty air. However, he snaps off an invisible cover of some sort—like opening up a remote to change the batteries, only you can't see the remote. He shows me a *V*-shaped box with mirrors on both its angled sides.

"The mirrored panels reflect the surrounding wall and ceiling, Danny—rendering the box, itself, invisible."

What's underneath the clever little box is even more interesting.

A gizmo of springs and wires hooked up to a pivoting mirror like you'd see if you tore apart your brother's kaleidoscope the day after Christmas to see how it worked. The pivoting mirror isn't much bigger than a postage stamp. It's anchored to the camera lens by a bent copper-wire contraption. Looks like somebody rearranged the parts to one of the plate hangers my mother used to display her Princess Diana collection all over our dining room walls.

Ceepak does a three-finger chop up the hallway to where it *T*'s into the corridor leading to the performers' suites. "The darkness at the far end of the hall matches the shadows near the authorized personnel only entryway."

He's right. I wonder if Rock's crew adjusted the overhead lighting fixtures to achieve the effect.

"See the small flip switch?"

I do once he points to it.

"The trip trigger is located *behind* the lens so a person in the camera's blind spot can activate it. Note also the angle of the mirrored glass. That slight canting creates a safe zone along the right-hand wall, all the way back to the door off the casino corridor. Think of a right triangle."

Fine. If I have to.

"If you know the angle of the mirror, the distance between the two side walls, and assumed a ninety-degree angle at the base of your triangle, you could compute the triangle's hypotenuse. Simple math, utilizing the Pythagorean theorem."

Wow. Pythagoras. Twice in one day. That hasn't happened since eighth grade.

"Triangulating from the camera lens, you would know the complementary triangle said hypotenuse created along the right-hand wall and, if you stayed within that triangle's confines, you could pass underneath the camera and enter the shielded area on the far side undetected." He turns and chops his hand up the hall again, up toward the *T* and Katie's room. "All movement beyond this point, including all activity at or around the real stage door, would remain unseen."

"And then somebody flips the mirror back—right after the show's over."

Ceepak nods. "Clarifying why you are seen as the first person entering this area. You were the first one to enter its field of vision after the mirror was flipped away from the lens at the conclusion of this evening's performance."

"I'll bet Tuiasopo flipped the switch! Right after I walked by the stage door."

"Perhaps. I suspect that, on closer examination, we might notice the slightest flash or jolt in the video playback prior to your entrance."

"If that little black-and-white camera is sophisticated enough to pick up something so subtle."

"Which they, most likely, are not," says Ceepak. "Remember, Danny: Mr. Rock is a master illusionist. He and his engineers understand physics. Trigonometry. Optics. All of this was taken into consideration when designing what appears to our untrained eyes to be nothing more than a miniature mirror attached to a thin metal spring."

The double doors at the far end of the hall squeak open.

"Thank you, Officer," says a familiar female voice. "Have your son give me a call the next time he's in Sea Haven."

Becca Adkinson.

One of my best buds from back home.

One of Katie's, too.

19

"Ceepak called me."

I nod.

Becca Adkinson and I are sitting backstage at the Shalimar Theater on a couple stools we found in the wings—back near the ropes and pulleys and counterweights they use to fly in the scenery. It's pretty dark. The only light comes from center stage, where a naked 300-watt bulb stands guard in a cage at the top of a pole.

The shadows here at the side of the stage are long and jagged, which is fine by Becca and me because we're used to sitting in the dark to talk about serious stuff. It's what we'd do back home: find a beach bench, sit under the stars, listen to the waves crash against the shore, and talk about all the things you can never really talk about under bright fluorescent tubes. It's easier for guys to talk in the dark because you can't see your listener's face; can't tell if she's yawning, staring blankly, or laughing. Darkness is why we have pillow talk, why we say stuff in bed we might regret saying anywhere else.

"I've been crying for hours," Becca says between sniffles.

I just nod.

I haven't had time to cry. Don't know when or if I will. I don't cry much. Except at movies about dogs that die before they should. Or when Mr. Gower, the drunken druggist in that Christmas movie, slaps George Bailey on his bum ear.

Becca sniffles and trembles out a small laugh. "I probably look like hell."

I nod again. Reflex.

"Gee, thanks, Danny-boy."

"Sorry."

Becca is blond, built, and, since she basically grew up on a beach, very concerned about outward physical appearances. Goes to the gym six days a week. Hits the tanning salon for a spray-on job in February. If you spend the majority of your working life in a bathing suit, this sort of body-obsession stuff happens.

Becca's folks own the Mussel Beach Motel back home in Sea Haven. She's been helping them run it since she was old enough to fold towels or put a plastic-wrapped toothpaste cup next to a sink. Instead of LEGOs or blocks, she built dollhouses out of little bars of hotel soap. Her Barbie's hair always smelled like Camay.

"Jess and Olivia wanted to come down," she says. "The Delianides sisters, too. I told them not to."

"Probably smart."

"Yeah." Becca shakes her head. "I can't believe the marshmallow crew lost another member." She digs in her tiny purse, searching for a fresh Kleenex. Finds a Starbucks napkin instead.

The marshmallow crew is what the six of us used to call ourselves when we were kids. Becca, Jess, Olivia, Katie, Mook, Me.

We would hang out on the beach all summer long, toast marshmallows on illegal bonfires we kept kindled way past midnight because we were toasted on beer and Boone's Farm wine.

Katie and Mook are now both dead.

"I saw her this afternoon," I say. "Katie."

Now it's Becca's turn to nod.

"I always thought that, you know, someday she and I would get back together."

Becca blows her nose into that napkin. "What?"

"Katie and me. I figured, one day, you know, we'd get married."

Man, does Becca shoot me a look. "No, you did not."

"Yunh-hunh."

"Ha! You did not!"

"Did too!"

Sometimes, when you hang out with friends you've known since the third grade, you revert to your third-grade level conversational skills.

"Get out of town! That is so bogus!"

"For real, Becca." I think we just leapfrogged forward to middle school.

"Danny, when was the last time you even talked to Katie?"

"I told you: this afternoon."

"Cha. Sure. But before that?"

"I dunno. After she left town. We talked on the phone."

"When?"

"This one time. I forget the exact date, okay?"

"You call her any time in the last twelve months?"

"I sent her a Christmas card."

"That e-card with the singing dogs you sent me?"

Busted. "Yeah."

"Danny, come on—what do you even know about Katie?"

"I might know more than you think I do. I met her new boyfriend this afternoon."

"No, you did not."

"Yunh-hunh. Did too." Yeah, I'm back to third grade. Maybe kindergarten. "His name is Jake. Jake Pratt. He's a dancer. Looks like he used to work at Chippendales." I don't mention that I think he killed Katie.

"He was a hunk?"

"Yeah. I guess." Becca has always been interested in the chiseled male physique. Buys a dozen hot-firefighters calendars every year, rotates them.

She shakes her head. "You don't know crap about Katie."

"What?"

"For your information, Danny Boyle, Katie never, ever dated hunks. Preferred a big brain and a sense of humor to bulging biceps or six-pack abs."

Okay. She did date me, and I'm not currently featured on any hot-cops calendars.

"And," Becca continues, "just for the record, her last boyfriend was not some guy named Jake. It was Ed Kaufman."

"Who?"

"Ed Kaufman. A sixth-grade teacher out there in San Mateo. They worked at the same school. They were hot and heavy for almost a year."

"A year?"

Wow. Katie probably showed this Kaufman guy my electronic Christmas card.

"They broke up a month ago. He wasn't ready to 'settle down.' His words, not Katie's."

"She wanted to marry this Kaufman guy?"

"I think so. We talked about it. Whether she should have a beach wedding out there or back here."

Becca wins. I know absolutely nothing about who Katie Landry is—or, I guess, was. All I know is who she used to be to me and who I made her out to be in my mind—all of it, of course, based on ancient memories and a big dose of present-day guilt.

"Why do you think Katie quit a job she loved and went to work for the Rocks? Do you think she was really working on her master's degree in elementary education so she could become a nanny to two spoiled brats? Well, one spoiled brat. She told me she liked the boy. What's his name?"

"Richie."

"Yeah. Little Richie Rich, she called him. Like in the comic books."

"You talked to Katie?"

"All the time, Danny. It's something girls do better than guys. We keep in touch with our friends—even after they move. It's how we stay friends."

My turn to nod again.

"Wow," is all I can say.

My mind is further scrambled.

Misperception meets reality. More mirrors, only this time, they're angled upstairs in my brain, reflecting back what I wanted to see.

Becca reaches over. Squeezes my hand. She and I dated once. A long, long time ago. Back when, for some reason I thankfully forget, we were all urging each other to "Get Jiggy Wit It."

Neither one of us speaks. Which is a good thing. Gives me a second to think about what she's been trying to say.

Don't tell Ceepak, but I've been seriously violating his code.

I've spent half a day lying to myself.

Imagining that Katie Landry was my soul mate. How could she be, when I haven't even talked to her for more than a year?

How could I pretend that one day she and I would get married when I don't even know what kind of cereal she likes for breakfast? She might prefer eggs. Maybe Eggos. Who knows? Not me.

So, I've been more or less moping around, hiding from the truth.

I don't love Katie Landry.

Hell, I don't even know who she really was.

Maybe that's why I feel so guilty about her dying.

I used to know every freckle on Katie's face, back, and chest. Used to trace constellations between them. But, with time, we lost touch with each other. It happens. Just ask Springsteen. He's sung all sorts of songs about people who swore they would never part and then, little by little, drifted from each other's heart.

"Danny?"

"Yeah?"

"You want to go home? Sit and sulk in your apartment?"

"No, thanks. My room here is nicer."

"Then grow up a little, okay? This isn't about you. This is about Katie. Somebody killed her."

"I know that. I'm the one who found the body."

"Good. Because you're a cop and that's exactly what Katie needs right now. She needs you and Ceepak to stand up for her and find out who the hell did this! She needs that a lot more than she needs you feeling ashamed about not calling her on her birthday last year."

Becca gets up from her stool.

"Where you going?" I ask.

"Wherever they take Katie."

"The morgue?"

"It's what I can do, Danny. You and Ceepak, on the other hand, can do a whole lot more."

True.

First off, we can go find Jake Pratt.

The guy who, according to Becca, wasn't Katie Landry's boyfriend.

But—he might've been her killer.

20

Becca Adkinson climbs into the back of an ambulance parked at a loading dock behind the Shalimar Theater—out where the casino crowds can't see it and think somebody had a heart attack when they hit the jackpot.

She's going to ride with Katie Landry's body to Shore Memorial Hospital, which leases morgue space to the Atlantic County medical examiner.

"Danny?" Ceepak flicks his chin toward the door.

We have work to do inside and Katie needs us in there doing it. The ambulance drifts away quietly. No need for sirens or speed, not on this run.

"Come on in, youse guys."

Detective Flynn motions for us to join him in something called the Golden Dragon Room. It looks like a corporate boardroom. Must be for business meetings to justify the tax deduction when a bunch of bond traders decide to take a quick junket down to Atlantic City.

A dozen red-leather rolling chairs are lined up on either side of a black-lacquer table as long and wide as an aircraft carrier. There are no windows—just thick, red drapes to make you think there might be one. The curtains match the carpet. So much so, it's hard to tell where one red sea ends and the other begins.

Two chairs on the far side of the table are already occupied. In one sits the skinny man with the greasy hair we met earlier in the theater lobby. The skeevoid Ceepak politely asked to stop swearing in front of all the little children. Krabitz. I think that's his name.

David Zuckerman sits in the other chair. He flips open his aluminum clipboard cover.

"Youse guys met?" asks Flynn, jabbing a backward left hook toward Krabitz and Zuckerman.

"I believe so," says Ceepak.

"You're that fucking meathead who gave me the fucking lecture in the lobby. What the fuck are you doing here?"

"Detective Flynn asked for our assistance."

"What?"

"They're cops, Kenneth," explains Zuckerman. "Police."

"Well, stay the fuck out of my way!"

Ceepak grins. "Excuse me?"

"Stay the fuck out of my way!"

"Why?"

"Because I'll find this guy before you two twits ever do!"

"That's not going to happen."

Now Flynn acts like a ref in the middle of the ring, holds up both hands.

"Breakitup. Everybodysitdown."

He tugs up on his suit coat. Does a couple shoulder dips. When the twitches subside, he rummages around in a pocket. Finds a scrap of paper. Roll of breath mints. Business card.

He squinches his eyes to read it.

"Deputies Ceepak and Boyle, meet Mr. Kenneth Krabitz." He flips the card over a few times, looking for more information. "Apparently, he's a PI. Private investigator."

"That's right," says Krabitz, leaning back in his chair. "I'm on a full-time floating retainer with Rick Rock Enterprises."

"Not for nothin'," says Flynn, "but you really ought to consider printing the PI information on your business card."

"Duly noted," says Krabitz. "I'll take it under advisement."

"I wanted this sit-down," says Flynn, "because Mr. Rock has asked his PI, Mr. Krabitz here, to aid in the search for his stolen property. The notebooks."

"We now suspect Jake Pratt was involved in their theft," says Zuckerman.

"You mind explaining how you made that logic leap?" says Flynn, leading with his chin a couple times.

"Easy," says Zuckerman. "Young Mr. Pratt has stolen things from the show in the past. Costume pieces. Stage props. Items from the souvenir shop in the lobby. In Vegas, he was suspended without pay for two weeks when we discovered that he had set up something of a Richard Rock emporium on eBay."

"So," says Krabitz, "I'm gonna go out there and find the little fuck."

"You, of course, know we're looking for Pratt, too," says Flynn. "He is a person of interest in the death of Ms. Kathleen Landry."

Krabitz tosses up both his hands. "Don't worry, Detective. I'll turn the chorus boy over to you guys just as soon as he gives me the fucking notebooks. Scout's honor."

"Have you checked his room at the Holiday Inn?" Zuckerman asks Flynn.

"Yeah. Pratt wasn't there. Our people talked to his roommate, dancer by the name of Mr. Magnum."

"That's his stage name," says Zuckerman.

"So I gathered. This Mr. Magnum says Pratt hasn't slept at the motel since Saturday. Didn't come home last night. Or tonight, of course."

"So," says Krabitz, "that means he must be hiding somewheres else."

F-ing brilliant deduction, Sherlock.

"Well, it's late," says Zuckerman, closing his clipboard holder. He and Krabitz stand up to leave. "We will, of course, keep you in the loop on anything and everything we discover in our burglary investigation."

"Appreciate it," says Flynn as the crack Stolen Notebooks Investigative Team heads toward the door.

Halfway there, Zuckerman stops.

Does one of those classic "oh-I-forgot-to-mention-something" pivots.

"Oh. By the way."

Here it comes.

"There's one more thing you gentlemen should probably know."

"What's that?" asks Flynn.

"Christina Crites, our stage manager, the one who helped you with the list of cast accommodations."

"What about her?"

"She just texted me. Said the prop pistol is missing."

"What?"

"The revolver. Silver barrel. Black handgrip. We use it in the bullet-catch number."

It was in the show tonight: Richard Rock has a volunteer from the audience load a bullet into the barrel. His wife shoots at him. He catches the bullet with his teeth. The bullets and the pistol looked very real. Sounded real, too.

"Is it a real revolver?" asks Ceepak.

"Yes," says Zuckerman.

Told you.

"Smith and Wesson. Five shot, thirty-eight caliber."

I remember it. Snub-nosed. Looked like something Dick Tracy might carry.

"When the stage manager locked up the prop room tonight, she noticed that both pistols were missing."

"Both?" Flynn is leading with his chin again, yanking at his shirt collar.

"We always travel with two. The hero and an understudy."

"What about the ammunition?" asks Ceepak.

Zuckerman nods. "That's missing as well."

21

"It's one AM," mumbles Flynn. "We should call it a night."

"Agreed," says Ceepak.

"Tomorrow, I'll follow through with MCU. Continue to coordinate the search for Mr. Pratt. We've got every cop in the state on the case. We'll find him."

"Where can we be of best use?"

"Lady Jasmine. Go talk to her up at Trump's place. I'll call ahead. Set it up for nine."

"Roger. Will do. We'll also attempt to identify the members of her entourage."

"How many were with her?" asks Flynn.

"Three. A dwarf, another female of Asian ancestry, and a rather large man whom I took to be her bodyguard."

"Dwarf?"

"Performer known as Mighty Mo-Mo. He is Lady Jasmine's costar at the Taj Mahal. According to the show's most recent advertisements in the *Atlantic City Weekly,* he lifts an elephant with one finger and flies on a magic carpet the size of a hand towel."

Ceepak. The man does his homework.

"Lady Jasmine and the others arrived well after Mr. Rock's performance had begun," he continues. "It is conceivable that they, somehow, gained access to the backstage area undetected."

Right. The dwarf. He could've crawled through an air-conditioning duct or something.

"You honestly think Lady Jasmine and her crew killed Katie so they could rip off Rock's notebooks?" I ask Flynn. "How'd that work? Jake barged in on Katie, sent the kids out for ice cream, made Katie put on the S and M gear, got busy with her, and then Lady Jasmine barged in on the two of them?"

This gets Flynn's neck popping again. "Maybe. Don't know. Need you two to find out."

Ceepak nods. "Danny, even if Lady Jasmine and her entourage had nothing whatsoever to do with this evening's incidents, eliminating them as suspects is a prudent course of action."

"Well, I don't think she'd murder Katie just to get her hands on a couple composition books," I say.

"Really?" says Flynn. "Why's that, Officer Boyle?"

I shrug. "First off, Lucky Numbers is just a frigging magic trick."

Flynn shrugs back. "A trick worth millions. Magicians? Fugghetaboutit. Very competitive individuals."

"Wait a second," I say to Ceepak. "Did you see the way Lady Jasmine shook her head and laughed at the end of the Lucky Numbers bit? She figured it out just by watching it."

"Or," says Ceepak, "she knew what was coming because she had just read all about it in Mr. Rock's journal."

Ceepak and I agree to meet out back on the boardwalk at 0845.

He and Flynn head left. I head right and follow the Xanadu's magic carpet back to the Crystal Palace Tower and my high-roller suite.

In a minor acknowledgment of what time it actually is, some of the shops in that fake Chinese town square are closed, even though the puffy clouds in the domed ceiling remain colored twilight pink. I notice, however, that the bars and nightclubs up on the second level are rocking. I can hear the beat reverberating through the walls. So, I head up the escalator on a beer quest.

Joe Mulligan has already started his final set at Yuk-Yuk-Ho-Ho's Comedy Club and I really don't want to walk in late so he can make fun of me. ("You're from New Jersey? What exit?") So I head over to the Pandamonium nightclub. The girl at the front is in one of those cat-suit body stockings the color of gray flannel. The way she looks at me? I'm not dressed properly to join the beautiful people inside sipping flirtinis.

So I try the Forbidden City.

Twenty-five-dollar cover charge. Champagne is fifteen bucks a glass. The waitresses don't wear very many clothes, just lacy undergarments.

So, on the beer front, I have one option remaining: Lip Sync Lee's.

The karaoke bar.

Sometimes, when he's thirsty, a man's gotta do what a man's gotta do.

It's dark and loud in here. There's a small dance floor in front of a giant-screen TV, which is currently playing what looks like the washed-out footage from a late-night commercial from 1975 for *Every Love Song Ever Recorded.* Guy and girl in meadow of flowers. Slow-motion hand-holding on beach. Playful car-wash hose-squirting action.

Song lyrics scroll across the bottom of the frame.

A tipsy sorority sister with half her dress sliding down one shoulder is swaying in front of the screen destroying a Carly Simon song: "You're So Vain." The "Don't you? Don't you? Don't you?" bit is all the same note repeated very loudly off-pitch.

This is worse than the first week of *American Idol* auditions.

Over at the bar, I see a pair of squirrely guys flipping through a three-ring binder the size of an airplane-maintenance manual. Must be the book where they keep the list of songs available to be karaoked.

"The Carpenters?" gushes one. "I *love* Karen Carpenter!" He is not drinking beer. His upside-down pyramid-shaped cocktail glass is turquoise blue.

His buddy flickers eyelashes. "Which song? She only sang like a hundred before she went all anorexic and died."

"You know." He sings a quick snatch. Something about birds suddenly appearing.

Meanwhile, the sloshed girl on the dance floor is attacking her chorus again: "Don't you? Don't you? Don't you?"

I'm ready for Karen Carpenter's birds. And a beer.

I see from the golf pencils and cards stacked in the rack where the beer coasters and peanut bowls ought to be that it costs $2.50 to destroy a song in public. The bartendress is over at a computer console, reading cards, punching in numbers—apparently programming my upcoming pain.

"So did you hear?" says one of the Karen Carpenter wannabes to my right.

"What?"

"The nanny. They think she and Jake were back there rodeoing sadie-masie style."

"Are they mental?"

"They say it's why he missed the show! And get this—just yesterday, Jake told me he was 'in love' again."

"Who was it this time?"

"An old flame."

His buddy clicks his tongue against his teeth. "That cheap child hops into more beds than a sleazy mattress salesman!"

"Uhm-hmm. This old flame, by the way, is currently *married*." He trills the word to underline it. "Their little reunion started with a Hawaiian Tropics bake-and-baste out by the pool."

"What can I get you?" shouts the bartendress who snuck up on me while I was eavesdropping. "What're you drinking?"

"Bud, if you got it."

"Bottle or mug?"

"Bottle."

"You want to sing?"

No, what I want to do is eavesdrop some more.

"No, thanks."

"Why not?" she says all coy and cuddly. She's cute. So's her low-cut top. She flashes me a flirty smile. "You afraid to make a fool of yourself?"

I tip my head toward the boozy girl clutching the mike and feverishly pumping her free hand over her head every time she chants, "Don't you! Don't you! Don't you!"

"I think you've already met your foolishness quota for the night."

My beautiful beer maiden laughs. "You're right. Hey, Blaine?" she hollers down the bar to the two gossipy guys.

"Yes, dear?" Blaine shouts back.

"You gonna sing?"

"Maybe."

"Come on! We need you!"

Blaine sighs. "Fine. C-fourteen. 'Close to You.' The Carpenters."

"Comin' right up!" The bartender fishes a frosty Bud longneck out of the ice chest. “Stick around. Blaine is good. He’s like a professional Broadway singer. Doing a show downstairs.”

“Is that so?”

“Yeah. Hey, Blaine?”

I’m glad she’s acting as a go-between. Otherwise, Blaine might think I’m hitting on him when he already seems to have a date for the evening.

“Yes, darling?”

“What’s your show called again?”

“ ‘Rock ’n Wow!’ ” He starfishes out his fingers on *Wow!*

I’m ready for Blaine and his buddy to leap into that hoedown number and whip out their bolo ties.

Because they’re Jake Pratt’s castmates.

In fact, the other guy is Jim Bob—the wiry little Lord of the Dance who escorted Richard Rock out of the theater during the Lucky Numbers bit.

I’m about to sidle over and ask them both a few questions when a blond bombshell stumbles into the bar looking so blitzed she wouldn’t be able to read song lyrics off the JumboTron screen at Shea Stadium.

Actually, on closer examination, I see it’s *the* blond bombshell.

Mrs. Rock.

22

Mrs. Rock stumbles over to the two guys.

"Blaine?" she slurs the word worse than Daffy Duck. "Have you seen Jake?"

"No, honey."

"I need to find him. The police!"

"We know."

I stand up. Time to make my presence known.

"Excuse me," I say. "I'm Officer Boyle. Sea Haven police."

Jim Bob curls up his nose. "Really? Here on vacation?"

"No." I dig in my pocket. Flash my badge. "I'm actually working for the Atlantic City police department. We're the ones looking for Jake Pratt. You guys know him, right?"

"Where's your badge?" asks Blaine, getting off his stool to shield Mrs. Rock.

"I just showed it to you."

"Funny," says Blaine, "I don't remember hearing Atlantic City recently changed its name to Sea Haven."

"Detective Flynn deputized me."

"Really? That must've been so special. Was there cake?"

"Don't tell this man anything!" Mrs. Rock blurts out. "Jake's in trouble!"

"Mrs. Rock?" I say. "We met earlier."

Back when you were sober, I want to add but don't.

"Remember? In your room? You talked to me and my partner, John Ceepak. Big guy. Muscles? Remember?"

She lizards out a dry tongue. "No." Her eyes loll up in her sockets as she staggers sideways.

Jim Bob stabilizes her with an elbow clutch. "Come on, honey. Let's walk you home."

"Did my wig slip?"

Now that she mentions it, her bangs do look a little longer than they did about ten seconds ago.

Blaine adjusts her hairpiece, slides everything up half an inch. "Good as new. Come on. We'll take you home, honey."

"Wait a second," I say. "Mrs. Rock?"

She pulls back her head. Tries to force her eyes into focus. "What?"

"We need to find Jake Pratt! If you know—"

"I'm sorry," says Jim Bob in his new role as Mrs. Rock's bodyguard. "We are not talking to you or any other members of the *Sea Haven* police department."

"I told you—I'm working with the ACPD."

"Prove it."

"Call the ACPD. Ask for Detective Flynn."

"Maybe tomorrow." He blows me a kiss. "Buh-bye!"

Blaine and Jim Bob grab hold of an arm each and ease Mrs. Rock toward the exit. She shin-bops a stump-high cocktail table.

"Take it easy, Sherry," Blaine suggests as he steadies her.

"Thank you, sweetie," she slushes. "I'll try."

"Put one foot in front of the other. That's the girl."

They leave. I puzzle.

I thought Mrs. Rock's first name was Jessica.

"Fascinating," says Ceepak when he and I meet up on the boardwalk at 0844 and I fill him in on my undercover bar crawl.

"Yeah. I don't think the two guys will talk unless we, you know, force them to."

"Come again?"

"They seem pretty loyal to Mrs. Rock. We might need to work them over a little to find out if they know where Jake Pratt is hiding."

"I see. Danny?"

"Yeah?"

"Torture, except in television shows featuring Jack Bauer, is seldom an effective interrogation technique."

"I wasn't saying we should torture them. Just, you know."

"No. I'm afraid I do not."

Yeah. Me, neither.

"Well, we should at least have decent ACPD badges."

"Detective Flynn concurs." Ceepak snaps open a flap on his cargo pants, which I guess he did pack because, like a true Boy Scout, he is always prepared. "He gave these to me earlier when we met for coffee."

Two silver and blue shields. I feel like when I was a kid and my parents took me to Wild West City over near Netcong. Without ever leaving New Jersey, we were able to visit Arapaho Indian Territory and the O.K. Corral, where the sheriff deputized everybody under the age of ten to help him tangle with the train robbers.

"We are to return these at the conclusion of the case," says Ceepak as I pin my new badge into the leather flappy thing where I store my Sea Haven tin. "He also gave me this."

He opens another leg flap and shows me what looks like a bloated cell phone with a stubby antenna and twist dial up top.

"Police radio. If Mr. Pratt is apprehended while we're at the Taj Mahal questioning Lady Jasmine, Detective Flynn will contact us ASAP."

"Cool."

Ceepak consults his Casio. "We should also contact Lisa Porter-Burt in a few hours."

She's the prosecuting attorney dealing with Ceepak's father up in Ohio.

"We need to make certain my father entered his guilty plea as anticipated and that Ms. Porter-Burt is satisfied with the terms of the deal."

"Busy morning."

"Roger that. Let's roll."

We head up the boardwalk. Ceepak sets a pretty brisk pace. The diagonal slats clip by. I smell creosote. Popcorn. We pass Andy's candy apples and overtake a few of those rolling chairs being pushed by Bosnians. It's early. I smell no BO.

"So what about Mrs. Rock?" I say. "How come the two dancers called her Sherry instead of Jessica?"

"Most likely because the blond you encountered in the karaoke bar was not Mrs. Rock."

Uh, yes it was. I'd recognize her, you know, distinguishing features, anywhere. Both of them.

"I recognized her!"

"I imagine you did."

"So why did they call her Sherry?"

"Remember that illusion where Mrs. Rock was instantly transported from a glass booth on one side of the stage to another booth situated on the opposite side?"

"Yeah?"

"That trick typically involves the use of a body double, Danny. I suspect this Sherry was the model hidden in the base of the second cabinet who popped into view as soon as Mrs. Rock exited her box via a trapdoor concealed in its floor and obscured from the audience's view by a series of mirrors set up underneath the platform."

Wow. More mirrors. Rock must need to buy a boatload of Windex.

We stroll past Bally's, the Rainforest Cafe, Dunkin' Donuts, Tattoo Tom's, more Oriental massage and therapy joints, several psychic-tarot card storefronts, the 88¢ souvenirs shop—which, by the way, sells hermit crabs *and* iguanas—a Skee-Ball arcade, a pizza-stromboli stand, and about a billion people inside rope-line switchbacks waiting to attack the sultan's feast, Donald Trump's "most spectacular breakfast buffet in the world" served downstairs at the Taj Mahal hotel and casino.

Nobody in the line is wearing a belt.

Trump's casino looks like a bleached white sand castle with gold trim—a glitzier version of that other Taj Mahal over in India. Lots of onion domes up top with tapered spindles that remind me of these very fancy Christmas ornaments my mother won't let me touch because they're made out of glass and I'm me.

"Lady Jasmine requested that we meet in her dressing room," says Ceepak as sliding doors whoosh open and we're hit with the first musty blast of air-conditioning mixed with eye-burning carpet chemicals.

"Does she know we're coming?" I ask.

"Indeed. Detective Flynn called ahead. Arranged our interview through her husband who also acts as Ms. Jasmine's manager and legal advisor. You'll recognize him, of course."

"Another body double?"

"No. Her husband came to the show with her last night."

"The bodyguard?"

"Slightly shorter," says Ceepak. "Mighty Mo-Mo."

23

"You Ceepak?"

"Yes, sir."

"This way."

We're being escorted backstage at the Taj by the four-foot guy we saw last night at Richard Rock's show. Mighty Mo-Mo. For someone so short, he has a deep, rumbling voice. Sounds like he smoked six stogies for breakfast.

"You guys need coffee?" Mo-Mo asks.

"It's kind of you to offer," says Ceepak.

"Hey, it's no sweat off my balls. We got a pot brewing, you know what I'm saying?"

"I'd like a cup," I say.

"Yeah," says Mo-Mo. "You look like you could use it. Rough night, kid?"

Not really. Just saw one of my best friends since forever trussed up like a kinky cow in a cattle-roping competition on a X-rated version of RFD-TV.

"Yeah," is all I say.

Mo-Mo nods sympathetically. "The nanny was a friend of yours, hunh?"

"Yeah."

"Hang in there, kid." He pats me on the butt. I think he was aiming for my back. "We'll help you out all we can."

"We appreciate that," says Ceepak.

"Detective Flynn is good people. Anything we can do, just ask. Here we go." He leads us through a door into another cinder-block corridor. As glamorous as show business is supposed to be, behind the scenes it's pretty dull. No tinsel and glitter. Just glossy white bricks. Looks like a junior-high classroom.

We approach a salmon-colored door with a homemade glitter star Scotch-taped to it. I hear a muffled TV set.

"I think Nicole's watching Regis and Kelly." He raps his knobby knuckles on the door. His fist is about an inch above the doorknob. "Yo, Nicole?"

"Just a second!" someone brays on the other side of the door. The TV snaps off.

"I take it Lady Jasmine is a stage name?" says Ceepak.

"Yeah. Nicole's a Jersey girl. From Flemington. Nicole Piscopo."

"I see."

Mo-Mo shrugs. "We figured Lady Jasmine was more, you know, exotic and what have you."

"Indeed."

The door opens and I don't recognize Lady Jasmine. Without the jet-black wig, angled eye makeup, or slinky silk kimono, she looks like my cousin Beth from Bound Brook.

"Hey, Morty."

"Hey, bubby. This is Officer Ceepak and his partner. What's your name, kid?"

"Boyle. Danny Boyle."

"Boyle," says Mo-Mo—in case his wife didn't hear me, I guess.

"Come on in," says Lady Jasmine who, offstage, does indeed sound and look like a Jersey girl named Nicole Piscopo, not a mysterious Asian sorceress called Lady Jasmine. I suspect the real Nicole has a *Got Beer?* T-shirt somewhere in her closet behind all the silk pajama suits.

We enter her dressing room. More cinder-block walls. There's a pink Formica makeup counter facing a whole row of mirrors ringed by dozens of clear fifty-watt bulbs inside cages. At least that part of her dressing room looks like showbiz is supposed to look. The chairs—the only furniture scattered around the otherwise empty floor—have faded vinyl seats and look like refugees from a banquet hall that got remodeled.

"You're sticking around, right Morty?" she asks her husband.

"You bet, bubby."

"Morty's my lawyer. Went to Rutgers. Up in Newark."

"Night school," says the little guy as he tries to unglue a grungy Mr. Coffee pot stuck to its hot plate. "You want that coffee, Boyle?" He pries the carafe free and I see all sorts of brown splotches on the lid. I don't think the pot's been washed since J. Lo played the Taj three Christmases ago.

"No, thanks. I'm good."

"Take a load off," says our hostess, pointing at the chairs. I pick one with foam poking up through a gash in the seat cushion and sit down; so do Ceepak and Mo-Mo. Actually, Mo-Mo sort of straddles his chair. His Nikes dangle about six inches off the floor.

"I'm so sorry to hear about the girl," says Lady Jasmine. "You guys figure out who did it yet?"

"No, ma'am," says Ceepak.

"It's why they're here, bubby," says Mo-Mo.

"Oh. Right. Duh. Guess we're suspects, hunh?"

Ceepak nods. "You did enter the auditorium rather late last evening."

"We were on a winning streak. At the blackjack tables. I love taking money from the competition." She cracks her gum. "What table were we at, hon?"

"B-forty-three," says Mo-Mo.

"Do you typically note the serial number of the table when you gamble?" asks Ceepak.

"Yo," says Jersey-girl Jasmine, "when we're racking up a stack of chips that big we do! Am I right, Morty?"

"Absolutely!" Mo-Mo leans out, slaps her five, and almost tumbles out of his chair on the rebound. "If a table's hot, we're not leaving till it goes cold."

"Your entire entourage was with you?" asks Ceepak.

"Yeah. Me. Morty. Lilani Lee. Ox."

"Ox?"

"My cousin Oscar. He's from up in Edison. Lost his job at the Ford plant. Used to bolt bumpers onto F-one-fifties."

"We hired him," says Mo-Mo with a shrug. "He's family, you know what I'm saying?"

"He's big," I say.

The lady snaps her Dentyne. "You noticed, hunh? We make believe I'm such a big-shot celebrity I need a bodyguard. Had Oscar shave his head. Told him he had to look the part, you know?"

"And Lilani Lee?" asks Ceepak.

"She's an . . . acquaintance."

"How so?"

"You know. Occasionally, we hang out. She likes the slots."

"The two of 'em met downstairs, what? Last week?" says Mo-Mo. "Sat side by side at these two incredibly hot machines. They're like each other's good luck charms!"

"Why did you choose last night to catch Mr. Rock's act?"

Mo-Mo and Lady Jasmine give each other this look. "What do you mean?" she asks.

"Why did you cancel your own show to see his?"

"We didn't cancel bupkes," says Mo-Mo. "You think Donald Trump is gonna let us play it that way? We'd be up in that boardroom of his, listenin' to him say, 'You're fired!' And there wouldn't be no taxi waiting for us downstairs, neither. We went to the Xanadu last night because we're always off on Monday nights."

"And last night was when his manager said we should catch the show. What's his name, hon? The manager?"

"Zuckerman. David Zuckerman."

"Yeah. Zuckerman."

"He called late afternoon," says Mo-Mo. "I remember we were upstairs in the room with sandwiches watching some show about penguins or whatever on Animal Planet. Remember, bubby?"

"Yeah. Good pastrami. Very thinly sliced. Not too fatty."

"Anyways," says Mo-Mo, "Zuckerman calls, says he knows it's kind of last-minute and all but since we take Mondays off anyways, do we want a VIP table for the eight o'clock show of 'Rock 'n Wow!'?"

"We comped them into our show when they first came to town. Rock, his wife, the kids, Zuckerman."

Mo-Mo nods. "Free tickets. Free booze. The whole megillah. We figure Zuckerman's ready to reciprocate. So we check the social calendar, Nicole calls Lilani to see if she's free and interested, we alert Ox—badda-bing, badda-boom. Seven-thirty, we're raking in the chips."

"So," says Ceepak, "if we were to examine the security tapes . . ."

"You'd see us at table B-forty-three," says Nicole. "Laughing our asses off. I couldn't believe the hot streak we were on. Maybe Lilani really is my good-luck charm. Cards kept comin' our way. Twenty. Twenty-one."

Mo-Mo laughs, remembering. "We almost missed the whole show!"

"But," says Ceepak, "you were there in time to see the Lucky Numbers illusion."

"Yeah," says Mo-Mo. "We saw 'the Big Trick.' " He stretches open his mouth, pretends to yawn.

"I take it you weren't impressed?"

"Come on. Nicole could do that Lucky Numbers *mishegoss* in her sleep if we had that kind of money."

"Why would you need money?"

"To, you know, rig it up."

"Morty?" Jasmine silences her husband with a head shake.

He holds up his hands in surrender. "I'm just saying."

"Well, just stop, all right?"

"Ma'am," says Ceepak, "my partner and I are investigating a murder. If you are withholding information—"

"On how a magic trick is done?" She smiles. "Come on, Mr. Ceepak. You're a cop. You know how to solve a mystery. Think about it for two seconds and I guarantee you'll figure it out."

Ceepak stiffens. "Perhaps, as you suggest, my partner and I would be able to unravel the illusion's secrets on our own. However, it might save us a great deal time if you were to elucidate further."

"Hunh?"

"The guy wants you to explain it to him," says Mo-Mo.

"I can't," says Lady Jasmine.

"Why not?" asks Ceepak.

"I took an oath."

Ceepak's left eyebrow shoots up an inch. "Pardon?"

"The Magician's Code." She raises her right hand. " 'I promise to never reveal the secret of any illusion to a non-magician, unless that one swears to uphold the Magician's Code in turn.' "

"I see," says Ceepak. I can tell: He's backing off. Johnny C. is a huge fan of codes. If he's gonna live his life by one, he has to let the magicians live by one, too.

Great.

No torture. Secrecy oaths that must be honored. Being an upright citizen can be extremely time-consuming.

"I will not ask you to violate your oath, ma'am."

"You don't need her to," says Mo-Mo. "That illusion is so lame, my two-year-old could tell you how it's done."

"We don't have a two-year-old, Morty."

The hands go up again. "I'm just saying, is all."

"So you didn't steal Mr. Rock's notebooks," I say, just to wrap this thing up. "You didn't go to the show to videotape his act, to try to rip him off?" I guess I sound pretty pathetic—Lady Jasmine gives me this very compassionate smile like I'm the kid who lost his parents at the mall.

"No, sweetie. That's part of the code, too. You don't do another magician's illusion unless he or she gives you permission. You absolutely don't sneak in with a camcorder to rip it off, not if you're legit."

"Which we are," says Mo-Mo. "Totally. Magic's been good to us, you know what I'm saying?"

Nobody says anything for a couple seconds. I can hear that nasty Mr. Coffee pot sizzling. It's been on the hot plate so long, it's starting to smell like my socks.

"Tell 'em about Lilani," says Mo-Mo.

"You think?"

"Yeah."

"Okay, this is like a total, you know, gut feeling."

"Go on," says Ceepak.

"I think Lilani being in the audience freaked Rock out."

"How so?"

"I don't know. It's just a feeling I got. When he walked past our table on his way to that bar in the middle of the auditorium—you know, to get that Shirley Temple."

Ceepak nods. "We were seated in the box next to you."

"Good seats, hunh?"

"Yes, ma'am."

"Anyway, when Rock walked by, he hesitated. I'm sure he could see through that silly hood he had on."

"Really?" I say.

Now Mo-Mo swings both hands out wide. "C'mon, kid. It's a magic show. What? You think bunnies really live inside hats, too?"

"Anyways," says Lady Jasmine, "I swear he was looking down at Lilani. That's what made him stop in his tracks like that."

Ceepak leans forward, rests his elbows on his knees. "Why?"

"That's exactly what I asked Lilani, after the show!"

"And?"

"Well, she tells me, for the first time since I met her here in the casino, mind you, that she runs this . . . *place*. On the boardwalk. Apparently, Mr. Rock has been a frequent visitor but he may not want anybody to know about it. It could, you know, taint his reputation."

"Big-time," adds Mo-Mo, crossing his arms genie-style across his chest.

"What sort of establishment does Ms. Lee operate on the boardwalk?" asks Ceepak.

"It's called Lucky Lilani's Stress Therapy," says Nicole. "It's very therapeutic. Very Chinese."

Mo-Mo snorts. "Come on, bubby. Call a spade a spade. It's a freaking massage parlor!"

24

Right across the boardwalk from the Taj Mahal Hotel and Casino is Atlantic City's world-famous family fun spot: the Steel Pier.

Used to be home to Rex the Wonder Dog and the diving horses.

I kid you not.

Real, live horses would clip-clop up this forty-foot ramp, and do a four-legged half-gainer into the Atlantic Ocean. Kids lapped it up.

These days, the Steel Pier's home to a bunch of rides: bumper cars, crazy mouse, flip 'n fly trampolines, jump cycles, pumpkin wheel, rock-n-roll, wet boats. But the ride they really need, in my humble opinion, is a mind scrambler because right now my brain is all kinds of jumbled up.

David Zuckerman invited Lady Jasmine to the show? So how come he and Richard Rock made such a big stink about her coming and begged Parker for extra security?

And what's with Mr. Wholesome Family Fun being in the frequent rubdown program of a cheesy massage parlor? Does he throw out his back on a regular basis sawing his wife in half? Or does he go there looking for the proverbial "happy ending?"

And don't forget last night's drunk blonde—Sherry, the body double. Why was she searching for Jake Pratt, who is currently our only suspect in the murder of Kathleen Irene Landry because Lady Jasmine and her entire entourage have an airtight alibi for the time of death, not to mention no motive and no desire to steal Rock's notebooks for Lucky Numbers since they figured out how the trick was done just by watching it?

My mind is beyond scrambled. It's a frittata.

We come out of Trump's Taj, squeeze our way past that breakfast buffet line and head back the way we came.

Ceepak fishes that police radio cell-phone deal out of his thigh pocket.

"This is Ceepak for Detective Flynn."

He releases a button. Waits.

"This is Flynn."

"We just met with Lady Jasmine. Apparently, she and her guests were invited to Mr. Rock's show last night by his manager, Mr. David Zuckerman. She reports having no interest in illegally acquiring the secrets to the Lucky Numbers illusion, stating that she and her husband were able to decipher said secrets simply by watching it."

"Why were they so late?"

"They informed us they were playing blackjack at table B-forty-three in the main casino."

"Okay. Easy enough to verify. I'll ask Parker to check it out."

"Roger that. Officer Boyle and I are currently en route to an establishment called Lucky Lilani's Stress Therapy."

When Ceepak says it, it sounds like a legitimate spa for athletes with meniscus disk issues.

"What's there?" asks Flynn.

"According to Lady Jasmine, Richard Rock has been a frequent visitor to the establishment."

"Do you think there is some sort of connection between Mr. Rock's, uh, therapy sessions and the murder?"

"Uncertain. However, I feel we should take a statement from Ms. Lilani Lee. Verify Lady Jasmine's statement."

"Yeah. Okay. She gives you any grief, give me a holler."

"What's your twenty?"

"Hunh?"

"Where are you currently located?"

"Oh. Right. We're, uh . . ."

I hear muffled scratchy sounds. Wind.

"Where are we, Mike?" Flynn asks someone off radio.

"Carolina and Atlantic Avenue," the other guy says back.

"Carolina and Atlantic," Flynn repeats into the radio. "Liquor store."

I glance at my watch. Ten-oh-five AM. A little early for cocktails. Unless, of course, you're Joseph "Six-pack" Ceepak. Then it's Jim Beam and Bud for breakfast.

Flynn crackles on: "Big plate-glass window. We're surveiling Krabitz."

"May I ask why?" says Ceepak.

"I'm wagering Krabitz knows more about Jake Pratt's whereabouts than he lets on. Detective Mike Weddle and I have been tailing him since he and his son came down around nine, hit the Xanadu breakfast buffet."

"Mr. Krabitz is in Atlantic City with his son?"

"I'm assuming that's who the kid is. Boy. Eleven. Maybe twelve. Came down from their room in the Crystal Palace Tower, headed straight for the Xanadu's buffet chow line. Forty-five minutes later, they returned to the Crystal Palace Tower and Krabitz came back down solo."

"Where is Mr. Krabitz now?"

"In a deli across the street from the liquor store. Eating a jelly doughnut."

The guy must love his breakfast foods. Never wants it to be lunch.

"Ten-four," says Ceepak. "We will interview Ms. Lee, check back in as soon as the interrogation is completed."

"Okay. Gotta go. Krabitz is on the move."

"Roger that."

Ceepak pockets the radio. His conversation with Detective Flynn took us all the way up to 1508 boardwalk. Lucky Lilani's Stress Therapy.

Through the windows, I see about a half-dozen Asian ladies lined up near a half-dozen padded tables. Way in the back, I see velvet drapes partitioning off what I figure must be the "special" private rooms, booths stocked with baby oil, erotic candles, and fruit-flavored condoms.

A couple of older women near the front are kneading the necks of weary gamblers in those massage chairs where you stick your face in the leather hole that always reminds me of a hospital bedpan; looks about as sanitary, too. There's a poster taped in the window, right above the MasterCard and Visa decals: *Full Chinese Body Massage: Back, Arms, Legs, Neck, Hands—Just $20.*

I'm wondering if they left off any more interesting body parts. The ones I suspect Mr. Rock came here to have a young Asian girl rub-a-dub-dub.

"Many of these establishments are actually bordellos," whispers Ceepak, gesturing toward a green neon sign: 24 HRS OPEN. "Oftentimes, illegal immigrants from Korea and Thailand are forced to work in these places as prostitutes to repay the cost of their transpacific passage."

I pretend like I didn't know.

We go in.

The air is hot and moist. Three girls in the kind of low-cut slinky dresses you don't see too much at 10:00 AM on a Wednesday are kneeling on the floor behind one of the empty massage beds, eating breakfast from bowls: steamed fish, rice, and some kind of slimy green vegetable. Looks like a few of the ladies brought their kids to work with them today. I see two boys, a little girl. One of the kids has powdered sugar all over his shirt, like he's been eating funnel cakes for breakfast. Guess this is one of those progressive workplaces with on-site day care. Either that or it's "Bring Your Kids to the Bordello Day."

"We're looking for Ms. Lee," Ceepak announces.

The breakfast bunch stares at us. The chair women stop working on their clients. The girls waiting for victims at the tables give us terrified stares.

I don't think any of them understand much English.

"Is Ms. Lee here?" Ceepak tries again.

"She no here," says a woman coming out from behind those velvet curtains at the back of the store. "Miss Lee not here."

"Yes you are," I say, because I recognize her from last night at the theater.

"Ms. Lee?" says Ceepak, flashing his new deputy badge. "I am Officer Ceepak. This is my partner, Officer Boyle."

"Is there going to be trouble?" asks one of the guys in a chair with his face smooshed through a leatherette doughnut hole.

"No, sir," says Ceepak. "We just need to ask the proprietress a few questions. Perhaps we should step into your office."

"What questions?" snaps Lee.

"Do you have an office? This might be best done in private."

"What questions?"

I jump in: "Does Richard Rock come here a lot?"

The folks who were eating fish and stringy greens for breakfast are kind of cowering on the floor now. Bowing down so we can't see any faces. I'm figuring our badges just made us look like INS agents.

"I don't know no Richard Rock," says Lilani Lee.

Ceepak points to a poster taped to the front of her cash register counter: "Rock 'n Wow!"

"He's the magician pictured in that poster."

"I don't know no magician."

"Lady Jasmine says you do," I toss in. "Mighty Mo-Mo, too."

"She lies. He lies."

"No, ma'am," says Ceepak. "They have no reason to do so."

"They lie! You leave!"

Ceepak steps forward.

We're not leaving.

Lilani Lee balls up her tiny fists. She looks pretty tough, even if she is wearing stiletto-heeled sandals and a clingy gown slit up to her thigh.

"You leave now! I call police!"

"We are the police," I say, wiggling my badge to make it catch the light, just in case she missed it the first time.

"You have warrant? I call my lawyer!"

"Ms. Lee," says Ceepak, "we have no desire to—"

"You leave! You leave here now!"

She lurches toward the cash register. Why do I think she keeps an aluminum baseball bat underneath that counter?

"Ms. Lee—"

"You leave!" she shrieks.

The radio in Ceepak's pocket screeches.

"Officers down! Officers down! Oh, fuck. Fuck, fuck, fuck!"

I recognize the voice: Kenny Krabitz.

"Oh, shit. They're fucking dead!"

We don't measure the blood we've drawn anymore
We just stack the bodies outside the door

Who'll be the last to die for a mistake
The last to die for a mistake
Whose blood will spill, whose heart will break
Who'll be the last to die, for a mistake

—Bruce Springsteen, "Last to Die"

25

Ceepak and I monitor the radio chatter and race to the scene of the crime: the Royal Lodge, that shabby three-story motel directly across the street from the Xanadu.

I see about two dozen cops swarming all over the place: in the office, clunking up steel steps, patrolling the second- and third-floor terraces. The biggest cluster is on the second floor, bunched up outside a door near one of the rusty staircases.

Down on the ground, two cops in bicycle helmets are rolling out *Police Line: Do Not Cross* tape, penning in the cars crammed nose-to-bumper in the parking lot. Three boxy ambulances and half a dozen cruisers with their roof bars spinning are parked on the sidewalk, rear wheels hanging off the curb, shafts of colored light bouncing off motel windows.

More mirrors.

Ceepak flashes his deputy badge at the cop standing guard

near the access point in the barrier tape. Fortunately, it's one of the bicycle guys we met yesterday.

"We need to be upstairs," says Ceepak. "We were working with Detective Flynn."

The guy nods. "The chief is up there now."

"What room?"

"Two-twelve. On the left." He gestures toward that knot of blue uniforms on the second floor.

"How are Detective Flynn and his partner?" asks Ceepak.

The bike cop shakes his head. "They're not gonna make it. The Pratt kid, either. It's a mess up there."

Yeah.

It's a mess.

We wait outside on the concrete balcony. From our holding position outside the door, I can see Detective Flynn and his partner Mike Weddle sprawled out flat on the floor. Both their chests are soaked with blood. It looks like somebody performed a rapid-fire exercise on them with a semiautomatic weapon as soon as they stepped across the doorsill. They're still holding their badges in frozen fingers. Sidearms are holstered and strapped. They never went for their weapons. Probably means somebody told them to come on in.

They weren't expecting resistance.

They should've. Their torsos are so riddled with splotchy circles of blood, I'm guessing neither of the detectives put on his Kevlar vest when they set out to tail Kenny Krabitz, PI, this morning. I see a radio like the one Flynn gave Ceepak. Krabitz must've dropped it after calling in his "officer down." It spit up batteries when it hit the floor.

I lean to my right, look left, and now I'm guessing Jake Pratt was the one firing the semiautomatic pistol at the two cops who came knocking on his door. I can see a Beretta M9 gripped in his rigor-mortised right hand. The former dancer is sprawled on top of the bedspread. The garden of blooms on the floral-patterned comforter is slowly sinking beneath a creeping lake of blood. Someone took Pratt down with a single shot to the heart.

For that role, I'm nominating Kenny Krabitz.

Richard Rock's PI is seated directly across from the bed at a shiny table in what the Royal Lodge brochures probably claim is a kitchenette. I see a waist-high, dorm-style fridge, a microwave with Chef Boyardee splatter patterns on its window, and a rack of uneven wire shelves lined with coffee mugs, picnic basket salt-and-pepper shakers, and a half-empty roll of paper towels.

Kenny Krabitz, P.I. is casually smoking a cigarette. There's a snub-nosed Smith & Wesson Dick Tracy–type pistol sitting on the table in front of him, right next to the paper deli cup of coffee that doubles as his ashtray. It is, of course, the five-shot .38-caliber pistol reported missing from the "Rock 'n Wow!" prop room last night. There's also a small pocket-sized notebook on the table, between the cup and the magician's pistol.

Krabitz locks the soles of his scuffed shoes on a chair rung, leans back, and props himself against the maple-paneled wall.

"Douse the smoke," orders this tall guy wearing a faded navy blue raincoat even though there's not a cloud in the sky. From the sound of his voice, his snowy white hair, and the way he carries himself, I'm figuring he's the chief.

"My nerves are jumpy," claims Krabitz, sucking down a few more milligrams of tar and nicotine with a wet smack.

"Douse it."

"I believe that's Chief Maroney," whispers Ceepak. He must've gone to the ACPD Web site and memorized the chain of command after we were deputized by Flynn.

"Okay, Mr. Krabitz," says Chief Maroney. "Tell me again. What the hell happened here?"

"Jesus, Chief, I already told you. Six fucking times."

"So tell me again!" he screams. Then—and I'd give him a medal for this, even though he's contaminating a crime scene—he rips that ash-dripping cigarette right out of Krabitz's smug mouth and grinds it out on the floor in the threadbare quarter-inch carpet. "Tell me how the hell two of my best cops waltz in here, sidearms holstered, and get themselves blown away by a goddamn chorus boy!"

"The kid had the Beretta," Krabitz says with a shrug. "Maybe he's ex-military. The M-nine is a military sidearm."

"So why didn't this ballerina take target practice on your chest, too?"

"Like I said, we were negotiating. He had Mr. Rock's notebooks there." He gestures toward some Mead composition books stacked on the edge of the bed. "Even had the one for the Lucky Numbers trick, which he knew was worth a fucking fortune. We were working out his asking price when your boys showed up."

"That when Pratt handed you the snub-nose thirty-eight?"

"He didn't 'hand' it to me. Like I told you, your two boys knock on the door, announce their presence. Pratt whips out his Beretta and tells them to come on in."

"And you don't contradict him? You don't warn my officers to stay out of harm's way?"

Krabitz flicks his head toward the bed. "Did I mention the putz had a fucking pistol?"

"Go on."

"He starts blasting away at your guys. They do not return fire. So, I dive for the thirty-eight I see sitting on the bedside table there and proceed to take Pratt down with a single shot to the chest. Guess I hit the bull's-eye, hunh?"

The chief jams his hands deep into the pockets of that trench coat—I guess so he doesn't strangle Krabitz.

"You're telling me, this kid, Jake Pratt, is sitting on the bed, squeezing off a full magazine of fifteen rounds from an M-nine. Meanwhile, you're tiptoeing around the bed to the night table, grabbing his other gun. Then you nonchalantly stroll back here to the front of the bed, position yourself directly in his line of fire, and take him down with one shot to the heart? What'd you do, count the bullets? Jump in and fire between his trigger squeezes?"

Krabitz shrugs again. "What can I say, Chief? I'm nimble."

"Why the hell didn't you just shoot the punk as soon as you got your hands on his other gun?"

"Come on—I can't shoot a man in the back. That's what cowards do."

The chief shakes his head. "Where's Dr. McDaniels?" he shouts to one of his men.

"On her way."

In my peripheral vision, I notice Ceepak nodding. He's relieved to hear that Dr. Sandra McDaniels, the top CSI in the state, is on the way. Since Detective Flynn helped her write her most recent field manual, you know Dr. McD's going to have a personal stake in nailing down the truth about what the hell really happened here because I'm with Chief Maroney: Krabitz's story sounds like total horse crap.

"Make sure Sandy does the trajectory work. See if it matches up with the bullshit Jack-be-nimble here is trying to sell us."

"You got it, Chief."

"And show her those two shopping bags. Could be connected to the other thing over at the Xanadu."

"Could be?" snorts Krabitz. "Come on! The Pink Pussycat Boutique is where Pratt bought that S and M underwear for the nanny. Hell, the credit card slip is still in the bag! His credit card! Got his name engraved on it and everything."

"You looked, hunh?" Maroney asks Krabitz.

"Yeah. While I waited for you boys to show up. It helped pass the time."

Ceepak, of course, was right once again: Katie's death and the theft of Richard Rock's notebooks are linked.

"And don't forget this," says Krabitz, tapping his finger near that small spiral notebook on the dinette table. "It's practically a confession. Love notes to the Landry girl. Detailed running time of the show, each bit's start and finish time. He knew exactly when everybody would be too busy to give a shit about how he was diddling the nanny back in that suite."

Now I wish I had my weapon to make Krabitz shut up.

"This bastard Pratt knew exactly how much time he had to dress her up, do the whole 'strangle me when I come' bit."

"Mr. Krabitz?" says the chief.

"Yeah?"

"Shut the fuck up."

Amen, Chief.

"Jesus," moans Krabitz, "why you being such a hard-ass here? I solved the fucking burglary and the murder. I did your whole fucking job for you."

"You got two cops killed!"

"Well, maybe if these two numb nuts hadn't been illegally surveiling me, hadn't busted in here like Rambo and Schwarzenegger."

"Enough! Lock this schmuck up. Put Mr. Krabitz in our smallest cell until Dr. McDaniels tells me what I already know: This slimeball is lying through his teeth."

Krabitz leans back and laughs. "You can't arrest me, Chief."

"Really? Watch me."

"What's the fucking charge?"

"Violating municipal ordinance twenty-three nineteen of the Atlantic City hotel-motel code. This is a nonsmoking room."

"Let's go," says a uniform who grabs hold of Krabitz's arm and helps him up out of his padded seat.

"I want to talk to my lawyer."

The chief is the one who shrugs this time. "So call him."

"I want to talk to David Zuckerman. Now! Right now!"

"We'll see what we can do about that," says the uniform as he escorts Krabitz around the two dead bodies blocking their path to the door.

"Hold on, hot shit," Krabitz says to the cop, which, by the way, is never a wise thing to call a person who has a loaded weapon strapped to his hip when you don't. "I can call him right here."

"Confiscate Mr. Krabitz's phone," barks the chief. "Now! It's evidence."

"Of what?" snaps Krabitz.

"Whatever the hell really happened here! Give me his goddamn phone and get him the hell out of my sight. He's contaminating my crime scene!"

The uniform tosses Krabitz's cell to another cop, who drops it into a paper sack. We spectators step back an inch or two from the doorway so the cop can shove Krabitz out of room 212 and onto our terrace.

Krabitz sees us. "Officers," he says with a grin. "I told you I'd find Pratt."

Yeah. He just didn't mention anything about killing him, too.

26

"You the two cops Brady deputized?"

"Yes, sir."

Chief Maroney came out to the second-floor motel terrace to catch a breath of fresh air. He unwraps a HALLS Mentho-Lyptus, pops it in his mouth. Nothing like that vapor action to jolt the stench of death right out of your nostrils.

"I'm John Ceepak. This is my partner, Danny Boyle. We're with the Sea Haven police department."

"What are you doing down here in Atlantic City? R and R?"

"No, sir. Our original objective was to take a deposition from a witness for an upcoming murder trial."

The chief nods. Clacks the lozenge against his teeth. "And then all hell broke loose."

"Yes, sir. Detective Flynn indicated that his investigative department was somewhat short-staffed. He asked that we assist him."

"Sea Haven let you do that?" the chief asks.

"We are on administrative leave from our duties for the remainder of the week."

The chief steps toward the edge of the terrace and rests his hands on the railing, leans out so he can squint up at the bright blue sky. "Flynn told me you guys knew the nanny."

"Yes, sir."

"Well, at least we know who killed her."

"Do we?"

The chief turns around so he can eyeball Ceepak. "Jake Pratt. The kid in there dead on the bed. He did it. Dropped a whole clump of pubic hairs on the carpet."

"You made the match?"

"Last night. We also ran a fingerprint check on that love note smeared across the bathroom mirror. Again, it comes up Pratt. Inside here"—he jabs a thumb toward room 212—"we find Pink Pussycat shopping bags with an itemized credit card receipt, listing the, you know, the merchandise Ms. Landry was wearing."

"The bondage costume that did not fit," says Ceepak.

"Yeah—because Pratt was the one who purchased the garter belt and what have you. Yesterday. Paid for it with his Visa card. It's all on the charge card. I figure Ms. Landry forgot to tell him her size. Women do that. Act like we should know."

"That's one possibility," says Ceepak, who's not as willing as Chief Maroney to wrap up the Katie killing and pin it on Jake Pratt.

Chief Maroney sighs. "You also got Jake Pratt's bolo tie as the murder weapon."

"There's no way of knowing whether—"

"Also, you got the fact that Mr. Pratt missed the show last night, the fact that he gave the two Rock children fifty bucks to go buy ice cream, the fact that he's holed up here in the Royal Lodge instead of down at the Holiday Inn where he's supposed to be. And then there's his diary."

"Diary?"

"That little spiral notebook we found."

"Have you analyzed and authenticated the handwriting? Is it Pratt's?"

"Matches a postcard we found on the nightstand. He was writing his mother. Telling her not to worry. Letting her know he was okay."

Guess he was—when he wrote it.

"Might I inquire as to the diary's contents?" says Ceepak.

Maroney reaches into his raincoat, pulls out his own memo pad. "First couple pages it's more or less his daybook. Rehearsal dates. Call times. Breakdown of the show." He flips forward a few pages. "He also scribbled a couple to-dos in a list. Tell wardrobe he needs a new dance belt. Get his tap shoes repaired."

Ceepak pulls out his own spiral book and starts jotting down notes.

"Things get extremely interesting on page six," says the chief. "I wrote it down verbatim."

Ceepak leans in so he can write it down verbatim, too.

" 'Katie. I am moving into the Royal Lodge as suggested. Being closer is better. I love you. I can't wait to be so close we melt into each other.' "

I must've flinched. Maroney is giving me the once-over.

"You okay hearing this?"

"Yes, sir."

Chief Maroney starts reading again: " 'I will get what we need. Ball gag. Hood. Harness. Handcuffs. I love you. The danger excites me. We were meant to be together forever.' "

Ceepak finishes writing, closes up his notebook. "If Jake Pratt loved Ms. Landry so much, why would he kill her?"

"How many times do you guys need to hear this? It was an accident. Erotic asphyxiation. Kinky sex that got out of hand."

Okay. My turn to speak up: "No way, sir."

"Excuse me?" This from the chief.

"No way did Katie Landry willingly allow Jake Pratt to strangle her with a bolo tie so she could, you know, have a heightened orgasm."

"Says who?"

"Me. And Detective Flynn. He figured that Pratt surprised Katie while she was drawing a bath for the boy. Then he kicked out the kids, forced her to put on that getup. Come on, if Katie Landry was really into breath-control games, she would've told Pratt what size S and M gear to buy. Katie was a kindergarten teacher! She knows how to order supplies!"

Okay, that didn't come out exactly the way I wanted it to, but I think I made my point.

"Has Dr. McDaniels examined the forensic evidence from Ms. Landry's murder scene?" Ceepak asks.

"Look," says the chief, sounding pretty annoyed with his newest deputies, "two of my best cops, two guys I play softball with, whose kids I know, two extremely good men were killed this morning. Figuring out what really happened inside that motel room is priority number one. For me. For Dr. Sandra McDaniels. For the entire ACPD. As far as we're concerned, the thing across the street is closed. Mr. Jake Pratt accidentally killed Ms. Katie Landry, even if she wasn't a willing participant in the sex games. Then Pratt stole Rock's notebooks, the ones we found in his room here, so he could extort some cash and finance his getaway. End of story. It's why that imbecile of a PI Krabitz knew where to find the kid. I figure Pratt contacted Rock's people. Made his demands known. They were haggling over price when my guys busted up their confab. So, I'm sorry, Officers, but I do not have the time, the manpower, or, frankly, the inclination to investigate the Landry murder further."

"We do," says Ceepak. "As I indicated, we're free all week."

The chief exhales noisily. I smell eucalyptus.

"You really think I'm missing something?"

"I think," says Ceepak, "that we owe it to Detective Flynn to ascertain the truth. It's what he was attempting to do. It's what made him follow Mr. Krabitz up here to this motel room."

That gets the chief sighing again. "Fine," he says. "Do it."

"Thank you, sir."

"But remember: resources get allocated my way first. Do not even think about dragging Dr. McDaniels away from what I need her to be doing."

"Of course not. You have our word."

"I can't give you weapons. Liability issues."

"Understood."

"So why the hell are you still standing here? Go on. Get to work."

Ceepak straightens up. Stands at attention. "Yes, sir. Danny? Let's roll."

"Where we going?" I ask as we clank down the steel steps toward the parking lot.

"Motel office. If, as Mr. Pratt's diary seems to imply, he and Katie were romantically involved, that he took this room across the street from the Xanadu at her suggestion, she would have undoubtedly spent some time over here with him."

True. You don't ask your boyfriend to secure a love nest if you don't intend to feather it with him from time to time.

We hit the tarmac and head for the motel office. We push open the door and it smells like they use sour milk instead of

Freon for air-conditioner coolant. There are two uniformed ACPD cops standing guard near the plate-glass windows.

Ceepak and I nod at them; they nod at us and hike up their gun belts because they actually have weapons even if we don't.

The desk clerk could care less about all the nodding and belt-hiking going on. He's sitting on a stool behind the counter, eyes glued on the morning newspaper, studying the sports pages, probably trying to decide who to bet his life savings on today.

"Sir?" says Ceepak.

"Yeah?" The guy doesn't look up. All we see are the three strands of oily hair straddling the fleshy summit of his bald dome.

"We need to ask you a few questions."

"So ask." He runs a finger across the box scores.

"Are you familiar with the tenant in room two-twelve?"

"Not really." He flips over a sheet of newsprint. "He the dead guy up there?"

"He's one of them."

The helpful clerk flicks his hand sideways, still doesn't look up from the paper. "These two showed me his picture."

"And?"

Now, finally, he looks up. "And what?"

"What can you tell us about him?"

"Who are you?"

"Special ACPD Deputies Ceepak and Boyle."

"Deputies?"

"Yes, sir."

"Like that Barney Fife character from Mayberry?"

"Yeah," I say. "Just like Barney. So, what can you tell us about Jake Pratt?"

The guy shrugs. "He checked in Sunday. Didn't pay for the room."

"Come again?" says Ceepak, stepping closer to the counter.

"He didn't pay for the room."

"Who did?"

"His girlfriend." He winks at us. "Older chick. A real cougar."

"Pardon?"

"You know—an older woman who digs the young stuff. This Pratt kid looked to be right out of high school."

"How old was the woman?"

"I dunno. Thirty. Forty. Hard to tell. She's had some major work done. Boobs. Nose. Face. You can tell, you know? No wrinkles when they raise their eyebrows. Using that Boflex stuff."

"What color hair did she have?"

"Blond."

Great. Means it wasn't Katie.

"But it was a wig," the guy says. "I don't think she wanted me to know who she was when she came in with the credit card but I could. Easy."

"By reading the name on the card?" says Ceepak.

"Nah. That was bogus, too. Janice Stone. It was a legit credit card. AmEx. Probably one of those *aka* deals. 'Also known as,' you know? I swiped it through the machine, everything comes up copacetic. But come on—you'd think she'd pick a better alias. Anybody could see right through that one. Janice Stone. How lame is that? She should'a gone with Betty Rubble, you ask me."

"Who was she?"

"Jessica Rock." He bobs his head toward the window. "The magician's wife from across the street."

27

We head across the street to the Xanadu.

We need to have a little chat with Mrs. Rock, find out why she was bankrolling Jake Pratt's secret motel room. I'm remembering what she said yesterday, that bit about "Nanny Katie, like many women, wasn't immune to the allure of a younger man, especially one as attractive as young Jake Pratt."

Then Mrs. Rock basically confessed to her own predatory cougarness: "Many of the gals in the show felt the same way."

Yep. One even paid for Jake's hotel room across the street.

It's no wonder the Rocks' private investigator found Pratt so easily: all he had to do was ask Mrs. Rock where she was warehousing her boy toy.

She probably even slipped Krabitz her copy of the card key.

We figure she might be at the theater rehearsing, seeing how they have to work in a new dancer to take Jake's place, so we head through that *Authorized Personnel Only* door off the main casino corridor.

"Aloha, dudes!"

Our ponytailed pal Tupula Tuiasopo is on the other side, guarding the backstage entryway in his *Event Staff* windbreaker. It's noon. Toohey starts work early.

"We're looking for Mrs. Rock," says Ceepak.

Toohey nods.

"Do you know where we might find her?"

"Where?"

Ceepak sighs. "I am asking you."

"Oh, right. Sorry, dude. What was the question again?"

"Where is Mrs. Rock?"

Tuiasopo shrugs. "Don't know. But, hey—you know who might?"

"Who?" asks Ceepak. He's clenching his jaw so tight I think his temples might pop open.

"Mr. Rock!"

"And where might we find Mr. Rock?"

"Swimming pool on the second floor. It's totally awesome up there, dudes. Tropical as shit. They call it 'the Garden of Delight' because it's like so totally delightful. And, it's a garden, too."

"Thank you."

"*Mahalo*. Later, dudes."

Yeah. Hopefully, a lot later.

Ceepak and I take an elevator up to the second floor, weave our way through some more slot-machine alleys, and stop to ask a cocktail waitress for directions, even though we're both guys. Finally, we find the Garden of Delight Spa and Pool.

It's this atrium made out of hothouse glass. The sun glares

down the way it does on an ant frying underneath a magnifying glass. The air's muggier than August back home in Sea Haven. I hear gurgling water and see steam rising up behind a bank of palm fronds.

We make our way through the jungle of sweaty greens and I hear a splash. When we come into a clearing, I see a solitary, dark-haired kid swimming in the narrow lap pool. There's some kind of modern art statue shaped like Tibetan tattoos on one side, a row of chaise lounges on the other.

Richard Rock is kicking back in one of the recliners. He's scribbling something into a marble-covered composition book. On the small table beside his chair are a neatly folded bath towel and a bottle of Hawaiian Tropic suntan lotion.

"Mr. Rock?" says Ceepak.

Rock closes his notebook.

"Hello again, Officers."

"We're looking for your wife."

"Really? Why?"

"Jake Pratt is dead."

Rock gives us what he must think is a very sincere and mournful head bob. "Heard about that. Tragic. Gonna miss him. Mighty fine dancer. Good little showman."

"Your private investigator, Ken Krabitz, is the one who shot him."

"Heard 'bout that, too." He gestures toward the swimming pool. "That's why I'm keepin' an eye on Kyle—Kenny's son." He leans forward, whispers, "Might be best if we don't talk about what happened across the street in front of the boy, hear?"

The kid swims to the edge of the pool, hauls himself up out of the water. He looks to be eleven, maybe twelve. Olive complexion. Dark hair. He might be five feet tall but probably only weighs about eighty pounds soaking wet, which he is right now.

"Is everything okay, Uncle Rick?" the skinny kid asks, toweling off his hair with a bath sheet he found on the foot of the chaise lounge closest to the pool ladder.

"Everything's fine, son. Why don't you run on inside there." He gestures toward what I'm assuming is the spa's clubhouse. "Go grab us a couple Coke-Colas."

"Are these guys cops?"

"Go fetch us them Cokes, hear?"

"Are they the assholes who arrested Kenny?"

"Kyle?" says Rock, sitting up in his recliner. "Watch your language, boy. What happened to your daddy don't give you no excuse to talk to your elders that a'way. It's time to paint your butt white and run with the antelope."

"What the fuck is that supposed to mean?"

Yep: he's Kenny Krabitz's kid all right.

"It means it's time for you to stop arguing and do as you're told! Go fetch us them Cokes!"

"Jesus. All right already."

Kyle pads away sullenly, his bare wet feet smacking like flip-flops on the tile floor the whole way.

"Poor boy," says Rock when the kid is out of earshot.

"Where is your wife?" Ceepak asks again.

"With David Zuckerman. They're hoping to post bail, help Kenny out of this jam. He only did what he had to do. Crazy Jake came at him with a military pistol!"

"We'd like to talk to Mr. Zuckerman as well."

That surprises Rock. "Really? Why?"

"It seems he is the one who invited Lady Jasmine to last evening's performance of your show."

"Shoot, son. Who's trying to sell you that pile of cow pies?"

"Lady Jasmine."

"Really? Well, Officer Ceepak—she's lying."

"Perhaps. However, her husband corroborates her statement."

"The midget man? Mighty Mo-Mo?"

"Yes, sir. If they were invited to the show, why were you so concerned about security last night?"

"You know, I don't spend that much time worrying about Lady Jasmine. I truly am not that concerned about her."

"Yesterday—"

"This is today, Officer Ceepak. No sense playing Monday-morning quarterback when we got us bigger fish to fry."

Ceepak sighs again. It's like everybody we meet in Atlantic City is determined to keep us spinning around in circles underneath a dark dome.

"Are you a frequent visitor to an establishment known as Lucky Lilani's Stress Therapy?" he asks Rock.

"Lucky who?"

I help out: "Lucky Lilani's. It's a Chinese massage parlor on the boardwalk."

"Now why the blazes would I go to a massage parlor? There's a Jacuzzi right over yonder, behind them palm bushes. If I get a crick in my neck, I can just go soak it in the whirlpool. Don't need no masseuse if you got you a Jacuzzi."

"We might need to examine your credit card bills to verify your statement."

"Fine. Just talk to David. He handles all the bookkeeping."

"Then we'll ask him about your wife's credit cards as well. Particularly the one issued under the alias Janice Stone."

"Sure. That there's the name Jessica uses when she needs to protect our privacy. Keeps the paparazzi from houndin' the kids."

"It is also the credit card your wife used to pay for Mr. Pratt's motel room across the street at the Royal Lodge."

"Uhm-hmm. Makes sense."

"Why was she renting a room for Mr. Pratt?"

"Because she is a very compassionate woman."

"Why didn't you or your wife tell us where we might find Mr. Pratt last night?"

"Because we didn't know where he was holed up."

Ceepak arches an eyebrow. "You didn't?"

"No, sir. I know I sure didn't."

"You both knew about the room. Across the street."

"Yes. We sure did. But we didn't think he'd be there. See, Jake knew we knew about his room so he also knew not to go there."

"But he did."

"He sure 'nuff did. Reckon he outfoxed us. Won't happen again. Trust me."

"Why did your wife think it was necessary for Jake Pratt to move into the Royal Lodge motel?"

"She heard tell that the fellow Jake was bunking with over at the Holiday Inn, this other dancer, Mr. Magnum, was a homosexual. Jessica didn't think Jake ought to be sharing a room with such a person, since the Bible says homosexuality is a sin. I reckon you can see why I love my Jessie so darn much. Good Christian woman. Been together fifteen years. Lookin' forward to fifteen more."

Man, talk about oblivious. This guy's wife is across the street shacking up with one of his hunky Chippendales dancers and he buys her recycled Dr. Laura crap about saving Jake from the vast gay recruitment conspiracy?

"See, fellers," says Rock, "Jake Pratt don't need any more sexual deviations like he might pick up from a radical-gay-type roommate. So my wife did the right thing, booked him a solo room across the street. She has what they call maternal instincts. Mother hens the whole cast—even the odd ducks like Jake Pratt."

"Why didn't you tell us about Pratt's new accommodations when you discovered your notebooks were missing and you suspected Jake Pratt was the one who stole them?"

"I reckon we're just not as sharp as you fellers. But this morning, Kenny-boy finally put two and two together. That's how come he got the notion to go check out the room over at the Royal Lodge."

"Why didn't you alert Detective Flynn, as you promised you would."

"Promise? I know I never promised anything to Mr. Flynn."

"Did you ever consider that the real reason your wife rented the room was because she and Mr. Pratt were romantically involved?"

Rock narrows his eyes. "You be careful, son, hear? You watch what you say about my wife and the sanctity of our marriage. Mrs. Rock has always been one hundred percent faithful. We made us vows. In front of Jesus and God almighty!"

I butt in: "Is Mrs. Rock at the ACPD building right now?"

"If that's where the jail is, that's where she and Dave Zuckerman went. I hope they spring Kenny-boy soon. I don't want to be babysittin' little Kyle all day long! Boy has a mouth on him."

Ceepak gestures toward the composition book, now serving as a coaster for the suntan-lotion bottle. "Working on a new illusion?"

"Might. Never know when inspiration's gonna mule-kick me in the head." He stands. Wraps his things up in a towel. "Now, if you two will excuse me, I best escort young Kyle up to his room so he can change out of them wet swimmin' trunks before his butt cheeks wrinkle up into a pair of prunes."

Great. Another image I don't want in my head.

Maybe the new trick Rock's working on can make it disappear.

Just like his PI made Jake Pratt disappear before he could contradict anything anybody said about him.

28

I'm thinking we should rent one of those Bosnian rolling-chair pushers for the day.

We came to Atlantic City on the Coast City Bus. We have no cop car. No motorcycles. We don't even have a trail bike like those two ACPD cops who showed up last night to guard the crime scene. The Atlantic City police department and jail are over in the Clayton G. Graham Public Safety Building on Atlantic Avenue, one of the yellow properties on the Monopoly board. I'm wondering if Ventnor Avenue and Marvin Gardens will be next door.

Anyhow, to talk to Mrs. Rock or David Zuckerman, we need to be a mile and a half further south, but first we need to find a casino exit, something the Xanadu makes extremely difficult because they don't want you to take your money down the street to somebody else's hot slots.

After a few false turns, we make it outside to the transportation center—a concrete-and-pillars parking garage like you'd find in any New Jersey mall, except it's been classed-up with a rubber-backed red carpet and velvet ropes clipped to brass stanchions. Swanky. Except the place still reeks of wet concrete mixed with exhaust fumes.

We inch forward in the taxi line while Ceepak works his cell phone.

"So her story checks out?" He's talking to Cyrus Parker. "Roger that." He covers the phone's mouthpiece. "Danny?"

"Yeah?"

"Those dancers you met last night with Mrs. Rock's body double. Do you remember their names?"

I wrack my brain. "Jim Bob and Blaine."

"Cyrus? Could you please check with Christina Crites, the stage manager, and determine the lodging accommodations for two dancers from Rock's show? Jim Bob and Blaine. Right. We're on our way to ACPD headquarters. Come again?" Ceepak grins. "Roger that." He snaps his clamshell shut.

"What'd he say?" I ask.

"He verified Lady Jasmine's alibi. She was at the blackjack table from nineteen-thirty hours until twenty-thirty. Cyrus's team was then able to track her on a series of PTZ cameras as she moved from the casino floor to the Shalimar Theater. She and her entourage took no detours. He also confirmed our suspicions about the backstage camera. When viewed in super-slow motion, a slight visual glitch is noticeable at precisely nineteen-fifty-five, immediately after David Zuckerman passes underneath the lens."

And goes around to the other side to flick the switch on that mirror contraption.

"So what'd he say that made you smile?" I ask.

"Cyrus requested that we inform Mr. Zuckerman that the Xanadu Hotel and Casino intends to bill 'Rock 'n Wow!' for the overtime pay due the extra security personnel he called in under false pretenses."

In the taxi, Ceepak makes another phone call. Ohio.

"Thank you, Ms. Porter-Burt. Appreciate it. He pled guilty? Then it's all good. Come again?"

I can't hear what the prosecuting attorney is saying but it's making Ceepak clench his jaw.

"Does he have that right?" he asks as he white-knuckles his cell phone. "Very well. I'll expect to hear from him."

He snaps the clamshell shut. Hard. I hope his brand-new LG unit came with hinge insurance. When he flipped it shut, it sounded like he was slamming a screen door made out of brittle plastic.

"Trouble?" I ask.

"According to assistant prosecuting attorney Lisa Porter-Burt, as part of his plea-bargain agreement, my father insisted on being granted the right to call me. Today."

"And Porter-Burt agreed?"

"No. Her boss did."

The rest of the cab ride is pretty quiet, unless you count the sound of Ceepak's jaw popping in and out of its socket. We pay the driver four bucks for hauling us the one and a half miles from the Xanadu to 2711 Atlantic Avenue.

Our deputy badges get us past security and into the processing room where Zuckerman is standing at a counter, signing papers.

"Mr. Zuckerman?" says Ceepak.

He grunts but doesn't look up from whatever it is he is so busy affixing his name to.

"Mr. Zuckerman?"

He turns around. When Ceepak uses that "don't-make-me-say-your-name-again" voice, folks usually listen.

"Yes?"

"Where is Mr. Krabitz?"

"Released on bail. Left me with all the paperwork."

"Where did he go?"

Zuckerman sets his smirk on annoyed. "I have no idea. He is a private contractor."

"Where is Mrs. Rock? We were told that she was here with you."

"She was. However, since the Rocks are currently without a nanny, she went back to the Xanadu to make arrangements for ongoing child care. She also needs to sort out their new accommodations since their previous living quarters are currently considered a crime scene."

"Very well," says Ceepak. "We'll talk to her back at the Xanadu."

"And why do you need to talk to Mrs. Rock?" Zuckerman snaps. "Surely she and her family have been put through enough in the past twenty-four hours. If you have any further questions, kindly address them to me."

"Fine. Why did Mrs. Rock rent a room for Jake Pratt at the Royal Lodge Motel?"

"Who says she did?"

"The motel desk clerk."

"Did he take her fingerprints?"

"Doubtful," says Ceepak. "Why?"

"How can he be certain it was Jessica Rock and not Sherry Amour?"

"Who?"

"The body double," I say. "Her first name is Sherry, remember?"

Ceepak nods.

"Put on the right wig," says Zuckerman, "they could be identical twins. Miss Amour and Mr. Pratt were the ones spending time together at that sleazebag motel."

"Mr. Rock told us his wife paid for the room," says Ceepak.

"And I'm sure Jessie had her reasons for doing so. Probably to protect Sherry. The two women are, as you might imagine given their work relationship, close. Unfortunately, Sherry is an alcoholic and a sexual deviant."

"What makes you say that?" asks Ceepak.

Zuckerman's lip sneers up toward his nose. "Did you watch any pay-per-view porno in your room last night?"

The hairs on the back of Ceepak's neck bristle. "Why is that relevant?"

"Check out the Classics channel. In her day, Sherry Amour was quite the adult movie star. A very talented and agile performer."

"And now you're suggesting that she and Pratt were intimate?"

Zuckerman's still shooting us his snide I-know-more-than-you grin. "Such was my understanding. And now, he's dead and she's missing."

"Missing?"

"Skipped town. Stage manager can't locate her. She's not in her room, not answering her cell. Listen, you're cops. You've seen this sort of thing before. Older woman. Younger man. He finds the relationship satisfying so long as the older women isn't grossly unattractive and has enough money to buy him gifts. But, being nineteen, Jake Pratt isn't going to remain exclusive to Miss Amour, not if he meets an attractive girl closer to his own age, a girl who's into the same kind of kinky sex he's into."

"Katie?" I say—just to make sure I know whose reputation the sleazebag is sliming now.

Zuckerman nods. "Ask the kids. Talk to Britney. She'll tell you. Nanny Katie and Jake Pratt were hot and heavy. A classic backstage romance. Happens all the time when we go on tour."

"I don't think that's what was going on," I say.

"So?"

Guess Zuckerman doesn't care what I think. He turns to Ceepak. "The nanny was murdered during the Lucky Numbers routine, correct?"

Ceepak nods, somewhat reluctantly.

"Well, Miss Amour isn't onstage for that one. In fact, after the transportation scene, which usually goes up at eight-twenty-five, Sherry's done for the night, leaving her free to roam around backstage, maybe sneak into room AA-four and interrupt an assignation between her young male companion and her younger, more accommodating competition—Kinky Katie."

I want to tell Zuckerman to stick a plug in his piehole but Ceepak shoots me a look. Shakes his head. Guess Zuckerman's still not worth it.

"Of course," Ceepak says, "we have no way to confirm who was in the backstage hallways during last evening's performance because you activated the mirror switch to disable the solitary surveillance camera."

"I sure did!" snaps Zuckerman. "It's imperative that our secrets remain just that. Secret."

"Did you tell Cyrus Parker?"

"Of course not. If one's goal is to maintain security, you do not alert those who would spy on you as to your intentions."

Ceepak changes his tack.

"Why did you request extra security in the auditorium last night when you were the one who invited Lady Jasmine to attend?"

"Who told you that?"

"Lady Jasmine."

The smirk broadens. "And you believed her?"

"She has proven truthful in other areas of her testimony."

"Right. Did she also tell you that crap about the massage parlor?"

Ceepak remains mute.

"She did, didn't she? She told you that Mr. Richard Rock spends all his downtime at some exotic Asian whorehouse on the boardwalk? You don't have to answer. Jasmine and her husband have been trying to smear our good names ever since we pulled into town. They even hired that Lilani Lee, a convicted sex peddler, by the way, to back up their cock-and-bull story because Richard Rock's well-known Christian values threaten Lady Jasmine's ticket sales. We're Disney. She, on the other hand, appeals to the same people who rent Sherry Amour movies up in their rooms."

"Thank you for your time," says Ceepak.

He's smiling.

He knows something. Something he's not telling Zuckerman or me.

"That's it?"

"Thank you for your time."

We head out into the hall; Ceepak spies an empty office.

"In here, Danny."

"What's up?" I ask.

"He's lying. If, as Zuckerman suggests, Ms. Lee is being paid to tarnish Mr. Rock's reputation, why did she insist that she had never met the man?"

Good point.

Ceepak pulls out his cell. I guess he didn't break it. "We need to talk to the two dancers. You say they escorted Ms. Amour home last evening?"

"Yeah."

"They might know something closer to the truth regarding her relationship with Jake Pratt."

He speed-dials Parker.

"Cyrus? John Ceepak. Do you have that motel information?" He jots down an address in his spiral notebook. "What's that?" he says to Parker. "Interesting. Roger that. We'll keep you posted."

He closes up his phone.

"What's up?" I ask.

"They are rooming at the Super Eight Motel on Tennessee Avenue."

"And?" I ask. I know there's more. Ceepak only says "interesting" when there is.

"Parker says we're not the only ones attempting to locate the two dancers. Apparently, Mr. Krabitz just contacted the stage manager and requested the same information."

29

The Super 8 Motel is, of course, located back near the boardwalk, on Tennessee Avenue.

We need to move from the yellow properties all the way to the oranges.

"It's pretty close to Caesars and all the other casinos," says Sergeant Lisa Knauf, the ACPD cop in charge of their motor pool as we sign her clipboard for our loaner vehicles. "Sorry this is all we have available right now," she adds.

"It'll work, Sergeant Knauf," says Ceepak. "In fact, they appear quite similar to the M-Gators John Deere provided for us over in Iraq."

"Probably because that place is full of sand, too," cracks Sergeant Lisa.

Our police vehicles for the day? A pair of four-wheel all-terrain vehicles typically employed by the ACPD beach patrol.

"Danny?" says Ceepak. "Do you know how to operate a Kawasaki 750cc quad-bike?"

"Yeah. Like a motorcycle."

"Exactly."

Of course, the beach patrol four-wheeler looks more like a supercharged riding lawn mower with humongous knobby tires, but the throttle is on the handle just like on a dirt bike and you squeeze the brake grips like on a ten-speed. This should be fun.

"Helmets, Danny. Helmets."

Right. I strap mine on.

"Head up Atlantic," says Sergeant Knauf. "Take the right on Tennessee." She doesn't add, "Do not pass Go, do not collect two hundred dollars." Before we leave town, I want to check out Mediterranean and Baltic. See if the rents really are that cheap.

Ceepak hops on his thunder-blue bike. Starts it up. I straddle mine. Goose the throttle. Get that whole zoom-zoom thing going.

"Let's roll!" Ceepak shouts over the din of our throaty four-stroke engines. These things sound like lawn mowers, too—angry ones that chewed too many weeds.

We scoot out of the parking lot and head up Atlantic Avenue. The four-wheelers are equipped with spinning lights up front but we don't flick 'em on. The word POLICE painted on the windscreen does the trick and people pull over to let us pass.

When we near Tennessee Avenue, Ceepak goes into one of those cocked-arm left turn signals I remember seeing in this safety bicycle-riding coloring book we hand out to kids back in Sea Haven. So, I do the same thing, even if it does make me look like a dork.

Up ahead, I can see the bright yellow and red Super 8 sign. The building is four stories tall, maybe half a block long. Looks like an adobe ranch house with cranberry trim. There's a fenced-in pool where the Royal Lodge would have a parking lot and white vinyl railings on all the floors so college kids don't use their terraces as diving boards.

"Danny?" shouts Ceepak.

Now his left arm is chopping straight ahead. Pointing toward the second floor.

I see it.

Kenny Krabitz, the scrawny PI, is kicking at a door. Pounding on it with his fist.

Good thing we borrowed the motorbikes. We got here just in time.

Ceepak gives his throttle a quick twist, pops a wheelie. "Head right," he yells. "I'll go left."

Ceepak fishtails his four-wheeler into a sharp turn and hops over the curb at one end of the sky blue swimming pool. He'll roll in to block the western staircase up to the second floor. I'll head up the street, swing in, and block the east. We'll cut off Krabitz's two escape routes, prevent him from kicking down the door into what I'm assuming is Blaine and Jim Bob's room.

"Krabitz!" I hear Ceepak scream. "Stay where you are!"

I glance left and see he is off his bike, pounding up the steel steps, two at a time, tearing off his helmet. He'd probably be reaching for his Glock right about now if, you know, Sergeant Lisa Knauf and the ACPD had issued us sidearms along with our ATVs.

I zip past an Aquafina machine and aim for the second set of steps.

"Freeze!" Ceepak screams as he starts running up the extremely long terrace.

"Fuck you, you fucking fuck!"

Yeah. It's Krabitz. He spins on his heels and heads for the staircase behind him: the one I'm aiming for.

"Freeze," I scream over my whining engine, so he knows we have this staircase blocked, too.

Krabitz grabs a railing and swings into a flying turn on the landing, halfway down the steps.

He is not going to stop.

He's going to run right past me and my ATV before I even dismount.

So I goose the throttle and aim for the steps.

Hey, steps are a type of terrain and this is supposed to be an all-terrain vehicle. The big balloon tires bump with a sharp jolt when they bite the metal lip of the first stair tread and haul me up. The shock-absorber springs boink up and down, making me do the same thing in the hard plastic seat.

"Shit!" Krabitz screams when he sees me gunning up the stairs for him.

Now the rear wheels of my golf cart on steroids dig into that first step and I heave forward. Krabitz retreats a step. My whining drive train torques, finds traction, and hauls me up another step. Krabitz retreats to the landing. I hear Ceepak clanking down the metal staircase behind our target.

This is a good thing.

Because I think I just exceeded the Kawasaki's maximum angle of attack. Four bouncing steps up, I start stuttering back down. I think I should've worn a dance belt with a cup today.

"Got him!" Ceepak hollers while he does something I can't see because the handlebars and gas tank on this thing are currently in my face and blocking my view. "Well done, Danny!"

As the pain in the Boyle family jewels subsides and my ride levels out, I can see that Ceepak has Krabitz pinned against the railing in a jujitsu armlock deal that looks pretty painful.

"Let me go, you fucking fuck!"

Oh, yeah. When Ceepak fully extends your arm, presses down on your elbow while simultaneously pulling up on your wrist—it'll hurt.

And when Krabitz is all splayed out like that, I can see the other missing prop pistol, the second Dick Tracy .38 caliber. It's tucked into the waistband of his pants. I know it's the second one because the ACPD still has the first snub-nosed pistol, the one he used to kill Jake Pratt, in their evidence room. Looks like Krabitz aimed to use this one on the two chorus boys if they didn't tell him what he wanted to hear.

"Awesome diversionary tactic, Danny," says Ceepak as we watch the ACPD cops haul Kenny Krabitz away for the second time in one day.

Mr. Zuckerman has probably been called back to the jail at the public safety building. He needs to post some more bail for his private investigator. As you might guess, it's against the law to kick open somebody's hotel room door after they tell you to go away. While we were busy corralling Krabitz, Blaine and Jim Bob were upstairs dialing 911.

"Let's go see if the two gentlemen in room two-twenty-four will talk to us," says Ceepak.

I follow him up the staircase.

We march to their room. Knock.

"Mr. Brisco? Mr. McMillan?"

Apparently, Cyrus Parker gave Ceepak last names to go with Jim Bob and Blaine.

"Go away!" says a voice on the other side of the door.

Ceepak holds his deputy badge up to the peephole.

"We're with the Atlantic City police. We'd like to ask you a few questions."

"That's what that other jerk-face said, too!" It's Blaine. I recognize his voice from last night. "He said he was with the police. He showed us his pistol to prove it!"

"Did he show you a badge?"

"Yes!" comes the indignant answer. "And it looked just like yours. You can buy those things for fifty cents on the boardwalk."

"I assure you, sir, these are legitimately issued deputy badges."

"Look, musclehead!" Jim Bob jumps into the act. I'm guessing he checked out Ceepak's chiseled male physique while peeping through the hole to examine his badge. "We don't want to talk to you! So go away!"

"It is, of course, your prerogative to refuse to speak to us," says Ceepak.

"But, come on!" I say. "We're just trying to help your friend."

"What friend?" asks Blaine.

"Ms. Sherry Amour."

"She's gone," says Jim Bob. "Left town late last night."

"What time?" I ask.

"We don't know. We haven't seen her since the show came down."

"Now who's lying?" I say.

"What?" The door sounds like it's in a snit.

"Come on," I say. "You guys escorted Ms. Amour out of the karaoke bar last night. Lip Sync Lee's. I was there, remember?"

There's this pause.

"We don't remember you," says Jim Bob.

Ceepak sighs. Me, too. So far, I don't think a single person in Atlantic City has told us the truth.

"I'm going to slip my business card under the door," says Ceepak. "I suggest that you call the Atlantic City police department. Ask them to verify our authenticity. Once you are confident we are who we say we are, perhaps you will reconsider your position and speak with us. You can call me on my cell at any time, day or night."

"And why would I want to do that?" says Jim Bob.

"Because we are very interested in ascertaining the truth about your two friends. Jake Pratt. Sherry Amour."

"Really? Or are you boys being paid to find Mr. Rock's stupid notebook, too?"

"Come again?" says Ceepak as he and I both lean in closer to the door.

"That asshole who was just here? He said he was going to 'wring our faggy fucking necks' unless we told him where Jake Pratt hid 'the last goddamn notebook.' "

"What did he mean by the 'last' notebook?" asks Ceepak.

"How the hell should we know? The man is psychotic."

"Does he think Jake Pratt gave this last notebook to you or Ms. Amour for safekeeping?"

No answer.

Ceepak presses on: "What can you tell us about their relationship? Were the two of them romantically involved?"

The door continues to give us the silent treatment.

Ceepak's cell phone rings. "Excuse me, gentlemen," he says politely. "I need to take this call."

Man, you make a plea bargain up in Ohio, your wishes get granted fast.

Ceepak steps away, snaps open his cell.

"So what's in the 'last' notebook?" I ask the door. "Another one of Rock's magic tricks? Did Pratt steal it so he could finance his getaway? That's what everybody keeps telling us. They say that Jake Pratt killed the nanny, my friend Katie Landry, then he stole some of Mr. Rock's secret notebooks so he could extort a million dollars, buy a couple plane tickets to Mexico or something. Then, about an hour ago, Mr. Zuckerman tried to make us believe that Jake and Sherry were hot and heavy and that Sherry was the one who killed Katie in a wild fit of jealous rage. I figure Zuckerman watches too many soap operas, how about you guys?"

No reply. I thought they might want to trash *The Young and the Restless* with me.

"Danny?" Ceepak returns to our mute metal door. "That wasn't my father. We need to roll."

"Where?"

"Back to the Royal Lodge. Dr. McDaniels has arrived on scene."

"Has she figured out who shot who up in room two-twelve?"

"Not yet. She tells me she's still working the trajectory angles, counting cartridges."

"But?" I know there's a but.

Ceepak hesitates. "Earlier today she was able to examine Katie Landry's body."

"And?"

More hesitation.

"Come on? What's up?"

"Dr. McDaniels paid particular attention to the ligature markings around her neck."

"And?"

"It seems Katie wasn't just strangled. She was tortured first."

We motor our ATVs over to the Royal Lodge Motel.

I hear something scraping along the pavement under my ride, like one of those dangling mufflers you sometimes see dragging along the pavement under an old clunker. Those puppies shoot up such a shower of sparks it looks like there's a tiny welder strapped to the chassis.

This is what I think about when I don't want to think about Katie being tortured.

It almost works.

Fortunately, the first crime-scene motel is only a few blocks away from the Super 8.

We pull up to the police tape at the far end of the parking lot, kill our engines.

"Where's Dr. McDaniels?" Ceepak peels off his helmet and asks the bicycle cops still standing guard.

"Upstairs with the chief."

"She asked us to swing by. She has new information pertaining to the incident across the street."

The bike-patrol guys tug up on the yellow ribbon, allowing us to scoot underneath and enter their crime scene. We cross the asphalt parking lot and start clunking up the metal steps. I'm glad I'm not riding up on a supercharged garden tractor this time.

When we reach the terrace, I see Dr. McDaniels standing outside room 212. She's scowling up at the sun, sucking in some fresh air, maybe wishing she still smoked. She's over sixty. I figure she used to be a smoker. In the olden days, everybody smoked. Constantly. Watch a movie.

New Jersey's (and maybe America's) premiere forensic expert sort of looks like a garden gnome without the ski cap or beard. Dr. McDaniels is short, under five feet tall, with bony matchsticks for legs and arms. She keeps her prickly white hair short, too. Wears a female buzz cut that reminds me of a bottle brush.

The last time we worked together, Dr. McDaniels was decked out in cargo shorts and a Hawaiian shirt from the Tabasco Sauce Collection. Today she's wearing a somber black pantsuit over a black blouse. Maybe because it's October. Maybe because she wants to show her respect for all the dead. She met Katie Landry in Sea Haven a couple summers ago; came to visit her in the hospital. She knew Detective Flynn, and probably his partner, too.

Dr. McDaniels sees us. Nods. "Ceepak. Boyle."

Usually, Dr. McD delights in busting our chops—zinging Ceepak with some wisecrack about his bulging muscles or telling me how my abs remind her of Irish oatmeal. Lumpy.

Today, all we get are our names.

"I went to the Shore Memorial morgue early this AM, prior to receiving the call on this incident," she reports without a trace of emotion, sounding more like Ceepak than Ceepak sometimes does. "During my examination, I paid particular attention to the ligature markings circling Ms. Landry's neck. The numerous abrasions and indentation marks made it readily apparent that the strangulation device had been repeatedly tightened, then loosened. As you know, all it takes to cause unconsciousness is eleven pounds of pressure applied against both carotid arteries for a period of ten seconds."

Ceepak nods so I do, too—even though I never knew any of that.

"If the pressure is subsequently released, consciousness will be regained rather quickly, usually within ten seconds. We hypothesize, then, that her assailant choked Ms. Landry at least a half-dozen times, undoubtedly intending to terrify her by making her think she was dying—in much the same manner that waterboarding gives a torture victim the sense that he or she is drowning. It is no wonder Ms. Landry involuntary urinated during the ordeal, which is often the case during strangulation." She stops. "Are you gentlemen okay hearing this?"

We both nod.

"Then you are better men than I'll ever be," she says with a tight crinkle of her pale blue eyes. "It made me sick. I haven't tossed my cookies like that in fifteen, twenty years." She shakes her head. "Torture sucks. You have any MP buddies still doing it down in Gitmo, tell them to knock it off."

"Yes, ma'am," says Ceepak.

McDaniels sucks in some more fresh air, pushes on: "I also noted the pronounced presence of petechiae—tiny red spots caused by ruptured capillaries—around the eyes, under the eyelids, and on the neck above the area of constriction."

"I noted that as well," says Ceepak. "She also presented with extremely bloodshot eyes due, no doubt, to similar capillary rupture in the whites surrounding her pupils."

"Right," says Dr. McDaniels.

My shoulders sag and my legs tremble with some sort of horror palsy. I hate hearing this kind of gory detail about a girl I was once head-over-heels in love with.

"Danny?" This from Dr. McDaniels.

"Yes, ma'am?"

"The phenomenon Ceepak and I noted, this pronounced petechiae, typically suggests a particularly vigorous struggle between the victim and assailant. In other words, Katie Landry did not give up easily."

Even though she was bound and gagged. So much for all the consensual sex-play theories.

Dr. McDaniels turns to Ceepak. "As you undoubtedly know, John, sexual humiliation, as evidenced by the ill-fitting S and M costume Ms. Landry was forced to wear, is another indication that she was tortured before she ultimately succumbed to asphyxiation."

"Yes," says Ceepak sadly. "It is, unfortunately, a common technique."

I remember the photos from the Abu Ghraib prison. Pyramids of naked Iraqi men with women's panties draped over their heads. That girl leading the nude Muslim man around on a dog leash, shooting the camera a smiling thumbs-up.

"The killer wanted information from Katie," mutters Ceepak.

"Yeah," says Dr. McDaniels. "He or she sure did. And you know what? I don't think Ms. Landry cracked. I don't think she gave the bastard what he or she was looking for." Now Dr. McDaniels knuckle-punches me in the arm like she used to do when we first met. "Irish girls? We're tough, Mr. Boyle. Fighters."

"Thank you." It's all I can say over the lump in my throat.

"I gotta get back in there," she says, gesturing toward room 212.

"Thank you for the update," says Ceepak.

"We'll keep you posted. We're close to pegging a more precise time of death using the virteous humor formula."

Eye jelly, they call it. A neat bubble of viscous fluid sealed off from the rest of the body inside the eyeball. You measure the levels of nitrogen, sodium chloride, calcium, and potassium in the postmortem eye and you get a pretty precise T.O.D. I took notes the last time Dr. McD worked a crime scene with us.

"You know," she says, "if Katie held out, didn't give whoever strangled her what they were looking for, the search is, most likely, still continuing. So find this bastard, boys. I've examined enough dead bodies for one day."

Ceepak responds with a very slow, bobble-head nod. Usually, that means he just figured something out.

Dr. McDaniels disappears into room 212. "Okay, guys," I hear her say to her team. "Finish the photographs. Chief Maroney? Dollars to doughnuts, Mr. Pratt was dead on the bed before your two detectives even walked through the door."

"You sure?"

"No. I'm damn sure. This thing only plays one way. Krabitz killed Pratt, then ambushed your guys."

Orders get barked. Radios crackle. I don't think Kenny Krabitz will be released on his own recognizance any time soon.

Wow.

Krabitz killed Pratt.

Then he, not Pratt, killed the two ACPD detectives.

And what did he do the minute David Zuckerman and Jessica Rock sprang him from his jail cell?

He headed over to the Super 8 Motel to knock on Jim Bob and Blaine's door. Actually, I think he meant to kick it in until we showed up.

Because he was looking for the "last notebook."

The one Jake Pratt didn't have.

"The last notebook," I mumble.

"Roger that," says Ceepak, who no doubt reached that same conclusion back when he was bobble-heading. "I believe it has been missing since yesterday and that whoever hired Krabitz had initially suspected Katie knew where it might be located."

"Did Krabitz kill Katie, too?"

"It's a possibility."

"That's why Krabitz was skulking around in the lobby before the show, demanding to see Zuckerman, wondering 'what the big problem' was. He's their hit man!"

Ceepak's eyebrows slant quizzically over his nose.

Doesn't stop me. "He could've gone backstage. If he knew about the security camera, how they disabled it, he could've gone into Katie's room. Killed her."

"Why?"

"I don't know. Because somebody told him to? Why'd he kill Jake Pratt?"

"Unclear at this juncture. And, Danny, we must still account for the presence of Mr. Pratt's pubic hair on the floor in Katie's room."

Yeah. I've been trying to deal with that for nearly twenty-four hours.

"Not to mention the sales receipt found in the shopping bag and the love note scrawled on the fogged bathroom mirror," Ceepak continues.

"*U* could be Sherry Amour," I say. "It's kind of an ambiguous love note, you know?" Then I remember: "Katie said she'd found something!"

"Come again?"

"Yesterday afternoon, when Katie left me that voice mail, she said she needed to talk to me about Jake Pratt. Said she'd found something."

"Did she elaborate further?"

I shake my head. "No. She couldn't. She had to hang up. Some woman kept calling for her. Probably Mrs. Rock. Could've been Sherry Amour."

"Interesting," says Ceepak as he begins drifting back toward the staircase. I follow behind him. "Perhaps Katie had found the 'last notebook.' "

"So what was in it?" I ask. "More magic-trick plans like the ones they found in Pratt's room?"

"Doubtful," says Ceepak.

"How come?"

"Because, so far, Danny, that is exactly what everybody has insisted *was* in them. No, I suspect that the missing notebook or notebooks contain something of a more personal, potentially incriminating nature."

"Like a diary or something?"

"Precisely."

His cell phone chirps. He whips it off his belt.

"This is Ceepak. Go."

He covers the mouthpiece to clue me in to who's calling: Cyrus Parker. Not his dad.

"Fascinating." Now he glances at his watch. "We'll be there in five."

He closes up the phone.

"What's up?"

"Cyrus has requested that we return to the control room and take a look at some footage his team recently isolated."

"More on Lady Jasmine?"

"Negative. Jake Pratt, riding in an elevator with a blond woman. Either Mrs. Rock or Ms. Amour."

"Parker can't tell which one it is?"

"Affirmative. He hopes you might be able to help them make

that call, since you saw Ms. Amour up close in the karaoke club."

"What were they doing on the elevator?" I ask. "Pratt and the blonde?"

"Holding hands."

31

We abandon our motorbikes with the ACPD officers guarding the Royal Lodge and dash across the street to the Xanadu.

Actually, Ceepak insists we go up the block to the crosswalk and wait for the light to change. Then we look both ways and proceed across the avenue when the red palm switches to the sideways ambling man. I'm just glad Ceepak doesn't make me hold his hand while we cross the street.

That's what Jake Pratt is doing with one of the two busty blondes on a video screen inside the security office.

"This footage was captured a little after thirteen-hundred hours on Sunday," says Cyrus Parker. "It's from elevator twelve. Over in the Crystal Palace Tower."

That's where my high-roller room is located.

Parker taps the TV screen. "They're holding hands pretty tight. The blonde seems to be the one initiating the squeeze."

"Roger that." Ceepak agrees. Me, too.

In fact, at one point the blonde grips Pratt's hands so tight, his fingers splay out. It looks like she's milking a goat udder. I think the only reason the two lovebirds aren't tearing each other's clothes off and leaping into a *Fatal Attraction* sex-in-the-elevator scene is because there's one of those slot-machine-loving Italian grandmothers in a flamingo-print muumuu riding with them.

"Watch this," says Parker.

The elevator stops, the doors slide open, and muumuu woman waddles off. When she's gone and the doors glide shut again, the blonde gives Pratt a soft, maybe teasing, peck on his cheek. She raises her left hand so she can nibble on his ear or whisper something dirty. Pratt just stands there, grinning like a horny idiot.

They don't do much else, at least not in the elevator. Since they work at the Xanadu, they must know about the eye-in-the-sky surveillance cameras recording their every move in every corner of the building. Apparently they were savvy enough to save their triple-X action for across the street at the Royal Lodge.

"Who is she?" Parker asks. "Mrs. Rock or Ms. Amour?"

"I can't tell," I admit.

"Rewind it," Parker tells the woman twisting the control knobs. "Take one more look, okay, Boyle?"

So we watch it all again and my eyeballs get the front-row seat. It's tough. The two women could be identical twins. Same hair. Same face. Same impossibly rotund boobs.

"I'm sorry," I say. "I can't tell."

"Okay," says Parker. "At least I only have two people to keep tabs on today. One of them, Ms. Amour, nobody can find. The other one, she's getting her nails done. Bring up seventeen, Kim." The woman at the controls punches some keys and we're looking at the Xanadu's luxurious spa. Mrs. Rock, wearing a bathrobe, her hair in a towel turban, is sitting in a padded chair while servants in nurse uniforms buff her hands and feet.

"Who is currently watching the Rocks' children?" Ceepak asks. "Mr. Rock?"

"Kim?" says Parker.

"The kids are in the candy shop off the main lobby," says the woman at the console as she clacks a couple more keys. "They have a new nanny and she's pretty lame. I think she's one of the chorus girls from the show. Young. African American. She keeps yawning. Needs coffee. Anyway, she's letting the rug rats run wild."

She clicks her mouse. The camera zooms in.

"Britney just shoplifted a pocketful of gummi fish."

"Gentlemen," says Parker gesturing toward his day-shift super-snoop, "I suggest you do not get on Ms. Kim Hammond's bad side. She'll see every bad thing you've ever done and then send a videotape of it to your mother *and* your wife."

"Now the girl's pawing through the malted milk balls," Hammond reports.

Parker heaves a sigh. "Have one of the guys suggest to young Miss Rock that she put her goodies in a paper sack and pay for them up front. About time someone taught that child some manners."

"You got it," says Hammond. "Jeremy? This is Kim upstairs. Go have a word with the young girl in the LA Dodgers baseball cap moving toward the caramel apples inside Kubla Khandy. Ask her to show you the inside of her pockets."

"You want me to escort her upstairs?" a voice comes back over the radio. "Hold her in the room?"

Parker shakes his head. "Nah. Just tell that damn babysitter to wake up and pay for what the kid tried to rip off."

On the screen, I watch a beefy man in a sport jacket step into the picture and tap Britney on the shoulder while her hand is literally in the cookie jar. Well, the jelly bean jar.

Britney, of course, throws a hissy fit. Pouts. Stomps on the floor. Throws a fistful of Jelly Bellies up in the air.

The new nanny looks like she's awake now.

When Britney won't show the security guard what's crammed in her pockets, the nanny digs inside them to see for herself.

Now Britney is screaming. Probably threatening to sue the casino, sue the new nanny.

I see her brother, little Richie. He's still wearing that tiger backpack but now he's pounding his fists on the babysitter's butt.

"Dammit! Haul those two brats up to their mother!" says Parker—almost loud enough for his floor man Jeremy to hear him without the aid of his radio. "She's in the spa."

"Ten-four," comes the reply.

We see the kids being escorted out of the store.

"Let's bring the nanny up here," suggests Ceepak. "She's in the show. Works with both Ms. Amour and Mrs. Rock. She might be better able to ID who it is on the elevator with Jake Pratt."

"Good idea. Kim?"

"I'll tell Jeremy."

"Thanks," says Parker. "Damn kids had me fooled."

That's right. Yesterday, he told us he'd had dinner with the whole Rock clan. Thought the kids were a couple of cuties. Another illusion shattered.

"Cyrus?" says Ceepak.

"Yeah?"

"Yesterday, you indicated that you had helped Mr. Rock with his act but had signed a confidentiality agreement that prevented you from revealing what it was you had done."

"True and true."

"Given recent developments, do you now feel at liberty to divulge what it is you did for Rock?"

"You mean will I go back on my word?"

"Circumstances have changed."

"Yeah. They have a way of doing that on a regular basis, don't they?"

"People have been murdered," Ceepak adds. "Katie Landry. Jake Pratt. Detectives Flynn and Weddle."

"I didn't sign any damn confidentiality agreement," says Ms. Hammond from her control console.

"True," says Parker. "However, Kim, since technically, you work for me—"

"Hell's bells—you can't swear me to secrecy just because you swore it."

"Ms. Hammond?" says Ceepak.

"Yeah?"

"Mr. Parker and I attempt to live our lives by a very strict, perhaps overly rigid, moral code."

"Tell me about it," says Hammond as she gulps a slug of coffee from a lipstick-rimmed mug. "The big man won't even let me lie to myself about how many doughnuts I had on my break."

Ceepak makes a finger tent under his nose. "Allow me to advance a theory. If I am wrong in the particulars, I trust, Cyrus, that you will cut me off and, thereby, prevent me from spreading further falsehoods."

"Yeah. Okay. I could do that," says Parker. "Because I won't lie or tolerate your lies, either. So, if you get it wrong, I'd be duty-bound to tell you. Cool."

"Very well. I presume you primarily assisted the show's stage technicians, helping them gain access to your security-camera feeds, that you wired them up to all pertinent cameras arrayed along the route Mr. Rock follows when he leaves the Shalimar Theater and proceeds to the high-roller room."

Parker doesn't correct or contradict Ceepak. In fact, he doesn't do anything. He just stands there like a six-foot-two brick wall.

"I also assume that Mr. Rock has his own backstage control room where the show's technicians switch between your camera feeds and determine the sequencing of images to be shown to the audience on the video screen."

The room is quiet, except for the constant clack and tap of computer keys, the whirr of hard-drive fans.

"Is that it?" asks Parker.

"Yes," says Ceepak.

"Good. Next issue: how are we going to find Ms. Sherry Amour? You got any theories on that one, Lieutenant Ceepak?"

"Not yet, Colonel Parker."

The two former soldiers are addressing each other by their old military titles. That means, as far as they're concerned, it's all good. Nobody violated the Code today.

Well, nobody in this room.

Out there in the rest of Atlantic City, they're trashing it every chance they get.

32

"Can you guys like arrest me or something?"

The shapely young dancer is throwing herself on the mercy of the security control room, hoping we'll lock her up and put her out of her misery: working with the Rock children. Her name is Kathy Young and she still looks like what she told us she was until she graduated from college last spring: a "FoXXy Dancer" with the Morgan State University marching band.

"I can't babysit those two monsters one more minute." She sips some coffee out of a paper cup Kim Hammond fetched from the break room. "Well, the boy is okay. At least he was until he started banging on my butt."

She raises her injured rump half an inch off her seat so she can rub the sorest spot. Like I said, she's very shapely. "We want you to look at this surveillance-camera clip," says Parker. "Can you tell us who that is?"

He replays the elevator love scene

"Ohmigod." Young giggles. "I had no idea."

"No idea of what?" asks Ceepak.

"That Jake was, you know, hooking up with an older woman. Someone in the show!"

"Does that surprise you?"

"Well, uh, yeah. He's what? Nineteen? She's got to be at least forty. Maybe forty-five. Who knew Jake was into the whole MILF scene, hunh?"

"Excuse me?" This from Ceepak.

I translate. Loosely. "Mothers I'd like to . . . fool around with."

"I see."

"Who is the woman with Mr. Pratt?" asks Parker.

"It's a pretty big secret."

"Did you sign a confidentiality agreement?"

"No."

"No?"

"Unh-unh. 'Cause we weren't supposed to even know about Mrs. Rock's body double, this lady named Sherry, who they keep like hidden upstairs in the hotel until the very last second before the show, but we're not supposed to know that because we're just dumb girl dancers and they don't trust us with any of their big-deal, super-duper secrets. We were hired to look pretty and kill time between tricks. None of us even get to work on the magic stuff, which, like, totally sucks."

"I see," says Ceepak.

"Except the big opening where the kids fly in. But everybody already knows how they do that."

They do? Ceepak and I couldn't figure it out.

She taps the glass on the video monitor. "That looks like this Sherry chick. The body double."

"Are you certain?"

"No. It could be Mrs. Rock. They both wear the exact same wig. Oh, wow. How weird would that be? Jake messing around with the boss's wife? Talk about fishing off the company pier where you eat."

Ceepak puzzles up an eyebrow as the chorus girl mashes up her clichés.

"Look hard." Parker presses on. "Is that Mrs. Rock or Ms. Amour?"

"I can't tell. They look so much alike, you know?"

Uh, yeah. That's whey they call 'em body doubles.

"You were only hired recently?" asks Ceepak.

"That's right. The same with all the girls. We're locals. I was dancing down at the Trop, saw the casting notice in the trades. This show pays better. We still get to go on, tonight, right? They're not going to shut us down on account of, you know—what happened to the other nanny?"

"It is my understanding," says Parker, "that all performances of 'Rock 'n Wow!' will go on as previously scheduled."

The way he says it? I think Security Chief Cyrus Parker lost that round with the PR people. Must be why there hasn't been much about the murder of Katie Landry on TV or in any of the local papers, why nobody seems to care that a beautiful woman was murdered last night, that a troubled dancer and two cops went down today. Either that, or no one in Atlantic City reads a paper or watches the news, just that in-house TV channel where they explain how to play baccarat.

"What can you tell us about Ms. Sherry Amour?" asks Ceepak.

"Is that her last name?"

"Yes, ma'am."

"Sounds like a porno name, you know? My porno name is Fuzzy Hemlock because Fuzzy was my first pet's name and I grew up on Hemlock Street."

"Fascinating," says Ceepak because he's very polite that way. "What can you tell us about the body double?"

The chorus girl shrugs. "Not much. Like I said, we weren't even supposed to know she existed. They kept her hidden away until like eight every night."

"I see," says Ceepak.

"But one night . . ."

Here we go.

"Me, Chandra, Monica, and Jodi—those are the other girls in the show—we were at this bar, the Forbidden City, which is this totally hot club over near the Crystal Palace Tower. We were all looking good, flossin'. I had on this like plunging bandage minidress."

She uses her hands to illustrate just how low and just how high.

I'm sorry I missed it.

"Anyhow, we're just marinating there . . ."

"You were just hanging out?" I translate so Ceepak and Parker will stop looking so confused.

"Totally. All of a sudden, I see this extremely tanked brunette eyeballing us. She stumbles over to the table where we're like, you know, just trying to chill. I'm thinking: 'lesbo alert.' Figure she's coming over to hit on us because we look so fine and there's no guys with us. Anyway, she's totally trashed. Slurring her words and stuff. She tells us she's in our show and we're all like, 'Uh, no you're not.' Long story short, she totally blows her cover. She shows us this blond wig she keeps stashed in her skanky canvas tote bag and tells us how she's like this body double for Jessica Rock because that's how they do the whole transporting trick, even though none of us know what this drunk woman is babbling about because we're off-stage when they do that trick, too."

"While intoxicated, did Sherry mention being romantically involved with Mr. Pratt?"

"No. After she like sampled all our drinks and totally spilled her guts, Blaine and Jim Bob, two of the boy dancers, came over and gently hauled her ass out of there. I think she has a drinking problem, you know?"

Yeah. I thought the same thing up in the karaoke bar.

"The three of them knew each other back in LA and Vegas. Chandra, Monica, Jody, and me? We're all Jersey girls." She pauses. "Hey, you know what?"

"What?" I say, since I'm a Jersey boy.

"I just now remembered: before the two guys showed up, Sherry asked us this totally random question."

Ceepak looks extremely interested. "What was it?"

"Well, I guess she knew we were locals, because she asked if any of us had ever worked at a place on the boardwalk called Lucky Lilani's Stress Therapy."

"Had you?" asks Ceepak.

"Hello? Excuse me. It's a massage parlor."

"We know."

"What? You think all showgirls are like hookers or something?"

"No, ma'am."

She waves her hand to let Ceepak know it's no big deal even if he did. "Whatever. After we totally laughed our asses off at her lame question, she mumbled something even lamer: 'That's where Richard Rock does all his casting these days.' "

We're back on the boardwalk.

"I'm beginning to suspect that Mr. and Mrs. Rock had an arrangement," says Ceepak.

I know where he's going with this: Mrs. Rock gets to play with Jake Pratt in exchange for looking the other way every time her hubby heads off to Lucky Lilani's for a happy ending courtesy of one of the Asian ladies in the back rooms behind those curtains.

"You think that's what's in the notebook?" I ask. "Details about what Richard Rock's been doing at the massage parlor?"

"Perhaps," says Ceepak. "We cannot be certain that the object being sought so arduously is actually a notebook. We only have Mr. Krabitz's word on that."

Yeah. So that means it's probably not true.

"However, whatever it is, if there is some form of physical evidence clearly linking Richard Rock to women smuggled into this country for the purposes of prostitution it could severely tarnish his family-friendly brand image."

No wonder seeing Lilani Lee at the show Monday night freaked Rock out.

"Good afternoon, Officers!" a voice calls out as we hustle up the boardwalk.

It's the Great Mandini again. His silk robe flutters in the breeze as he stands behind his folding table shuffling a deck of cards with one hand, rubbing his bunny's ears with the other.

"Have you figured it out yet?"

Ceepak stops. So I do, too.

"Come again?" he asks.

"Have you figured it out?"

"Figured what out?" asks Ceepak.

"Lucky Numbers."

"Mr. Rock's featured illusion?"

"Yes, sir." Mandini manipulates his deck of cards. "What's your favorite card, Mr. Boyle?"

"What?"

"Pick a card."

What the heck. I reach for the deck.

"Not that way. That's the old-fashioned way. Just name it."

"Jack of diamonds," says Ceepak.

Mandini moves the deck over toward Ceepak since he seems more eager to play than me. "Kindly pull out the jack of diamonds, sir."

A crowd starts to gather around the table.

Ceepak extracts a card from the deck. Who knew we had time for this? I thought we were hotfooting it down to Lucky Lilani's.

"Two of clubs," says Ceepak after examining his draw.

"Rub it on the rabbit," says Mandini. "That two of clubs will magically turn into your jack of diamonds."

Ceepak strokes the rabbit with the edge of his card. The bunny wiggles its nose. Sniffs the card. The crowd chuckles.

"Take a look," says Mandini. "Did it work?"

Ceepak flips his card over, shows it to the magician.

It's still the two of clubs.

"No, sir."

"Of course it didn't work!" Mandini snatches the card out of Ceepak's hand. "You're not the magician. I am!" More laughs from the crowd.

Mandini rubs Ceepak's two of clubs against the rabbit's fur.

"See, when I do it, it always works."

He flips the card over.

Jack of diamonds.

"Tricks always work for the magician, my friend. Always." He shuffles the jack of diamonds back into the deck, then holds the stack of fifty-two cards underneath the bunny's nose. It twitches and wiggles its snout. Sneezes a tiny bunny sneeze.

"Bless you," Mandini says. Then he taps the deck and pulls out a card from somewhere near the middle.

It's Ceepak's two of clubs again.

"Remember: the magician not only holds all the cards, it was his deck to begin with."

Ceepak nods thoughtfully. "Thank you, Mr. Mandini."

"Happy to help, my friend. Semper Fi. Semper Fi."

Okay. That was one of those extremely weird Ceepak moments where I just wait for him to tell me what we learned in class today because I have absolutely no idea what the heck the magic-bunny detour was all about.

We pick up our pace and march through the teeming crowds, hundreds of people in no particular hurry. It's after 5:00 and the boardwalk is packed. Rolling chairs keep rumbling by. Gaggles of guys and girls giggle past. Weird pinball machine noises surround us. We have to hike a couple more blocks to Lucky Lilani's Stress Therapy so I go ahead and jump-start the conversation.

"That was pretty neat." It's the best I can do on such short notice.

"Indeed," says Ceepak. "I sense that Mr. Mandini knows how frustrated we are in our quest to determine what really happened backstage at the Shalimar Theater during Mr. Rock's performance. Therefore, his simple yet elegant demonstration served to remind us of a basic truth regarding illusions. They are just that. Something that deceives the senses or mind."

"Okay, but how'd he turn that two of clubs into your jack of diamonds?"

"Elementary sleight of hand, I would imagine. While I was distracted with the rabbit antics, he undoubtedly extracted the jack of diamonds from the deck."

"But how did he know what card you'd pick?"

"He didn't. However, as a professional, he had ample time to locate said card while we wasted time rubbing our two of clubs against the rabbit's fur."

"He did?"

"Yes, Danny. Remember: he's the magician. He holds all the cards and, as Mr. Mandini so astutely pointed out, it was his deck to begin with. He decides what will be."

Ceepak is channeling a Springsteen song about the political magicians who manipulated America's reality for eight years. The folks who magically turned anyone who disagreed with them into cowards or traitors because they had the power to shape the truth into what they wanted it to be. Especially on FOX.

We reach 1508 boardwalk. Lucky Lilani's Stress Therapy. The glass door flies open. Out comes David Zuckerman.

"Good afternoon, Officers," he says, his voice clipped and efficient—not to mention snide and snarky. "Great minds think alike, eh?"

"How do you mean?" says Ceepak.

"I followed up on Lady Jasmine's repeated accusations regarding Mr. Rock. I am pleased to report that no one inside this establishment or in any way connected to it remembers him ever coming here. Have a good day, gentlemen."

33

Ceepak stands outside Lucky Lilani's door, right underneath the flickering CHINESE FULL BODY MASSAGE neon.

He's smiling.

Me? I'm mad.

I want to run up the boardwalk, tackle Zuckerman, and rifle through his wallet because that's where I usually file my receipts. Just wad 'em up and stuff 'em in, empty it all out once a year, usually around April 14.

But, then again, maybe when you buy somebody's silence, pay them to act dumb, to back up your big lie, maybe you don't ask for a receipt, even if hush money is somehow tax deductible.

Ceepak and I haven't discussed this yet, but we both know what just happened inside the sleazy rubdown joint ten seconds before we got there. David Zuckerman, Richard Rock's extremely resourceful go-to guy, headed us off at the pass where he simultaneously beat us to the punch. After a visit from the magician's money man, nobody inside Lucky Lilani's is going to remember anything about Richard Rock's seedy rendezvous with assorted Asian temptresses.

"You want to go in?" I ask Ceepak anyhow.

His smile broadens. "I see no need to do so at this juncture, Danny."

Up the boardwalk, I can see Zuckerman pressing his iPhone to his ear, no doubt calling in a status report to Mr. and Mrs. Rock, something like "mission accomplished." They should hang a banner off the side of the Xanadu Hotel.

"Come on! Let's go have a word with that bastard! Nail his ass!"

"No need, Danny."

"Oh. Okay."

"There is also no need for that sort of language."

I fume for a second and try to think of something else we could do because I'm tired of standing around being out-tricked by the magician and his crew.

"We should go inside and lean on Lilani Lee!" I suggest. "If we scare her enough, maybe threaten to shut her down, she might give up the truth and tell us why Richard Rock just sent Mr. Z over here to buy her off!"

Ceepak still has his placid Buddha face going.

"I understand your frustration," he says, way too serenely. "But such an interrogation would also be a waste of our time."

I give up. "You're right. It's Atlantic City." I say it like I'm in a Jack Nicholson movie and it's all anybody needs to say to sum up the whole sorry situation. There's no way we're going to uncover the truth in this man-made Glitzburgh erected to hide the ugly underbelly of a town where the mayor sometimes goes missing for three weeks at a time.

"Danny?"

"Yeah?"

"There is no need to question Ms. Lilani Lee or any of her massage technicians because Mr. Zuckerman's presence already tells us everything we need to know. It is an implicit confirmation that what Lady Jasmine claimed and what we suspected is true: Richard Rock was, indeed, a client here and, most likely, involved in unsavory not to mention illegal sexual activities on its premises."

Oh. Right. That's why we don't need to talk to anybody. I thought it was because they'd all lie to us anyway.

"Thirsty?" Ceepak asks, gesturing toward an open-air pizza stall squeezed in next door to the stress relief center.

Okay, a beverage break is a somewhat screwy choice right now but I follow Ceepak up to the food booth with signage boasting of stromboli and stuffed slices, not to mention funnel cakes and chicken cheesesteaks.

At the marble counter behind the glass display cases, there's a beefy Italian guy, what we sometimes call a Guido down the Jersey shore. His nappy hair is cut close, his muscles bulge, and even though there's an October chill in the air, all he wears up top is a sleeveless T about the size of one my six-year-old cousin would wear. The tighty-whitey shows off Guido's tan, his gold chain, his hairy back, and his swirling arm tattoos—all at the same time. Right now, this guy is extremely focused on his work: hand-slapping and punching a dough ball—forcing it to lie down flat on a dinged-up pizza pan.

I'm wondering if the dough ball is somebody he knows.

Ceepak examines the sample bottles of Snapple and Pepsi products lined up on top of the tallest showcase, the one displaying yesterday's funnel cakes. Their white powdered sugar has gone semigloss gray.

"I sometimes find that a cold beverage helps me focus," Ceepak says as he sizes up the drink selections.

I sometimes find the same thing. But my cold beverage of choice is typically a beer.

"What'll you have?" the Italian guy asks without looking up. He's knuckling the dough like mad, stretching it out thin, forcing it to the edge of his pie pan.

"Something without caffeine, please," says Ceepak.

"We got Sierra Mist."

"What's that?"

"Lemon-lime. Like Sprite or Seven-Up only it isn't."

"Sounds good. One Sierra Mist, please."

"What about you, chief?"

Guess that's me. "Red Bull."

"All we got is Amp."

"Great." Amp is from Pepsi. It's like Mountain Dew but even more caffeiney.

The pizza guy goes to the cold case, gets our drinks. Ceepak hands him a $10 bill. The guy slams down some keys on a register. Bells ding, a drawer pops open, he finger-scoops up our change, slams the drawer shut.

Ceepak slips a dollar bill into the blue paper tip cup.

"I was wondering," he says to Guido, oh-so casually after a sip of soda. "My friend and I are from out of town and would like to catch a magic show at one of the casinos."

"So?" says pizza man.

"Can you make a recommendation?"

"What? Do I look like the fucking chamber of commerce here or something?"

"No, sir. I simply thought—"

"Yeah, yeah. Whatever. You could check out that 'Rock 'n Pow!' they got over at the Xanadu."

"Is it good?"

Pizza man shrugs as best he can while twisting his pan and

stretching his dough. "How should I know? I work nights. But I met the star. This Richard Rock character. He's the big-shot magician. That's why they call it 'Rock 'n Pow!'."

"I see."

"He's kind of a prick. Thinks he's hot shit. The 'most amazing illusionist in the Western world,' whatever the fuck that's supposed to mean."

"Does he eat here often?"

"Three or four times this week, he stops in for something sweet. Likes the funnel cakes."

Ceepak subtly tilts his head, directing my attention to an autographed black-and-white publicity photo taped to the wall behind the pizza man: Richard Rock in his tux and cowboy hat.

"That's him, I take it?" says Ceepak.

Pizza man glances over his shoulder. "Yeah. Guess he's a magic cowboy or whatever."

"I think I've already met him."

"Next door?"

Ceepak can't lie, so he doesn't. "No. Elsewhere."

We get another shrug as pizza man reaches for a ladle to scoop tomato sauce out of a five-gallon tin drum. "This *strunz* Rock? He's next door a lot. Comes here after going there. Sometimes before—takes the ladies a little treat. He tells me Lucky Lilani's has the best Chinese massage chairs, as if I got time to have some Oriental chick knead my neck. Rock says it's therapeutic, like visiting a chiropractor. All that sawing his wife in half gives him muscle cramps. Wish he'd saw my wife in half, you know what I mean? That would definitely take care of the pain in my neck, not to mention the one in my ass."

Ceepak gives our Italian fountain of information a two-finger salute. "Thank you again for the cold beverages. Very refreshing."

We walk up the boardwalk, away from the pizza stand.

"You saw Rock's photo, right? Behind the counter? That's why all of a sudden you were thirsty?"

"Indeed, Danny. It is circumstantial evidence, but the pizza parlor employee more or less corroborated our prior suppositions."

"Yeah."

"We also learned something else quite valuable on this seeming detour."

We did?

I wish I knew what it was other than the fact that Richard Rock is a jerk, can't stop talking about himself, and likes funnel cake more than zeppole.

"We now know," says Ceepak, "that whatever the killer is so desperate to locate has little or nothing to do with Mr. Rock's activities at the massage parlor."

Really? We know that?

Ceepak reads my face. "If, Danny, Ms. Lilani's silence can be purchased so easily, the incriminating evidence must not be related to her or her establishment."

Got it. Why go through all the trouble of torturing and killing people when all you have to do is write a check or drop off a bag of cash?

"So what do we do next?" I ask.

"Since Cyrus is keeping an eye on Mrs. Rock, I think we should redouble our efforts to locate her doppelgänger."

"Her what?"

"Sorry. It's a German word. Means double or look-alike—most commonly an evil twin. The literal translation is 'double walker,' meaning someone who is acting the same way as another person."

With Ceepak, you get beverages and a Berlitz lesson.

"We could go talk to her pals, again," I suggest. "The two dancers. Blaine and Jim Bob. They always seem to be the ones hauling Sherry Amour home when she gets plotzed."

"Roger that," says Ceepak as he rocks his wrist to check his watch. My $10 Swatch knockoff tanked the last time I did dishes and discovered that it really wasn't water resistant to fifty meters so I scope out my cell-phone window instead. Six-twenty-four PM. The sun is starting to set behind all the casinos towering to the west.

"When's your dad supposed to call?" I ask.

"No set time was given."

"That's a pretty weird thing to ask for in a plea deal, isn't it? A phone call to your son."

"My father, as you may recall, Danny, is an extremely manipulative man. He is playing mind games. Making me wait. Hoping he can, once more, ruin my day. These murders, however, beat him to it."

I nod. Ceepak keeps staring at his watch. People breeze past us on the boardwalk. A couple rolling chairs. I fiddle with the green tab on top of my Amp can.

Ceepak's head snaps up. He's back.

"We could reclaim our ATVs, ride back to the dancers' motel," he says. "However, Blaine and Jim Bob should be arriving at the Shalimar Theater within the hour. Backstage might prove a more advantageous location for our next conversation."

Yeah. We can talk to their dressing-room door this time.

"Remaining close to the theater will also allow us to monitor Mr. Zuckerman's movements."

I nod. That oily dude is definitely worth continued monitoration.

Now Ceepak's cell phone chirps. He flips it open.

His asshole dad?

"This is Ceepak. Go."

He shakes his head to let me know it isn't Joe Six-pack.

"Yes, ma'am. That is how I typically answer my phone. Sorry. Will do." He covers the mouthpiece so he can whisper who it is. "Dr. McDaniels."

Figures. She's back to full chop-busting mode. Might be a good sign.

"I see. Interesting. What's your confidence level? Excellent. Roger that. Appreciate it." He folds up his phone. "Dr. McDaniels's team has worked up Katie's eye-jelly numbers."

That means they have a more precise estimate on her time of death.

"And?"

"Dr. McDaniels states with what she would label a 'very high degree of certitude' that Ms. Landry died at approximately nine-oh-five PM. About ten minutes before the conclusion of 'Rock 'n Wow!' "

"During that last trick," I mumble. "Lucky Numbers."

"Roger that," says Ceepak.

A lightning bolt hits me. "That means Katie was murdered while Jessica Rock was onstage, working with the volunteer from the audience and her double, the dopple-whatever, Sherry, was nowhere to be seen!"

"Or," says Ceepak, "vice versa."

34

"Go away!"

We're backstage at the Shalimar. At least this door has a sparkly silver star on it. No peephole.

"We need to determine Ms. Amour's current whereabouts," says Ceepak to the cold steel panel two inches in front of his face.

The dancers on the other side of the door are unmoved by our requests for cooperation.

"Go. Away. Now."

Blaine sounds particularly peeved.

"We are not talking to you!"

"Gentlemen?" A new higher and even huffier voice is heard from. I'm figuring it's Mr. Magnum, Jake Pratt's former roommate and the only other male dancer still alive. "Please go away. We have a show to put on!"

And we have a murder or two to solve.

"Very well," says Ceepak. "If you gentlemen change your mind about discussing this matter, please give us a call." He slips another card under another doorsill. If this keeps up, he's going to need to hit Kinko's soon.

We're in the cinder-block hallways behind the Shalimar stage, to the left of that *T* in the corridor. If we had turned right, we would've wound up outside the crime-scene suites. The doors to AA-4 and AA-6 are still sealed shut with tape from the ACPD and the state major crimes unit. There are some other dressing rooms further up the hall, including two with gold stars affixed to the doors. I'm figuring that's where the Rocks dress.

David Zuckerman comes boot-heel-clicking up the hall. He wears a wireless headset and is once again carrying that sleek aluminum clipboard case. "Fifteen minutes, people," he announces. "Fifteen minutes.

It's 7:45. The curtain goes up at 8:00.

"You gentlemen need to clear this area," Zuckerman says.

"Actually," says Ceepak, "we still need to locate Ms. Amour. Have you heard from her?"

"No."

"Do you know how to reach her?"

"No."

"How will you do the show without her?"

"We'll manage." He flicks his wrist dramatically. Makes quite a show of examining the time on what looks to be one of those very expensive TAG Heuer jobs NASCAR drivers supposedly wear even though their wrists shake so much while they're doing 195 MPH I wonder how they could ever see what time it is.

"We also need to talk to Mrs. Rock," says Ceepak.

"Maybe after the show."

"Now would be better."

"Fourteen minutes, everybody. Fourteen minutes."

Okay. That last announcement was just to piss us off.

Zuckerman touches the talk button on the belt pack linked to his headpiece. "Toohey? I need you outside the boys' dressing room. We have a situation." He releases the switch, simpers at us. We're his situation. "Mr. Tuiasopo will escort you gentlemen out to the lobby." His voice is as buttery as an ear of corn at a county fair.

"We would like to see the show again," says Ceepak.

Zuckerman blinks. "Did you purchase tickets?"

"No. We have been otherwise engaged."

"Right. Did you stay at Lucky Lilani's long enough to enjoy a soothing neck rub?"

"Negative," says Ceepak.

"We had a cold drink, instead," I say, just to see if it makes butterman melt a little. "At the pizza place next door."

"Fascinating."

"What's up, boss?" The giant Samoan lumbers down the corridor toward us in his security windbreaker. He sees me and Ceepak. "Yo, dudes. You two stayin' loose and keepin' mellow?"

"Twenty-four-seven," I say.

"All right, little brother. That's what I'm talking about."

"Mr. Tuiasopo?" This from Zuckerman.

"Yes, sir, boss?"

"Kindly escort Officers Ceepak and Boyle out of my backstage and into the auditorium."

"House seats?"

"Fine."

"You got it, boss. You ready to lock it down back here?"

Another flick of the wrist from Zuckerman. "Yes. Gentlemen?" He extends his arm to the left, indicating which direction we should hurry up and leave in. "Enjoy the show."

Toohey ushers us up the corridor, under the single security camera, and out the authorized personnel–only door.

When we hit the hallway outside the Shalimar, Ceepak's the one checking his watch. "Mr. Zuckerman is now activating the security-camera cloaking device."

We move into the theater lobby. It's packed. Parents. Kids. Families. At the souvenir stand, I see a little redheaded girl slipping a bolo tie over her head, trying it on. It kind of breaks my heart. Katie was a redhead.

"You boys are living large tonight," Tuiasopo booms. "Emperor's row. Box three-oh-one. Mega-VIP section." He pushes open the auditorium doors. We follow. "You need a program?" he asks when we pass the usher handing them out.

"Yes," says Ceepak. "Thank you." He rolls up the mini-magazine, secures it in a cargo pants pouch. No need to read it. We pretty much know the cast list.

"Enjoy," Toohey says when we reach our seats, the same ones Lady Jasmine and her entourage occupied last night. "Yo, Valerie?" He snaps his fingers. A China-doll waitress struts over, balancing a tray of beer bottles. "Fix my friends up with whatever they want, dig?"

Valerie looks bored. Her tray looks heavy.

"What'll you have?" she asks, most of it coming out her nose.

I order for the table: "Two cranberry juices. Each."

We need clear heads.

"Later, dudes." Tuiasopo departs, undoubtedly to once again become invisible and stand guard outside the stage door.

"Pay close attention, Danny," Ceepak whispers once the cocktail waitress scribbles our order on a napkin and slumps away. "Particularly, note any discrepancies with what we witnessed last evening."

"Got it."

A minute after 8:00, the house lights dim.

"Ladies and gentlemen, boys and girls, are you ready to be amazed?"

The show begins.

A couple of things are different right away.

First of all, there are only seven dancers. Well, that's not really different. It was that way last night, too. What's different tonight is nobody looks like they expect Jake Pratt to show up. They've reconfigured the choreography so it doesn't seem so off-balance and out of kilter.

Second, little Richie Rock does not make his pajama-clad entrance. Only Mrs. Rock and bratty Britney float down to the lip of the stage tonight. I figure Richie is too distraught over the death of his nanny. He and Katie seemed pretty tight.

Then, of course, Nanny Katie doesn't make her entrance either. It's Nanny Maria. I think she's a seamstress with the show or something. Looks miserable being in the spotlight. Keeps acting like she wishes she could disappear.

The show moves on. They do the catching-a-bullet-in-the-teeth bit but tonight they use an old-fashioned musket since the Dick Tracy pistols are both currently tagged as evidence in an ACPD storage room.

They totally skip the whole transporting-Mrs. Rock-from-one-side-of-the-stage-to-the-other trick. Hard to do when your body double is AWOL. Instead, they work in a quick-change trick where Rock has the missus in and out of a dozen different outfits in under two minutes.

"Dang!" Rock cracked as his wife stepped into a curtained box wearing a shimmering red gown and, one step later, came out the other side in some kind of cheerleader outfit, complete with pom-poms. "Reckon I ought to take away her credit cards!"

Yee-haw. Family-friendly fun.

A few illusions later, Rock launches into his familiar patter.

"Ladies and gentlemen, boys and girls, I hope you and your families are enjoying your time here in Xanadu, a palace more incredible than the stately pleasure-dome the mighty Kubla Khan did decree."

I see Ceepak glance at his watch.

He jots down the time on the napkin coastering his cranberry juice cocktail.

2044. That's 8:44 PM in non-militarized time zones.

According to Dr. McDaniels, Katie died at 9:05 PM.

2105.

Twenty-one minutes from now.

Rock's sight gags about Marco Polo's exploding fireworks and falling spaghetti receive their *ooh*'s, *aah*'s, and groans from the crowd. He plucks a fresh fortune cookie out of thin air, launches into the whole Lucky Numbers spiel.

"I'll bet I could make a lot of money if I played my lucky numbers out on the casino floor! But I don't have any lucky numbers in my fortune cookie." The house lights, once again, come up a little. "Do you folks? Do any of you have a lucky number?"

Hands shoot up. People shout.

Ceepak jots down another time coordinate: *2048.*

Rock banters with a new volunteer. It's a man tonight, so I guess yesterday's lady wasn't a plant. Rock plucks at the air and conjures up another $50 purple poker chip.

"What's your name, sir?" he asks as the volunteer climbs the steps up to the stage.

"Larry Robert Bugal."

"Larry, have we ever met before?"

"No," he says.

Jessica Rock, dressed in that dazzling low-cut gown, strolls onstage like Vanna White, just like she did last night.

"Very well, Larry," says Rock. "Do you have a lucky number?"

"Yes."

"Is it between one and thirty-six?"

"Yes."

Mrs. Rock waltzes into the wings and pushes that rolling easel on stage.

"You know, numbers can be dadgum powerful," Rock says like he said last night. "Now, I know what you're thinkin': my cow died so I don't need your bull anymore. So, I'm gonna prove it to you. Larry, I want you think about your lucky number."

"Okay."

"You seeing your number? Visualizing it?"

"Yes."

"Good," says Mrs. Rock, beaming her brilliantly white beaver teeth. "Concentrate on it, Mr. Bugal."

"I am."

"Larry," says Rock, "I want you to stay here with Jessica."

"Okay."

"It'll be fun," says Mrs. Rock. "We're gonna make you rich!"

"Okay."

And that's when the second lightning bolt hits me.

Last night, Mrs. Rock didn't say a damn word during this whole entire bit. Tonight, she's Chatty Cathy.

35

I turn to tell Ceepak my major news flash.

As usual, he's ten seconds ahead of me. In fact, he's already standing, tilting his head to indicate that we should slip out to the lobby. Now.

Onstage, Rock announces, "I'm going out into the casino to make us some money! Jim Bob? To the high-rollers' room!"

"Don't forget your blindfold, honey!" Mrs. Rock says.

Who knew she had so many lines?

Ceepak and I slink through the shadows, slip past the usher, and head for the exit while Mrs. Rock places the black hood over her husband's head.

"Thank you, dear," says Rock. "But if I'm going to play with the high rollers, I need to look like I belong."

We exit the auditorium while Rock plucks his pinky ring and white lapel rose out of the air.

"All righty. Let's go win us some money!"

The door swings shut behind us.

"Is everything all right, gentlemen?" asks a young usher.

"Ten-four," says Ceepak.

"Hunh?" The usher, not being an off-duty cop, sounds confused. Ceepak is way too focused to respond.

"We're cool," I say.

The usher nods, makes his way over to the candy counter to flirt with the girl stacking her Goobers.

"Mrs. Rock didn't talk last night!" I whisper-blurt to Ceepak.

"I noted that as well."

"That means it was probably Sherry Amour onstage when Katie was killed!"

"Agreed."

"Mrs. Rock could've been in the room, torturing Katie! Murdering her!"

"It's a possibility."

"She had the opportunity and the means! Jake Pratt's bolo tie because he was back there waiting for her!"

"And her motive?" Ceepak asks.

M.O.M. Means, Opportunity, Motive. You need all three or you've basically got diddly.

"I dunno. Jealousy?"

Ceepak gives me an extremely thought-filled look. He's not convinced Mrs. Rock did it but he's not sure she didn't, either.

"What's our play?" I ask.

"We shadow Mr. Rock as he leaves the theater. Since Katie was killed during the performance of this illusion, I feel it is imperative that we completely unravel its secrets."

Makes sense.

"Meanwhile, we alert Cyrus. Have him intensify his surveillance of Mrs. Rock. Make certain we know where she is at all times, on- or offstage."

"How? The camera-blocking mirror dealio is already flipped on."

"Perhaps Cyrus can rectify that situation."

Ceepak reaches for his cell. Speed dials Parker. I glance at the digits on my phone: 8:50 PM.

"Cyrus? Ceepak. I suggest you send a uniformed member of your team to the backstage access corridor and disable the device Rock's people attached to the lens of your PTZ camera. We have reason to suspect Mrs. Rock was involved in the murder of Katie Landry. She must not be allowed to leave the building following the conclusion of this evening's performance. Roger that. We're on Mr. Rock. Right."

The floor starts shaking because the prerecorded track about Lucky Numbers has way too much bass in it.

That means Rock has his Shirley Temple and is headed for the door.

"Ceepak? He's coming."

He closes up his cell. "Parker's sending a team to deal with the camera."

We head out of the theater and blend into the crowd of casually dressed folks strolling up and down the corridor.

The Shalimar doors swing open and here comes Richard Rock, black sack over his head, moving like a blind Frankenstein. Jim Bob is leading him by the elbow. The camera guy with the video unit propped on his shoulder is walking backward in front of them.

"Show Larry and the other folks where we are, Fred."

The cameraman swings around to take in that wide-angle view of the glittering passageway sweeping off to the casino floor. The camera guy then swishes back around to frame up Rock again.

"All right, Fred. You can go back inside with that thing. Switch to the hotel security cameras, fellas!"

The camera guy heads back to the lobby. Inside the theater, they're watching the feed from the casino's PTZ cameras.

"Keep thinking about your lucky number, Larry! Think real hard on it, son."

We move past the *Authorized Personnel Only* door. The security guard, the guy who used to vacation up in Sea Haven every summer when his kids were younger, shoots me a wave. I vaguely wiggle a few fingers in response—I don't want to attract too much attention.

We're trying to tail these people.

So far, Jim Bob hasn't seen us.

"Ladies and gentlemen, boys and girls," Rock says as Jim Bob leads him on, "it was the ancient mathematician Pythagoras who once declared, 'The world is built upon the power of numbers.' Tonight, Larry, we will put his words to the ultimate test. We will witness just how powerful one number can be!"

The casino floor is dead ahead.

Jim Bob and Rock hang a left, head toward another side door also labeled *Authorized Personnel Only*. There's another private-duty security guard in another *Event Staff* windbreaker stationed in front of it.

Before the door glides shut, I can see Richard Rock whipping off his black hood and hear him say, "Do you believe one number can change your life, Larry?"

"Fascinating," Ceepak says, almost under his breath.

We head for the door.

"You can't use this door," says the guard, raising a hand to give us the halt sign.

"Yes. They can." Parker.

Guess he and his cameras were tracking us again. He brought

along more friends. About eight of them, none under two hundred pounds, all of it solid muscle. Two of the moose take hold of Mr. Event Staff's arms, haul him away from his guard post.

"Tail the husband," says Parker. "We're on the wife."

36

This is so weird.

Rock is saying all the stuff he said last night while he wound his way through the slot machines but, instead of moving across the casino floor, he's walking with Jim Bob down a dimly lit cinder-block corridor.

Ceepak and I are maybe thirty feet behind them, lurking in the shadows, moving as quietly as cats stalking a bottle cap.

"We're almost there, ladies and gentlemen. The Ming Dynasty Room," Rock declares.

To us, his voice sounds echoey, because it's reverberating off the slick brick walls. But the magician has that cordless head mike so folks in the theater hear him just fine. While he rambles on about high rollers winning and losing millions of dollars on a single spin of the roulette wheel, he makes a left turn. Who knew there was such a maze of backstage passageways for the use of authorized personnel only?

Who knew they were all connected?

Because when we make the left, still thirty feet behind Rock, I realize we're tippytoeing up the other end of the hallway that leads to the hotel suites reserved for the star performers—rooms AA-6 through AA-2. I can see the yellow crime-scene tape plastered on Katie's room. The Rocks', too. Ceepak glances at his watch again. Fortunately, the numbers on his Timex Ironman are pretty huge and sort of glow.

2100.

Nine PM. That means last night, around this same time, during the Lucky Numbers routine, Mr. Rock walked right past the door to his kids' room while somebody was inside it torturing Katie.

"Excellent," I hear Rock say up ahead. "Guess we had a little technical difficulty."

Or is that when his microphone went dead? Did an audio technician hear something horrible in the background and push the mute button?

"Glad you can hear me again," Rock says like he said last night after the *Please Stand By* disappeared from the screen. "We are now in the Xanadu's world-famous Ming Dynasty Room, Larry."

No, we're not.

Richard Rock and Jim Bob have come to a complete stop in the backstage hallway—beyond the *T*, on the far side of the chorus boys' dressing room. Jim Bob fishes into his dance pants and pulls out a key. He unlocks a door two down from where we tried to question him and Blaine. Rock and Jim Bob step into whatever room is behind the door. We hear a dead bolt strike its plate.

When Ceepak and I hit the *T* on this side of the dressing room doors, we duck into the main corridor. Press our backs up against the wall. Take a moment.

"Video control room," Ceepak whispers. "It's how they do the trick. Prerecorded. Thirty-six numbers."

Now I get it. We didn't see the real Ming Dynasty Room. Just its illusion. In fact, everything we saw on the screen after the camera swish-panned to the right to "show the folks where we're headed" then blurred back to the left was already on digital tape. They cut away to the prerecorded stuff while the live image was obscured by the motion blur.

That's why Rock made such a big deal about putting on the pinky ring, the boutonniere, even stopping at the cocktail bar for that stupid Shirley Temple. We saw him add those elements to his wardrobe before he left the theater and that made us believe what we saw on the screen was real when, in truth, all they had to do was pre-shoot footage using the same props.

Remember, there are no windows in the casino. No way for us to realize what time or even what day the footage we were watching was shot.

Even the "technical glitch," the audio signal cutting out from his radio microphone, was probably planned. You make it a little sloppy, a little less than perfect, we think your illusion is even more real.

Most likely, Katie already had that ball gag in her mouth at 9:00 PM because whoever was in AA-4 working her over knew Richard Rock would be strolling up the hall, armed with a live microphone. After all, Jake Pratt sent the kids out for ice cream around 8:20. The torturer had forty minutes to make Katie talk. When she wouldn't, when the killer knew the show was almost over—maybe because they heard Richard Rock rambling on about the Ming Dynasty Room as he walked past their door—they decided to kill Katie.

Now that we know how the trick is done, it's not that amazing. In fact, it only worked because we fell for it. All Rock had to do to convince us we were seeing what we thought we were seeing was keep up the patter over his cordless mike and address the volunteer by name.

Meanwhile, the JumboTron screen in the theater was showing prerecorded digital images of a fantasy high-roller room, which nobody in the audience had ever actually seen because they're not cattle barons or oil sheiks.

Clever.

Then, once Rock saw what number between one and thirty-six the volunteer from the audience had written on the marker board, the control room called up the footage showing his hand—the one with the sparkling horseshoe-shaped diamond pinky ring—placing the purple chip on the appropriate square. While we were amazed by that, they cut to a different angle—the overhead shot—and showed us another chunk of prerecorded digits, one of thirty-six different files, and we saw the roulette wheel's silver ball hop into the winning slot.

How did Rock and the control room crew know what number the volunteer picked, since they made such a big deal about her never saying it out loud? Easy. Inside the auditorium, probably hidden up in the catwalks with all the klieg lights, they have their very own PTZ camera focused precisely on the spot where Mrs. Rock (or Sherry Amour) rolls out the easel. The Great Mandini was right.

They hold all the cards. It was their deck to start with.

"Fancy meeting you boys back here."

Ceepak and I both whip to our right.

Parker again.

Ceepak puts a finger to his lips.

"Roger that," Parker whispers.

"Where's their stage-door security guard?" Ceepak asks, his voice barely audible.

"Mr. Tuiasopo is sharing a room with the other gentlemen my

team escorted upstairs. Kim Hammond is asking them both a few questions about who's been tampering with and disabling hotel property."

"You deactivated the mirror device mounted to the PTZ camera?"

"Nah. We just tore it down."

Ceepak grins. "That'll work."

"Where's Rock?"

"Up the hall in what I hypothesize is a video control room. That's why, last night, Lady Jasmine was unimpressed with Lucky Numbers, why she said she could do the illusion herself with the proper funding."

"It's all on tape?"

Ceepak nods. "The seemingly live events were prerecorded, utilizing the casino's security cameras as well as footage taped in a studio constructed to resemble your Ming Dynasty High Roller Room. Where's Mrs. Rock?"

"Last report, still onstage with the audience volunteer."

"Station a man at the stage door."

"Done." Parker gestures to his right. I peer down and see a linebacker in gray slacks and a blazer moving in to stand where Mr. Tuiasopo had been standing when I came back here to talk to Katie.

"Are there any other exits?"

"Another door, stage right. Also covered. Trapdoors in the stage floor."

"Leading to?"

"Basement. I have men down there, too."

"Excellent."

"When can we stop whispering?" Parker asks.

Ceepak checks his watch. "Approximately ten minutes. When the Rocks take their final bows at twenty-one-fifteen."

That means it's currently 2105. Katie's time of death. She's been gone a whole day.

"We need to arrest Mrs. Rock!" I say.

"What's the charge?" asks Parker.

"Murder!"

"The nanny?"

"It's a possibility," says Ceepak.

"Why? What's her motive?" Parker asks.

"Fear of discovery," I offer, sort of making it up as I go.

"Come again?" says Parker.

"We know either Mrs. Rock or Sherry Amour paid for Jake Pratt's motel room across the street," I explain. "We've seen one of them holding hands with Pratt on the elevator. Tonight, me and Ceepak figured out that Mrs. Rock wasn't onstage during the Lucky Numbers bit last night and that's when Katie was killed. So she did it!"

"For real?" Parker asks. I don't think he's buying my closing argument.

"Definitely! See, last night, the so-called Mrs. Rock didn't say a word to the volunteer onstage. Tonight, she wouldn't shut up. That's because last night the part of Mrs. Rock was played by Sherry Amour!"

"So Jessica Rock could come back here and kill Ms. Landry?" says Parker. "Why?"

I look at Ceepak. He nods. Encourages me to keep taking wild stabs at the truth.

"Well, I figure, Katie found out about Mrs. Rock's affair with Jake Pratt. A teenager. They were both afraid that if Katie told anybody, they'd have to stop seeing each other because what they were doing over at the Motel No-Tell kind of went against the whole family-friendly image of the Rocks' show. So, Mrs. Rock told Jake to torture Katie until she told him where she had hidden whatever it was they were looking for. I'm figuring it was a sex video. Like that one Pamela Anderson and Tommy Lee made, you know?"

Now Parker gives me the slow up-and-down head nod typically reserved for homeless people who swear the Chipmunks are planning a sneak acorn attack.

It doesn't slow me down.

"When Katie wouldn't talk, Pratt left the room at a prearranged time—probably right before Lucky Numbers started. But first, he ran into the bathroom, finally turned off the hot water pouring into the tub for Richie's bath, and scribbled that love note on the steamed-up mirror. *J luvs U*."

"How come the tub didn't overflow?" Parker asks.

"Hunh?" I wasn't expecting a plumbing sidebar.

"How come, if the hot water's been running since Ms. Landry came backstage with the kids, it never flooded over the sides of the tub?"

"It never does," I say. "Unless, you know, the water's totally gushing. There's an overflow drain deal built into the latch fixture. That's how high the waterline was."

"Hunh."

"When Lucky Numbers started, while her husband was super-busy, Mrs. Rock came back here, tried once more to convince Katie to give up the tape or whatever they thought she had. When she wouldn't, Mrs. Rock strangled Katie with Jake Pratt's bolo tie."

"I see," says Parker. Now he turns to Ceepak seeking confirmation for my harebrained hypothesis.

"It's a definite possibility," he says. "As Danny suggests, we should detain Mrs. Rock for further questioning."

"Wait a second," says Parker. "What about the, you know—the pubic hair the CSI guys found?"

"I suspect," says Ceepak, "that the material was harvested by the killer earlier and planted to incriminate Mr. Pratt. It's why there was a clump of it, not a strand or two."

Cool. Ceepak's on board with my whole theory. Maybe. At least the part about the pubic hair being planted, which, come to think of it, I didn't even mention.

But, now that Ceepak mentions it, it makes sense Mrs. Rock would try to frame Jake Pratt. The lady is most likely into spider sex. According to this show I saw once on the National Geographic Channel when the Mets game got rained out, female spiders have twisted ideas about dinner dates.

If a male hangs around too long after the sex is done, the female kills and eats him.

Or, they hire a PI to do the killing part the next day.

My father said "Son, we're lucky in this town
It's a beautiful place to be born
It just wraps its arms around you
Nobody crowds you, nobody goes it alone.
You know that flag flying over the courthouse
Means certain things are set in stone
Who we are, what we'll do and what we won't."

Yeah, it's gonna be a long walk home
Hey pretty Darling, don't wait up for me
Gonna be a long walk home

It's gonna be a long walk home

—Bruce Springsteen, "Long Walk Home"

37

I think my theory makes sense.

Mrs. Rock killed Katie because Katie had uncovered some sort of evidence that exposed her seedy affair with a barely legal boy.

I'll wager that Mrs. Rock, as the senior partner in the scandal, was the one who called most of the shots. Told Jake Pratt to buy the lingerie and force Katie to wear it. Told him to send the kids out for ice cream. She probably even lent him the fifty bucks.

She probably also suggested that Pratt use his bolo tie to choke Katie to the brink of suffocation, to scare her into telling him where she had hidden her evidence.

But, Katie didn't.

Okay. I have to wonder about that. Why not?

Why didn't she just give them what they wanted?

Maybe being forced to strip naked and pull on all that leather garter gear was just too humiliating, stopped her from thinking straight.

See, the Katie Landry I knew back in elementary school was a sweet and innocent Catholic kid. She grew up to become a sweet and innocent kindergarten teacher. Hell, she could've been a nun if, you know, girls still did that sort of thing. So if Mrs. Rock and Jake Pratt wanted to sexually humiliate Katie as part of their torture technique, man, they sure made a smart costume choice. I'm certain Katie Landry wished she could die before she actually did.

And then, clever spider woman that she is, Mrs. Rock used the same kinky sex setup to frame her disposable boy toy. She dropped a pile of his pubic hairs on Katie's carpet. I figure she harvested them earlier when Pratt was distracted. When Jessica Rock had him squirming on the mattress in ecstasy, he clearly wasn't paying very close attention to what her fondling fingers were actually doing *down there*.

And when her disposable boy toy was framed and ready for hanging, she paid sleaze-bucket Kenny Krabitz to nail him with a pistol she'd lifted out of the prop room.

"You really think she did it?" I ask Ceepak.

"I suspect she was somehow involved in the murder and/or its cover-up."

Okay. Not a ringing endorsement. But I'll take it.

We're still stationed in the hallway backstage. I can hear the canned music they use for the big finish seeping out through the stage door, which somebody on the other side just propped open in anticipation of the final curtain call.

Parker has gone off to help cover the other stage exits.

"But what about the diary?" I say this out loud.

"Come again?" says Ceepak.

"The spiral notebook the ACPD found in Pratt's room at the

Royal Lodge when they found the Pink Pussycat bags. Why'd he write her that love note?"

"I don't believe it was a love note to Katie."

"No?"

"Do you recall the actual wording?"

"Not precisely."

Ceepak reaches into a knee pocket on his cargo pants, pulls out his own little spiral-bound book.

"I took the liberty of cribbing it when Chief Maroney was reading the pertinent passage: 'Katie. I am moving into the Royal Lodge as suggested. Being closer is better. I love you. I can't wait to be so close we melt into each other.' " Ceepak closes up his notebook, tucks it back into his pants. "The punctuation after *Katie* is crucial."

Oh-kay. If Ceepak says so. Me? I let the computer check my spelling and grammar.

"It is a period, Danny. If Pratt had meant it as a missive to Ms. Landry, he would have used a colon. Perhaps a dash. Maybe even a comma. But by coming to a full stop, he is merely adding another item to his to-do list."

Got it. *Katie*. It's something to be dealt with. Like: *Laundry*. Read that way, this is a note to whoever told him to take care of Katie, agreeing with their suggestions on how the job should be done. Move into the Royal Lodge. Be closer to the scene of the crime. Have a place to hide immediately afterward.

And now I think we know who he really wanted to melt into. It sure wasn't Katie. She was way too young for this creep. That lover's spat I witnessed in the lobby? It wasn't one. It was Jake Pratt already hounding Katie to turn over whatever evidence she had uncovered. The guy was nineteen. Nineteen-year-olds are what they call impetuous. So even though he had been given his marching orders, Pratt probably wanted to wrap up the Katie problem without going through all the trouble of playing dress-up back in AA-4.

Now I hear thundering applause pouring out of the stage door.

"The show is over." I see Ceepak brush his hip, checking for his Glock, which, like mine, isn't there. Usually, when we apprehend a primary murder suspect, we're armed. Not tonight.

"Great show, guys!" gushes the nanny-dancer, the first one to bound out the stage door. "Awesome!" She and the three other chorus girls bounce up the hall dressed in their sexy cowgirl outfits—complete with white gun belts holstering pink pistols.

Next come the three remaining male dancers: Mr. Magnum (who, by the way, is kind of tiny), Blaine, and Jim Bob. The guys look like total doofuses compared to the girls: spangled Stetsons, bolo ties, cowhide vests, and chaps flapping against their legs.

Finally, here comes Richard Rock followed by David Zuckerman. Zuckerman is hugging his aluminum-clad clipboard. His face is flushed and his scalp is even pinker than the chorus girls' six-shooters.

Meanwhile, Rock is shaking his head and sighing heavily.

"How could you betray me like that, David?" he says as they march up the hall.

Zuckerman blinks. "She asked me."

"Son—never miss a good chance to shut up."

"Gentlemen?" Ceepak interrupts. "Where is Mrs. Rock?"

Rock dabs at his face with a towel. "What are you two boys doin' back here? This area is off-limits."

"We are here as part of the continuing investigation into the murder of Katie Landry. Again, Mr. Rock—where is your wife?"

"You boys should'a notified us first if you were gonna come nosin' around while we was onstage."

"We obtained clearance from hotel security."

Rock turns to Zuckerman. "David?"

"Yes, sir?"

"Get on the horn and call that Cyrus Parker fella. See if he really did give these two permission to snoop around back here." He puffs out his chest, goes nose to chin with Ceepak. "You boys see anything interesting while you were spyin' on me?"

"Yes, sir."

"Oh, really? What?"

"We now fully understand how the Lucky Numbers illusion is done."

"Say what?"

"We know it is merely a matter of you manipulating prerecorded digital video images inside a control room while narrating the footage in a manner designed to convince the audience that what they are seeing on-screen is actually happening."

Steam blasts out of Rock's ears. Well, it would if this were a cartoon. "David?"

"Sir?"

"Call the goddamn fucking lawyers. Sue this sumabitch. Sue the Atlantic City police department for being dumber than fucking dirt and deputizin' these two little shits in the first place. Slap an injunction on them."

"I believe," says Ceepak, "that what you should request is a restraining order."

"What?"

Ceepak is scanning the hallway behind Rock. "Where is Mrs. Rock?"

"Gone."

"Say again?"

"She's gone! Pulled up stakes and left me."

"I find that hard to believe," says Ceepak. "Mrs. Rock was just onstage."

"Hell, I know that, boy. I was out there with her. But she refused to come off this a'way with me. Apparently, somebody's been snooping around where they shouldn't ought to. Told Jessie what Lady Jasmine's been saying is one hundred percent true. Told her I've been frequenting a massage parlor up the boardwalk, ain't that right, David?"

"Mrs. Rock asked me to look into the matter, yes. After Mr. Ceepak reported that Lady Jasmine was continuing to make her allegations."

Rock shakes his head, walks on by. "If I was you, I would've taken a closer look at to who it was signin' my paychecks, Davey. I don't like this . . ."

"You always instructed me to do whatever Mrs. Rock asked me to do."

"David, I don't particularly like it when people put words in my mouth unless I say it!"

With that, Rock storms up the hall toward the *T*.

We turn to follow and I see that the chorus boys have been hovering around the corner, sponging up some hot gossip for tonight's dish session up in the karaoke bar.

"Where did Mrs. Rock go?" Ceepak now asks Rock's back.

Rock tosses up his hands and, without turning around or slowing his stride, says, "Who knows? Too bad she can't run across the street, cry all over her boyfriend's pillow."

Finally, dramatically, he stops and turns.

"That's right. I knew what the hell was goin' on over at that motel."

"With Jake Pratt?" asks Ceepak.

"Hell, yeah. I knew all about it."

"Yet you told us you weren't worried about your wife having an affair with the young dancer."

Rock shakes his head. "I know I didn't say she was one hundred percent faithful."

He disappears into his star dressing room.

Mind scramble alert.

Richard Rock flips and flops more than all those pancakes back home in Sea Haven.

At the far end of the hall, there's a blinding blast of white light as the *Authorized Personnel Only* door is shoved open.

"Did she come off this way?" It's Parker flanked by two ACPD cops.

"Negative," says Ceepak.

"Where the hell is she, then?"

"Mr. Rock claims she refused to exit with him. Marital difficulties."

Parker palms the top of his head. "Well, she didn't come out the door on the other side of the stage. And my guys in the basement didn't see anybody, either. Damn."

Ceepak turns to Mr. Zuckerman. "Where is she?"

"Gone."

"How?" demands Parker.

"I don't really know. However, Jessica Rock has been working in magic for well over two decades. Escape acts are her stock in trade. She does one onstage every night."

"Wait a second," I say. "You're telling us she magically transported herself out of the theater?"

"Perhaps."

"Well, how'd she do it without her body double?"

Another smug shrug. "I couldn't tell you. I will, however, tell you the secret to any successful illusion."

I take the bait: "What?"

"Preplanning."

We're frantically sending out search parties.

Coordinating with the video surveillance team.

And this is when Mr. Ceepak finally calls from Ohio.

We're still backstage, so we duck into that electrical closet for a little privacy. I go in with Ceepak because he gestures that I should.

He thumbs the speakerphone button on his LG cell so I can hear every rank thing his father has to say.

I think he wants a witness.

"Where'd I catch you, Johnny?"

"Where I am is of no consequence."

"It is to me. See, I'm in a jail, Johnny. No windows. Can't see shit except bars, a bunk, a crapper, and this ugly-ass gangbanger who thinks I'm gonna be his bitch tonight. Fuck you, my friend. Get the fuck out of my face. Asshole. He's backing off. Fucking pussy."

Ceepak closes his eyes. Drops his head.

I take the cell phone so his hands are free to cover his face.

"Can't talk long, Johnny. That assistant prosecuting attorney Lisa Porter-Burt might look hot 'n sexy in those tight suits she sashays around in but, I tell you son, the girl is one cold bitch. Only gave me five minutes to call my son."

Ceepak lowers his hands. I aim the phone at him.

"The clock is running," he says, slow and tight.

"You're down there in Atlantic City, hunh? How's that working out? You talk to that asshole Burdick, yet? You take his deposition, Johnny-boy? I'll bet that was fun." Mr. Ceepak laughs up a chest full of mucus. "Hey, you see him again, tell him to go fuck himself. For me. Okay? Then tell him my good news: I'll be coming to see him. Soon."

Ceepak stares at the phone.

"Yeah. That's what I wanted to share with you, Johnny. Guess how much the People and State of Ohio care about what I did all those fucking years ago? They could give two shits. Well, Porter-Burt might. She might give three or four. But her boss, this gray-haired geezer, he sure as shit didn't. He just wanted to push another pile of paper off his desk, clear his calendar, save the taxpayers the expense of a trial, wrap this sucker up."

I cannot believe what I am hearing.

"Yes, sir, son—the criminal justice system proved most merciful and wise today. Lenient, even. The top dog realized I've served time in my own private prison, torturing myself for years about what happened. He could see how remorseful I was. How guilt-ridden and repentant. He's a father, Johnny, just like me, so he knows about the mental anguish I've been through, especially after I told him about Billy being raped by a priest and all. I admit, I laid it on pretty thick for the old fart, but, hell—a man's gotta do what a man's gotta do, am I right, Johnny?"

Ceepak doesn't respond.

"Hey, too bad you weren't here to contradict me, hunh? But, well—you're always somewhere else, aren't you? Always running off to do your duty for god and country. Iraq. Atlantic City. Always eager to lend a hand, aren't you, Johnny-boy?" Another phlegmy laugh. "Jesus, how can you be my son and still be so fucking dumb? You don't have to answer that, Johnny. Not right now. We'll talk about it when I come see you. We'll go grab a couple beers. You'd like that, wouldn't you, son?"

Mr. Ceepak pauses. Waits for his son to say something.

Ceepak doesn't.

"Guess you can't talk 'cause you're all choked up to hear how good my plea deal worked out, hunh? That's okay. We'll be together soon. What is it? October. Hell, with a little time off for good behavior, I figure I'll be out by Christmas. Tell your mother. I'll be home for Christmas—just like in the fucking song! If not Christmas, Easter for sure. Like I said, Johnny—this lead prosecuting attorney or whatever the fuck they call him? He's a father. He knows how much grief comes with two shitty sons."

There's a knock on the closet door.

"Ceepak?" Parker. "We've got her."

"Roger that." Ceepak stands and gestures for me to hand him the cell, so I do.

He punches off the speaker button. Brings the phone up to his ear.

"Are you done?" He's standing at what I think the army manual calls *parade rest* with the phone cocked to his ear, waiting for his father to finish. "If any of what you said is true, trust me, sir—it is not going to play that way. You'll see. I'll hire lawyers." Another pause. Ceepak listens. I can hear a rant of some sort reverberating out of the earpiece.

Ceepak glances at his watch.

"Sir?" Ceepak interrupts his old man. "I believe the prosecuting attorney's office granted you five minutes for this phone call. Your time is up."

He slams the clamshell shut.

"Come on, Danny. Let's roll."

For someone who magically disappears on a regular basis, Mrs. Rock doesn't remain invisible for long.

Parker's security team monitoring the eyes in the sky spotted her at a "Cops and Donuts" slot machine on the main casino floor. She was the only woman in the three-acre playing field wearing a sequined gown. Sure, some of the Irish ladies had sequined leprechauns on their baggy green sweatshirts, but Mrs. Rock was the only one out there in formal wear.

It's a little after 9:30 PM when we follow Parker and two of his men into the crowded casino. The 8:00 shows and lounge acts just let out, so it's rush hour on the gambling floor. The place feels more crowded than an airport terminal in a blizzard when all the flights are canceled and everybody's already bored with the chicken-wings at the sports bar.

We're off the carpet, onto the shiny terrazzo tile.

"What'd your old man want?" Parker asks.

"Inconsequential at this juncture."

Parker and I both nod. We've known Ceepak long enough to know that when he uses two words like that in one sentence, his emotions are shutting down so he can concentrate on the job.

So we silently proceed up the lane of "Cops and Donuts" slots.

There's about a hundred of the machines stretching toward the horizon and every one is currently occupied.

We see the glittering gown.

"Mrs. Rock?" says Parker, his voice booming. We pick up our pace, close in on her stool.

"Just a second." She slaps her spin button again.

"Will you kindly come with me?"

"Hold on, hon. I get a bonus game."

"Mrs. Rock?"

"Dadgumit!" Mrs. Rock's bonus spin ends up paying off exactly nothing. "This machine was hot until you boys came along!"

"Let's go upstairs, ma'am," says Ceepak. He and Parker now look like polite bookends—both of them have their arms extended to the right to indicate which way Mrs. Rock should scoot off her stool.

"I can't leave. I have a fifty-dollar credit!"

"We will gladly issue you a voucher for the remainder," says Parker.

"But somebody else will come along and win after I've been the one feeding money into this machine!"

"Actually," says Ceepak in his robo-cop voice, "that is a fallacious assumption. Past wins or losses are not predictive of future wins and losses."

Mrs. Rock smiles up at Ceepak. Now she's impressed by his brains as well as his brawn.

Ceepak, however, is not smiling back.

"This way." He's still gesturing to his right.

"Fine." Mrs. Rock swivels around to rub the spin button. "I'll be back, big boy. I'll be back."

Yeah. She'll be back. In twenty or thirty years—if she gets time off for good behavior, like Mr. Joe "Six-pack" Ceepak.

39

We're in Cyrus Parker's office.

It's not much. A ten-by-ten room with a metal desk and a telephone—the kind with too many throbbing lights on it. There's a corkboard on one wall with "persons of interest" posters tacked to it. Card counters. Pickpockets. I recognize the two guys Ceepak and I tussled with on the floor in slots, row 42.

"So, how'd you get past my guys?" Parker asks Mrs. Rock.

"Should I call David?" She shifts in her seat to show us as much leg as she can without showing us everything up where the legs end. This is my first interrogation of a suspect dressed in a slinky cocktail dress with a slit racing up the thigh. It adds to the intrigue.

"Is Mr. Zuckerman your lawyer?" asks Ceepak.

She grins coyly. "He is our family adviser."

"We are not, at this time, pressing formal charges," says Ceepak.

"Charges? All I did was skip one silly autograph session in the lobby. I just couldn't face my adoring fans. Not tonight."

"How?" demands Parker. "How'd you slip out of the theater and into the casino without bumping into any of my men?"

"We have an exit."

"Where?"

"Downstairs."

"We had all the doors covered on the lower level."

"Not this one. Besides, it's not really a door. In fact, it's more of a hidden panel. Very ingenious. Slides to the side. It also won't appear on any of your blueprints or building schematics."

"Did you people put it in?"

"Yes," says Mrs. Rock, slinking into cutesy-poo baby talk. "We people put it in."

"Why?"

The grin grows more mischievous. "We needed it."

"For what?"

"One of our world-famous illusions."

Parker crosses his arms over his barrel chest and his bulging arm muscles almost rip through the seams in his shirt sleeves. "Mrs. Rock? I need to know specific details about this secret panel. . . ."

"For that, you will need to talk to Mr. Zuckerman. Unfortunately, I've signed several nondisclosure agreements." She focuses on Ceepak, leans forward in her chair. Most guys would at least glance down to see how much more of her big boob valley the dip revealed. Not Ceepak.

Cleavage scheme foiled, Mrs. Rock aims for Ceepak's weak spot: "Surely you gentlemen wouldn't have me violate my word of honor?"

"What about last night?" asks Ceepak.

"I didn't skip out last night. But today, I had to! You see, I had been playing that same 'Cops and Donuts' slot machine earlier in the day and it had proved quite hot."

Of course, when she says *hot*, she has to wiggle a little in her seat so we all take in the cheesy double meaning. But her cheesecake display isn't working on Ceepak.

Or Parker.

Or me, and I'm usually a pretty cheap date.

"I love 'Cops and Donuts'," she coos. "Especially when they're hot. The doughnuts, I mean."

Now I'm wondering if she's the one who rented the pay-per-view porno movie in AA-4. I think it's where she scrapes up most of her dialogue.

"Why weren't you onstage last night during the Lucky Numbers illusion?" asks Ceepak.

"Excuse me?"

"Last night. When your nanny was murdered. Your double was the one onstage."

"Is that what Sherry told you?"

"No, ma'am," says Ceepak. "It's what we deduced from your actions this evening."

"Look." Her back stiffens. Hands smooth out her skirt, closing up any visible slit. "I admit that I have something of a gambling addiction. Some nights the allure of all those machines whirling out in the casino is simply too much for me to resist. Especially after receiving confirmation that my husband has, indeed, been frequenting a cheap Chinese massage parlor where, I am told, one can have every part of one's body rubbed until it feels much, much better."

"Why weren't you onstage last night when Ms. Landry was murdered?" Ceepak asks again.

"I can't believe you fell for Sherry's idiotic insinuations."

"Again, I reiterate, we did not discuss this matter with Ms. Amour. In fact, we remain unable to locate her. However, during last night's performance, you did not speak to the volunteer onstage. Tonight you did. In fact, you were quite verbose."

Here comes that playful leer again. "You're very observant, Mr. Ceepak."

"Would you care to explain?" says Ceepak. "Why the vast discrepancy in your two performances?"

"I was doing Sherry a favor last night. For whatever reason, she asked me to remain mute during that particular number. Heaven only knows why."

Ceepak bristles. "We, of course, have no way to corroborate what you say. No proof."

"Yes you do. Just look at the show tapes. We record every performance. There's a video camera up in the light booth. You'll see this."

She wobbles her left hand, flashes her glittery engagement ring.

"I have one. My sister doesn't. She never married."

"Your sister?"

"Yes," says Mrs. Rock. "Sherry Amour is my sister. That's a stage name, of course. Our real family name was far too dull for her chosen line of work. Julia Pratt. Sounds dreadful, don't you think? Terrible porno name."

"Pratt?" says Ceepak.

"That's right."

"As in Jake Pratt?"

Mrs. Rock giggles. "Of course. Julia is Jake's mother."

40

My mind is way beyond scrambled now.

I think it's clotted. Poached. Hard-boiled. I know my head hurts.

"Jake Pratt is your nephew?" Ceepak presses on.

"That's right. As you may know, Richard has always insisted on making our show a family-friendly enterprise. It's why we put our own children in it. Why, the costume designer is a cousin. The set designer, too. Of course, Mr. Zuckerman isn't a blood relation, but he's been with us so long, we consider him family. It's the secret to our success. Family."

"You did the show tonight," says Parker, "even though your nephew was murdered this morning?"

"Of course. We did it for the rest of the family. The ones counting on us for their livelihood. It's what Jake would have wanted us to do. Julia—I mean, Sherry—too. We all believe in the unparalleled power of the family bond. It's why I know I will eventually forgive my husband his weaknesses and wanderings. We made a vow. For better or worse. Chinese massage parlors? They're just part of the bad you put up with for all the good."

Mrs. Rock slowly turns her sparkling diamond ring 'round and 'round her finger and I'm reminded of the flashing laser lights inside that mind scrambler ride back home in Sea Haven. I'm also reminded of how Mrs. Rock's rock, the size of a crystal salt shaker, nearly blinded me from the stage when the follow spot hit it last night.

"I find it hard to believe," says Ceepak, "that your body double would not wear a similar ring. You people are master illusionists. The true magic is in keen attention to details such as that—no discernible discrepancies between the principal player and the body double."

"I wouldn't allow it."

"Come again?"

"This ring symbolizes the eternal commitment Richard and I share. I would rather expose an illusion's secret than compromise my most cherished family values."

"I don't believe you," says Ceepak.

"It's the truth."

Bull. Shit.

I think it, don't say it. From the looks on Ceepak's face, he's thinking similar, if cleaner, thoughts.

Mrs. Rock, however, remains oblivious to our manure-filled minds. She spreads on a second layer.

"Of course, I can understand my sister being jealous of all that this ring symbolizes. My marriage. Our successes. Sherry's been something of a drifter all her life. Poor girl couldn't even tell you who Jake's father was. Seems there are several potential candidates for that dubious honor. When she got deeper into drugs and the whole pornography scene, we were forced to take Jake into our home. When she finally cleaned up her act, we gave her a job, worked in some transporting illusions. Julia and I aren't twins, mind you. She's years older than me. But with some cosmetic surgery, serious work with a personal trainer, a top-notch wig designer . . ."

"You say you will eventually forgive Mr. Rock for his dalliances at the massage parlor," says Ceepak.

"Yes. Eventually."

"Has Mr. Rock forgiven you for your affair with Jake Pratt?"

Mrs. Rock goes rigid. Closes up everything she can without resewing her gown.

"What?" She spits it out.

"We have evidence suggesting that you and your nephew were lovers."

"That is sick, Mr. Ceepak. Sick."

"Did you not rent him a motel room across the street?"

"I did no such thing."

"The desk clerk can identify you."

"He's a filthy liar if he says I ever spent the night there with my nephew! That's incest, isn't it? You can't sleep with your nephew! It's against the law."

"Wait a second," I butt in. "Yesterday, you hinted that you were not immune to, what'd you call, 'the allure of a younger man, especially one as attractive as Jake Pratt.' "

"I hinted at no such thing."

"I heard it. In your voice."

"Then you have a very filthy mind."

"Danny?" Ceepak shakes his head.

I shut up as suggested.

"Am I free to go?" Mrs. Rock asks, concealing everything she can because I'm totally skeeving her out.

"One of my men will escort you to the dressing room backstage so you can change into your street clothes," says Parker. "He will then escort you upstairs to your suite where he will remain, posted outside the door. You're not to leave the premises, ma'am. We'll need to see those show tapes you mentioned."

"Just ask David," says Mrs. Rock, refusing to stand up from her chair until I look somewhere besides at her. So I shift my eyes over to Ceepak.

He looks worried.

I don't blame him. Maybe Mrs. Rock has another secret escape panel inside her dressing-room closet.

"What will be, will be," mumbles Ceepak, channeling his inner Springsteen. "The more we listen to this cavalcade of lies, which can only be countered by those who have been silenced or remain unavailable for questioning, the more we are trapped inside their illusion."

We're actually with Parker inside the security command center, but I catch his drift. Kim Hammond is still on duty, seated at her console dutifully tapping keys, calling up that archived video clip from the elevator ride.

We've already checked out the show tape: you can, indeed, see the big diamond ring during the Lucky Numbers bit. Ceepak also rolled the tape back to the transporting illusion. When you zoom in, you can see that Mrs. Rock goes into the booth stage right wearing a ring and reappears stage left without it.

"I can't help but think we are being duped," Ceepak says. "Do we even know if Mrs. Rock and Ms. Amour are truly related? All we have is her word, which, in my opinion, is virtually worthless."

Unfortunately, Ceepak can't force the rest of the world to adhere to his code. They can lie all they want. Right now, we have no way of knowing what the truth is because it's been reflected through too many crooked panes of silver-backed glass by just about every person we've encountered since arriving in Atlantic City. The place is a fun house. Trick mirrors. Shifting floors. Losers who think they'll be winners after one more trip to the ATM.

"The ghost enemy," says Ceepak, and from the look in his eyes, I know he has temporarily drifted back to Iraq. "The truth of any dynamic situation is extremely difficult to ascertain. Enemies hide among the innocents. Innocents stumble into the wrong place at the wrong time."

I settle in against the edge of a desk. So does Parker.

"One night," says Ceepak, "we were stationed just north of Ramadi, on the main highway, a road riddled with booby traps and improvised explosive devices. Late in the afternoon, we were handing out soccer balls and candy to a group of kids. You've never seen such smiles. It had been some time since these children had been able to come outdoors and play and they were making the most of it. So were we."

A thin smile crinkles his lips for a half second before it evaporates.

"A Hyundai sedan comes up the road. Heads straight at our vehicle. No one is manning the gun in the turret topside. He's down, playing soccer with the kids. The car keeps coming. It's maroon."

Of course he remembers the color of the car. Probably still sees it in his nightmares.

"I step into the center of the roadway, wave at the car, signal for it to come to a full and complete stop. The driver responds by accelerating. I hear the engine roar. I assume it's another car bomb."

I nod. As if I have a clue.

"I was forced to make a split-second decision based only on what was readily observable: a maroon Hyundai racing toward the children and our military transport vehicle. Was it an innocent family sedan or was it a suicide bomber with a trunk loaded down with artillery shells?"

"What'd you do?"

"I raised my weapon and listened to the engine whine. Standard procedure would dictate that I first fire a warning shot into the air, then a shot to the tires, and, finally, a shot through the windshield to take out the driver. However, this particular vehicle was approaching far too rapidly for me to observe established protocol. The kill shot would need to be the first and only round fired. So I waited. Perhaps longer than I should have."

"What happened?"

"The Iraqi driver finally saw me. He slammed on his brakes, lifted both hands off the steering wheel, skidded to a stop. A moment later, he shifted into reverse and backed away. What I took to be an enemy combatant proved, in the end, to be a civilian driver who could not see me, our Humvee, or the children playing soccer due to the blinding glare of the setting sun behind us."

"Wow."

Parker nods in agreement. He served in the First Gulf War. "Perceptions and reality, Officer Boyle. The truth remains dynamic and all you can do is embrace the suck."

"Yeah." I have no idea what that last bit means but Ceepak's nodding so I figure it's military talk for coolly dealing with whatever crappy situation comes your way.

"Therefore," says Ceepak, "we must redouble our efforts to separate illusion from reality. We must be certain we know what we are looking at, not what we *might* be looking at."

"Here we go," says Hammond, who has found the elevator scene on her hard drive.

"Please fast-forward to where the blonde whispers into Mr. Pratt's ear."

"You got it."

The digits streak forward. She clicks her mouse. Things slow down to real time as the blonde raises her hand and whispers into Pratt's ear.

"It appears Mrs. Rock is being truthful in regards to this particular incident," says Ceepak.

"How so?" asks Parker.

Ceepak taps the screen with the blunt end of a pen. "Note how she brings up her left hand to whisper into Pratt's ear. The ring finger is bare."

No dazzling diamond flaring up at the camera lens.

"So," says Parker, sounding like somebody scrambled his mind, too, "this blond woman, the adult movie actress, is his mother?"

"On further viewing, it is safe to say we might have misinterpreted a mother's innocent hand-holding as something more lascivious. My wife, Rita, holds my stepson's hand from time to time. Not often and only when none of his friends are present."

"Why's the double all dolled-up, looking like Mrs. Rock, riding the elevator in the middle of the day on a Sunday?" Parker asks Ceepak.

"Not knowing, can't say."

Yeah. Me, neither.

"So," says Parker, "Mrs. Rock didn't do it? She was onstage when Ms. Landry was murdered."

"If," says Ceepak, "any of the rest of what she just told us is also truthful. We need to talk to Ms. Julia Pratt."

"That's Sherry Amour, right?" says Parker.

"Roger that."

"Okay. Just want to be clear." He shudders his head, trying to jangle his brain cells back into alignment. It's like whacking a TV to make the picture sharper. Sometimes, it works.

"Another *J*," I say. "Julia."

Ceepak nods. "Further complicating the true meaning of the

message written on the bathroom mirror." His cell chirps. At least we know it's not Ceepak's damn dad. That man's five minutes are up.

I glance up at the digital clock spinning on one of the security-camera feeds: 2210. Ten minutes after 10:00 PM.

"This is Ceepak. Go. Yes." He listens. Brings his hand up to his face so he can pinch his nose bone. Whatever he's hearing, trust me—it's all bad. "Remain in your room. Roger that. The police are on their way. We'll be there ASAP."

He closes up the clamshell.

"That was Blaine and Jim Bob," he reports. "The dancers. They have located Sherry Amour."

"Where?" I ask.

"In her room. Upstairs at the Super Eight Motel. Jake Pratt's mother is dead."

41

The medical examiner says Julia Pratt, aka Sherry Amour, has been dead for over eight hours.

I don't want to mention the flies up in room 332.

It's 10:30 PM. Dr. McDaniels is once more on the scene.

"Krabitz," she says out on the third-floor terrace, which is crowded with cops, when one of the CSI techs shows her the slug they dug out of the bed inside the room. "Thirty-eight caliber. He came up here before you boys collared him downstairs harassing the dancers."

That was this afternoon.

Sherry Amour was already dead when Ceepak and I were down below, storming the second floor on our ATVs, trying to stop Krabitz from kicking in Blaine and Jim Bob's door. The barrel of that gun I saw tucked into his pants was probably still warm.

"The dancers knew she was up here," says Ceepak.

"Yeah," says Dr. McDaniels, knuckle-punching him in the left arm. "So you two might want to go downstairs and talk to them about withholding evidence. Me? I've got another murder scene to process."

Ceepak nods.

Dr. McDaniels inhales as much fresh air as her lungs will allow and heads back to her grim task. I see her swatting at black specks before the door to room 332 swings shut.

She is, as Parker might say, embracing the suck.

Ceepak and I trudge down the metal staircase to the second floor.

This time when we knock on room 224, the two guys inside actually open the door. Fast.

"Gentlemen," says Ceepak.

Jim Bob looks like he's been crying. Blaine still is.

"Is she dead?" Jim Bob asks.

"Yes."

"We thought so. When we went up there. Found her like that. We hadn't heard from her all day so we decided we had to check in on her."

"We had a key," mutters Blaine.

"We called nine-one-one. Right away. Even before we called you. I swear we did."

Ceepak nods. "I'm certain you reacted as swiftly as you could."

"Oh, my god!" gushes Blaine. "She's dead! Sherry's dead?"

Ceepak nods again.

"Oh, my god. I need to sit down." He takes the foot of one of the twin beds.

"How long have you gentlemen known she was upstairs?"

"Since last night," says Jim Bob. "When we booked the room for her."

"It's in my name," says Blaine. "I put it on my credit card. It's why we had the second key."

"Thank you for being forthcoming about that," says Ceepak. "We appreciate it."

Yeah. Of course, we would have appreciated it even more if they had been forthcoming about it when we dropped by this afternoon. Or tonight, when we tried to interview them through their dressing-room door. Or after the show, when they were in the hallway, hanging on every word we exchanged with Richard Rock and David Zuckerman.

"We didn't know if we could trust you two," says Jim Bob. "We thought you might be working for them."

"Who?"

"The Rocks!"

"But then we heard you in the hall tonight!" says Blaine. "You drilled that man a new asshole."

"Come again?"

Jim Bob tries to clarify: "When you figured out how we do the Lucky Numbers trick and Richard got all mad—you didn't even care."

"You're my kind of man!" adds Blaine.

Ceepak doesn't flinch. I would have. "We need to ask you gentlemen a few questions," he says.

"Of course." Jim Bob gestures toward the one chair and then at the twin beds. "Please. Sit down."

We do. Ceepak lets me take the chair. He sits on the edge of the other bed.

"We were afraid to go upstairs and check in on Sherry," says Jim Bob. "Ever since that man came pounding on our door. We thought they had people watching us and we didn't want to give away her hiding place. See, she usually lives upstairs at the Xanadu. They sneak her backstage at eight, right when the show goes up."

"Who was she hiding from?" asks Ceepak.

"The Rocks, I guess. That man with the pistol, Krabitz, he works for them, right?"

Ceepak nods. "He is a private investigator in their employ."

"Last night, we brought Sherry here, straight from the karaoke bar," says Jim Bob.

"She could barely walk!" adds Blaine, placing a hand beside his mouth so he can confide a secret. "She'd been doing shots of vodka since the show went down. Since she heard. First in the lobby bar, then that lounge with the dreadful Motown music."

"Heard what?" asks Ceepak.

"That Nanny Katie was killed!" says Jim Bob. "Sherry felt horrible. She told us she was responsible."

Whoa. She confessed to killing Katie?

"How so?" asks Ceepak. "Is she the one who strangled Ms. Landry?"

Blaine sits up straight. Mugs this totally horrified face. "Sherry? Impossible. She wouldn't hurt a fly."

Again with the flies.

"She didn't kill Nanny Katie," says Jim Bob. "But, okay, this is extremely complicated. Sherry Amour was really Julia Pratt. Jake Pratt's mother."

"So we have heard," says Ceepak.

"Oh. Okay. Last night, when she couldn't find Jake and ask him what had happened to Katie, she started freaking out. She was afraid Jake was somehow mixed up in the murder because, remember, he skipped out and nobody knew where he was. That's why Sherry came up to Lip Sync Lee's still in her costume. She'd been looking for Jake since she heard the news about the nanny."

"Looking for him and drinking," adds Blaine.

"Did Sherry think her son killed Ms. Landry?" asks Ceepak.

"She knew it was a possibility. Jake Pratt was a hothead. He'd been arrested like a hundred times. Sherry blamed herself for that, too."

"Why?"

"Years ago, when she was doing way too much cocaine, she basically abandoned Jake. Sent him off to live with relatives."

"He was like ten or eleven when this happened," adds Blaine. "So this is only eight or nine years ago."

"Anyway," says Jim Bob. "Sherry sent Jake to go live with his rich aunt and uncle out in LA. Beverly Hills."

"His aunt and uncle being Jessica and Richard Rock?" says Ceepak.

"Exactly. Sherry *begged* Jessica to take the boy off her hands, said she couldn't handle raising a son until she cleaned up her own act. Jessica agreed. The Rocks didn't adopt Jake or anything, but they took him into their home."

"More like a mansion," says Blaine.

Jim Bob nods. "Seven bedrooms. Six baths. Maids. Five-car garage. Long story short, Jake *loves* it there!"

Blaine waggles a few fingers near his left ear. "Swimming pools. Movie stars. What's not to love?"

"So Jake lived with the Rocks," says Jim Bob. "Meanwhile, back in Las Vegas, Sherry kept churning out triple-X movies for Vivid Videos. But she also kept going to N.A. meetings. She worked hard, too. Got totally clean and sober."

"From the coke," Blaine clarifies. "Not the booze. You can't give up everything all at once."

"Anyway," says Jim Bob, "when she was clean for eighteen months, she flew out to LA and convinced the Rocks that she was ready to raise her own son. She brought Jake back to Vegas to live with her. Now, of course, he's turning twelve, thirteen. Hitting puberty. Has hormones screaming through his body, plus he's used to sleeping on three-hundred thread count Egyptian cotton sheets in a mansion, not on a lumpy Goodwill store couch in a lousy one-bedroom apartment.

"Before long, Jake starts getting into all sorts of trouble with just about every Las Vegas–based law enforcement agency. He's in and out of juvenile court so many times, all the bailiffs know Sherry by name and are constantly hitting on her, asking her out on dates. Jake eventually ends up doing some time inside the Clark County Juvenile Detention Center."

Blaine bats his eyes. "Some time? It was the boy's boarding school for four or five years!"

Jim Bob sighs. "Jake has serious anger issues."

"Gentlemen," says Blaine, like it's a royal pronouncement, "Jacob Pratt was nothing but trouble. Sherry told us he broke her heart on a daily basis."

"There's more to it," says Jim Bob. "Something bad happened to Jake while he was out in LA. Something horrible. At least that's what Sherry said."

"What?" asks Ceepak. "What happened?"

Jim Bob looks around. Whispers: "When he was ten, Jake Pratt was molested."

"By his aunt?" I ask because I'm the guy with the filthy mind.

"Maybe. That's what I think. But Sherry never got into specifics, never said who did what, only that it was somebody 'in the family.' And it wasn't a onetime deal, either. This went on the whole two years he lived out there in their mansion. It's why Sherry joined the show in Vegas when she learned Jake had finagled his way into the cast."

"How'd he do that?" asks Ceepak.

"Pulled some strings. Talked to his Auntie Jessica."

"When was this?"

"Maybe nine months ago. We brought the show to the MGM Grand. Sherry and Jake were already living in town. It was easy for Sherry to keep an eye on her son, especially when she agreed to do the plastic surgery and stuff so they could work in the transporting illusion."

"I think Sherry really wanted to keep an eye on her," sniffs Blaine.

"Mrs. Rock?" says Ceepak.

Jim Bob nods. "Don't let her wholesome family-values act fool you. Mrs. Rock enjoys spending time with young, muscular men."

"She even hit on *me*!" This from Blaine with both hands on his chest in horror.

"Anyway," says Jim Bob, "last night, when she was so drunk she could barely walk, Sherry blurts out how she dragged the nanny into it, too."

Ceepak leans forward. "How?"

"Saturday night when, yes, she was also drunk, she begged Nanny Katie to keep an eye on her son because Jake said he was falling in love again, that the 'relationship' was just as wonderful as it had been when he was out in LA, and his mean, miserable whore of a mother—that's what he called Sherry—couldn't stop him from doing what his heart told him was right."

"More like his dick." Color commentary courtesy Blaine. "He bragged to us in the dressing room Monday about hopping into the sack with his old flame."

"Can we go back to the weekend?" says Jim Bob.

Blaine bats his eyes. "Fine. Whatever."

"So, Saturday night, Sherry told Katie what had happened to Jake when he was living with the Rocks. She practically begged the nanny to protect her son. Katie didn't totally believe Sherry, of course."

"She's a sloppy drunk," adds Blaine. "Katie probably thought it was the vodka tonics talking."

"On Sunday," Jim Bob continues, "the male dancers had to do a photo shoot up on top of the Crystal Palace Tower. . . ."

"Just us chorus boys and Mrs. Rock," adds Blaine. "We posed

on the helicopter landing pad. Pretended like she was making this grand entrance out of a whirlybird. By the way—I am *terrified* of heights."

"Mrs. Rock, too," says Jim Bob. "So Sherry had to put on the costume, stand in for her."

"Jessica Rock is not afraid of heights!" Blaine protests. "She was too busy down in the casino to be bothered."

"Whatever. After the shoot, Sherry and Jake rode the elevator down together and, when they were finally alone, Sherry told her son how much she loved him and how Katie Landry was going to be his nanny now, too—making sure he didn't get into trouble again."

That explains the elevator ride.

And why Jake assumed Katie knew about his checkered past.

"Then," says Jim Bob, "yesterday afternoon, Monday, Katie found something."

"What?" asks Ceepak.

"We don't know. Around four-thirty, Katie called Sherry and said she had found something pretty horrible. She explained that she had some police friends who just happened to be in town."

"Is that you guys?" Blaine asks.

We nod.

"We're sorry for your loss," he adds.

"Katie told Sherry she was going to consult with you gentlemen first," says Jim Bob. "Figure out what to do with whatever it was she had just found."

"You think it was a secret sex video?" asks Blaine, all hushed and dramatic.

"We do not know," says Ceepak, even though that's my theory, too.

Blaine tortures his bottom lip into a twist. "Nanny Katie was a sweet person. Very, very sweet."

"Brave too," adds Jim Bob. "Sherry said that, when she called,

Katie promised she would do whatever she could to protect her son, no matter what."

No matter what.

It seems Katie Landry was the one person in Atlantic City who actually meant what she said.

Even if it got her killed.

42

"Earlier," says Ceepak, "you mentioned that, last night, Ms. Amour showed up at the karaoke bar 'in costume.' What, precisely, did you mean by that?"

"You know," says Jim Bob, "she was still wearing the platinum wig. Too much makeup. Had her boobs pushed up high."

"And she was wearing that hideous cubic zirconium ring," adds Blaine. *"Très gauche."*

"She only wears that thing when she fills in for Jessica during the last bit," explains Jim Bob. "Lucky Numbers."

"Why would Mrs. Rock request that Sherry take her place onstage during the Lucky Numbers routine?"

"Sometimes," says Blaine, "Mrs. Rock likes to sneak out a little early and hit the slots before the casino gets too crowded."

So.

Chalk up another lie for Mrs. Rock, that whole sanctity-of-the-engagement-ring BS she was shoveling earlier. The video clearly showing the diamond sparkling on her ring finger during the performance of Lucky Numbers on Monday night isn't much of an alibi anymore. Mrs. Rock could've left the stage early for a different reason besides spinning for "Donut" bonuses. She could've slipped out to help her young lover murder my old girlfriend.

"We should go arrest her," I say to Ceepak.

He holds up his left hand. "Hang on, Danny."

"She did it!"

"I don't think so."

"What?"

"I sense the diamond ring is the distraction we are meant to focus on. We need to ponder alternative possibilities a split-second longer."

Great. Ceepak's back in the middle of hell's highway over there in Iraq, playing chicken with a car bomber, taking his time to consider all potential explanations. Well, maybe this time he will take too much time and, instead of an innocent Iraqi driver in need of polarized sunglasses, we'll end up with Mrs. Jessica Rock getting away with murder.

Then again, Cyrus Parker does have security guys stationed right outside her hotel room door so—unless she has another secret panel in the closet—Mrs. Rock isn't escaping anywhere anytime soon.

I let Ceepak play through.

"Jim Bob . . ."

"Please. Call me James. Mr. Rock came up with that corny Jim Bob crap. Thought is sounded more Texasy."

"We think it sounds lame," adds Blaine.

"Very well, James. Do you always act as Mr. Rock's escort out of the auditorium after he puts on the hood?"

"Yes. And it's not really a blindfold. He can see right through that sack."

As Lady Jasmine suspected.

"The fabric looks thick, but it isn't. I'm just there playing seeing eye dog to help sell the illusion."

"You were with him on Monday night?"

"Yep. I've never missed a show since we opened."

"Was Mr. Rock's behavior different on Monday?"

"Sure."

"How so?"

"He was furious. Jake cut the show without any notice or telling anybody where he was and that ticked Mr. Rock off, royally. 'I'm docking his pay! I'm firing him! I don't care if he is effing family!' See, usually we make a big deal out of walking up that corridor in front of the theater even though, as you probably figured out, they cut away from the live feed the second Fred does the swish pan."

"Go on," says Ceepak.

"Well, like I said, typically we walk up that hallway so everybody can see us because, you never know, some of those people may have already paid a fortune to see the show and our stumbling blindly up the hall gives them permission to believe that what they thought they saw on the video screen really happened. It's also a great publicity stunt. Gets the buzz going."

"You won't *believe* how many people buy tickets just because they saw Richard Rock walking up the hall like a zombie," Blaine chimes in.

"Usually," says James, "we walk about a hundred feet with Richard pretending he can't see where he's going. When we get to the fountain, the one with the ducks, we head left, and go through a door that leads into a secondary backstage access passage."

Ceepak nods. We're familiar with the route. We took it with them tonight.

"Now, on Monday night, things were different! As soon as

Freddy pivoted into his swish pan, Mr. Rock froze. We weren't walking anywhere because he was furious, started reaming me out. 'Where the *F* is Jake? Do you effing know?' Of course, I didn't. We weren't really friends."

"Jake was an asshole," says Blaine. "I'm sorry. I know I shouldn't speak ill of the dead but forgive me, it's true. He was a first-class a-hole."

"What happened next?" Ceepak asks James.

"Fred, the cameraman, heads back to the lobby, per usual. Richard yells, 'We're taking the shortcut!' and heads for the door right next to the lobby entrance. There's a security guard standing there when we do the show, but he may not tell you much because he works for Richard Rock, Inc."

"Go on."

"We push through the door, head up the hall. Of course, that means we have to hug the right-hand wall so we're in the safety zone, the blind spot that'll take us under the security camera without it even knowing we're there. The Rocks are fanatics about backstage secrecy. I guess most magicians are. We have cast meetings about security leaks all the time. Anyway, while we're shuffling up against the wall single-file Indian-style, Mr. Rock tells me to hurry backstage and make sure that any setups in the wings or prop stuff Jake was responsible for are taken care of. I told him there wasn't anything, that Jake should just be out there onstage with the other dancers, doing the cowboy routine, killing time. Mr. Rock tells me to go wait in the effing wings anyhow."

Ceepak nods. Why am I getting the feeling he already suspected something fishy was going on with Mr. Rock during Monday night's performance of Lucky Numbers?

"Also," says James, "he's so busy yelling at me, I notice he isn't chatting with the volunteer from the audience as much as he usually does."

"He's not addressing her by name, correct?" says Ceepak.

"That's right."

So that's how Ceepak knew something was weird about Monday's show compared with tonight's.

"He didn't even do his standard patter," says Jim Bob. "In fact, he stopped doing it right after the swish pan."

"How do you think that was accomplished?" asks Ceepak. "How could Mr. Rock seem to be talking through his microphone when, in fact, he had switched it off?"

"I'm not sure. But, well, if they can prerecord the images, they can easily do the same thing with the words. They probably have an emergency audio track standing by in the control room they cut to the instant he switched off his head mike."

"He can do that?"

"Sure. There's a transmitter pack on his belt with an on-off switch."

Ceepak turns to me. "And that, Danny, is why, on Monday night, Mr. Rock did not mention the volunteer's name again until nearly the end of the routine."

Uh-oh.

I think I know what Mr. Rock was doing during those ten or fifteen minutes of dead air.

He was backstage in room AA-4.

Taking over for Jake Pratt. Killing Katie Landry.

43

We hitch a ride in an ACPD cruiser and head back to the Xanadu.

On the ride, Ceepak cell-phones Cyrus Parker.

"We need to apprehend Mr. Richard Rock. Roger that. We're almost there. ETA one minute. Ten-four."

I'm in the backseat, staring out the window. On our return trip to the glitzy Xanadu, we need to roll through the seedier side of Atlantic City first. Past the run-down apartment complexes where everything looks stained and rusty. Ditto for the dumpy motels.

We take a turn and I can see that billboard I first read from the window up in my high-roller suite.

CHRIST DIED FOR OUR SINS.

"Richard Rock killed Katie?" I mumble while wondering if Christ knew that particular sin was coming down the pike.

"Yes, Danny," says Ceepak—in answer to the question he actually heard.

"What about Jake Pratt's pubic hair?"

"Mr. Rock could have harvested it just as easily as Mrs. Rock. In fact, I believe it was Mr. Rock who molested Jake Pratt when he was a child. Furthermore, I suspect that, muddled in the emotional confusion such a relationship would undoubtedly engender in a preadolescent male, Pratt coped by giving the abuse incidents romantic overtones."

"*J Luvs U*," I say. "He smudged that on the mirror for Richard Rock."

"I believe so."

We pull into the Xanadu's covered driveway. It's after 11:00 but there are two bellhops on duty. Neither one comes over to help us with our luggage. Guess cop cars usually don't carry any.

The ACPD patrol car's tires screech on the concrete as it heads back to the Super 8 Motel and Julia Pratt's murder scene. I've almost lost count of how many people had to die for Richard Rock to fulfill his fantasies.

So many dead. Julia Pratt. Katie Landry. Detective Brady Flynn. His partner, Mike Weddle. Even Jake Pratt, Mr. Rock's onetime lover.

Then I think about how many people had to go along with whatever Rock told them to do so he could keep piling those bodies outside the door, to paraphrase Springsteen. His wife. His manager. The guys in the video control booth. Toohey Tuiasopo and the rest of the "Rock 'n Wow!" security team. Kenny Krabitz.

"Wait a second."

"Yes?" says Ceepak.

"Why did Rock have Krabitz kill Jake Pratt if they were falling back in love?"

"Perhaps the feeling wasn't mutual. Perhaps Pratt had grown too old for Mr. Rock's tastes."

Yeah. Nineteen ain't the new eleven.

We head through the automatic glass doors, pick up the geometric carpet, head toward the Crystal Palace elevators where the Rocks have taken up temporary residence.

Ceepak's cell phone chirps.

"This is Ceepak. Go. Roger that."

He halts.

So I do, too.

Now he heaves a sigh.

"Very well."

I can see the cogwheels spinning inside his head. I suspect the situation has gone "dynamic" once again.

"New plan," he says into the phone. "We are proceeding to the boardwalk."

We start walking again; Ceepak keeps the cell pressed to his cheek.

"Hmm? I'm playing a hunch, Cyrus. Right. Will do. I'll keep you posted."

He clips the phone back to his belt.

"Parker reports that Mr. Rock is no longer located here at the Xanadu."

"What?" We're hurrying up the never-ending carpet, trying to cut across the casino and make our way to the far side and the escalators down to the boardwalk exits as quickly as we can. It's like a half-mile hike. "They let Mr. Rock leave the building?"

"Roger that. But, as you recall, Danny, until minutes ago, Richard Rock was not considered a suspect or accomplice for any of the crimes that have been committed over the past two days."

"We were supposed to arrest Mrs. Rock, right?"

I know that's what I wanted to do until Ceepak stood in the middle of the road a little longer—metaphorically speaking, of course—to see if another solution might reveal itself.

"They knew we'd be able to eventually learn about the second diamond ring from somebody in the show, right?"

"Yes," says Ceepak as we bustle past the "Cops and Donuts" slot machine lane. "I imagine that in the final act of the illusion as originally conceived by Mr. Rock, we were meant to arrest his wife. At her murder trial, irrefutable evidence as to her actual whereabouts at the time of Katie's death would have been presented, some proof stronger than that which she initially proffered."

"Maybe they know there's a PTZ surveillance-camera shot of Mrs. Rock out in the casino hitting the 'Cops and Donuts' machines on Monday night, too."

"Of course. Well done, Danny! Excellent analysis."

Hey, I took a shot.

"The prosecutor would, most likely, not think to search for such evidence," says Ceepak. "The defense attorney's investigators would. They could also demonstrate with testimony from a handwriting expert that it was Sherry Amour who had signed autographs in the lobby on Monday."

"They could call you as a witness," I say. "Make you bring the stuffed tiger you got autographed for Rita."

"Indeed. The charges would have been dropped during the exchange of evidence phase—before the case even went to trial."

"Too bad Kenny Krabitz is in jail. He could've drummed up all kinds of PI work once he became famous for uncovering the dramatic evidence that proved Mrs. Rock's innocence."

We reach the escalators and head down to the boardwalk exits.

"Mr. Krabitz is not a licensed private investigator, Danny."

"No?"

"No. It is why his business cards did not specify his occupation."

Oh. I just thought he was stupid. "So who is he?"

Ceepak grimaces. "I suspect Mr. Krabitz is the individual

charged with the unseemly task of procuring underage sex partners for Mr. Rock's amusement."

"What?"

"That boy. At the swimming pool. I do not think he is Mr. Krabitz's son. It's why the boy called his supposed father 'Kenny' instead of 'Dad.' "

"So Katie found out about all this?" I say as we swirl out the revolving doors and hit the boardwalk.

"I'm afraid so."

"Why didn't she just tell me?"

"I believe she intended to."

But they got to her before I did. Jake Pratt. Richard Rock. She couldn't talk about it in her phone message to me because Mrs. Rock came into the room.

"So where the hell are we going now?" I usually don't talk like that with Ceepak, but I'm not usually this pissed off, either.

These bastards killed Katie.

"Lucky Lilani's Stress Therapy."

"The massage parlor?"

"Roger that."

We head south.

The boardwalk isn't crowded. Just a few stray drunks whoohooing it all the way home to their hotels.

"Can I ask why? They don't want to talk to us."

"Because Zuckerman solicited their silence for a fee," says Ceepak.

"Wait a second. Rock just jumped ugly all over Zuckerman for running down to Lucky Lilani's to spy on him for his wife."

"No, Danny. The altercation in the hallway between Mr. Rock and Mr. Zuckerman was another bit of business staged solely for our benefit. All part of the illusion."

"So why was Zuckerman down at Lucky Lilani's?"

"Our initial supposition was correct. Mr. Zuckerman was there to make a payoff. It is a public space—the one element of the illusion not under the illusionist's total control."

"Rock went there to hire prostitutes?"

"I suspect so. Danny," says Ceepak somberly, "do you recall the young boy we saw at the massage parlor this morning? He was sitting on the floor, huddled with several women and children."

"Sure. They were all eating breakfast."

"This particular boy had powdered sugar all over the front of his shirt."

"Yeah. He looked like he'd been eating funnel cakes."

Ceepak doesn't say a word.

Because he doesn't have to.

I'm remembering what the guy at the pizza stand next door to Lucky Lilani's told us: Richard Rock preferred the funnel cakes to the *zeppole*. *"He's next door a lot. Comes here after going there. Sometimes before—takes the ladies a little treat."*

The ladies or the boys?

44

It's nearly midnight.

The pizza man is rolling down his iron security gates, closing up shop.

"Officers?" a voice cries out from the shadows near another candy-apple stand to our right—the ocean side of the boardwalk. "Officers?"

The Great Mandini steps into the glow of fluorescent light illuminating the candy stall's steel counter.

"Might I have a word with you, Officers?" he calls out.

"Not right now," says Ceepak. He's focused on Lucky Lilani's Stress Therapy. A customer comes out the door looking the same way guys do when they try to slink undetected out of an adults only DVD store on Route Nine.

"We're kind of busy," I holler over to the street magician.

He bows gracefully. "I will wait, gentlemen. Semper Fi."

We head for Lucky Lilani's. That green neon still sputters in the window: 24 HRS OPEN.

"Danny?"

"Sir?"

"I'm heading for the back rooms. If necessary, counteract any interference up front."

"Right."

Usually, Ceepak is in charge of the counteracting interference department. Tonight, he's a man on a mission and needs me to cover his back. This is when you really wish you packed your pistol.

Ceepak uses both hands to shove the front door. It flies open with a bang that nearly rips down the tasseled pagoda bells hanging off the hydraulic hinge.

"Hello!" tweets the woman behind the cash register. She stands underneath the only weak-wattage lightbulb in the place that isn't red or blue. "Welcome to Lucky Lilani!" Tweetie at the counter wears a tight silk minidress that shimmers and ripples like swells on the ocean.

It's dark in here. Smells like yesterday's fish mixed with baby oil and patchouli candles. Ceepak keeps marching toward the velvet curtains in the rear.

"Hey, mister! Where you go?"

She reaches under the counter.

"Don't," I say.

"He no go back there!"

"Don't!" This time I raise both arms to indicate that she shouldn't do what I know she's thinking about doing. She's definitely got a bat under the counter. Aluminum, no doubt. The kind that makes your skull ring.

"He no go back there!"

Ceepak pushes through the curtains.

Down ducks Tweetie. Up comes the bat.

"We're with the police," I yell. I reach for my back pocket to find that damn deputy badge. I shove it forward. "We're with the police!"

She swings for the tin star.

I pull back before the bat whacks my hand and sends it over the left field fence.

She whiffs. Misses by a mile.

I make my move, jump in and grab hold of her arm while the momentum of the swing pulls her into a lopsided follow-through.

"Police!" I'm screaming this in her ear. "ACPD!"

"He no go—"

"Police!" I squeeze her left wrist hard. She hisses and cat-paws at me with her right, because I forgot to grab hold of that wrist, too. You know those curved nail extension deals? They're like bear claws when they scrape down your cheek. The pain gets my adrenaline pumping and gives me nearly Ceepakian strength, making it possible for me to do that yank-up-and-twist-down move I saw him execute on Krabitz earlier.

"Fuck you, mister!" the petite Asian princess screams before the pain in her popping arm socket cuts her off. The baseball bat clinks to the floor.

I grab it and cock it up over my shoulder like a caveman.

"Stay back," I snarl, letting her know I intend to swing at the first pitch she sends my way. "Put your hands on top of your head! Now! Do it!"

She does.

"Danny?" This from Ceepak somewhere behind those curtains. "Bar the door. I'm calling this in."

Armed with the softball bat, I back toward the entrance. Block the only exit. The guys who had been sprawled out on the rubdown tables before I screamed "Police!" are now sitting up, their eyes wide. Panic is written all over their faces. I wonder if any of them are governors from New York.

The drapes ruffle open and Ceepak steps out of the back room, his hand gripped tightly to the elbow of a middle-aged man who needs to zip up his fly. The guy—whose hangdog face could be on the cover of *Guilty* magazine next month—is using his free arm to clutch at the gap in his unbuttoned Sansabelt slacks.

The young boy we saw yesterday comes out behind Ceepak.

He looks even more ashamed than the dirty old man.

An ACPD patrol car, lights flashing, cruises up the boardwalk. Two cops go inside to process everybody.

Ceepak is curling up his copy of the "Rock 'n Wow!" playbill into a tube again. He tucks it back into a side pocket on his cargo khakis.

"I showed the young boy Richard Rock's photograph."

"And?"

"He started crying. He subsequently lowered his trousers and showed me the welts and bruises on his buttocks."

I feel another boiled-dumpling-sized lump rise up in my throat. It's not enough that Richard Rock preys on young boys. He has to rough them up, too?

"Officers?" The Great Mandini hurries across the boardwalk.

"Yes?" says Ceepak.

"Tell me, are you gentlemen currently seeking the whereabouts of Mr. Richard Rock or are you otherwise engaged?"

He's got Ceepak's attention. Mine, too.

"Do you know where we might find him?"

"Indeed. You see, I was closing up shop on the boardwalk when I saw Mr. Rock and his son come storming out of the Xanadu. I thought it rather peculiar that the young boy was going out at this late hour. Therefore, I secured my rabbit in his carrier and followed after them."

"Where did they go?"

"First stop was that snack bar across the way." He points to where we saw him ten minutes ago. "Mr. Rock does not know who I am. Therefore, I was able to get quite close to them. He was attempting to bribe the boy with sweets. Snow cone. Caramel corn. Candy apple. Anything little Richie wanted. But the boy kept shaking his head. He didn't want any of it. In fact, he seemed sad. Scared. When the boy continued to refuse his entreaties, Mr. Rock grew angered. Snatched the boy's arm, tugged it hard. 'Did you bring your swimsuit like I told you, Richie?' I heard him say."

"And?"

"The boy said the bathing suit was in his backpack. Mr. Rock pulled his son away and they headed up the boardwalk. I was going to follow, but I saw you two gentlemen approaching at a rather rapid clip and, therefore, I decided it might be more prudent to remain here so I might relate what I had observed."

But we didn't have time to listen. Now Richard Rock and his son have at least a five- or ten-minute head start on us.

"Where did they go?" Ceepak asks, his voice urgent.

Mandini points up the boardwalk. "Toward Trump's Taj Mahal. I heard Mr. Rock say it was time for a midnight swim."

45

"He's going to slay his son," says Ceepak matter-of-factly.

"What? Why?"

"I'm assuming little Richie found what his father has been searching for."

Oh, shit.

"He'll make it look like a drowning." Ceepak does a three-finger hand chop to the east. "Be on the alert for any indication as to where they left the boardwalk and accessed the beach."

Ceepak is scanning the horizon. Checking out all the ramps down to the sand, the alleys between buildings, the railings. I'm eyeballing the rolled-out beach fencing down in the sand, looking for breaks in it. We're approaching the Taj on the left, Atlantic City's famous Steel Pier on the right.

"He is hoping to create another illusion, Danny," says Ceepak while still scrutinizing every inch of the boardwalk to his right.

"Mr. Rock obviously understands that homicidal drowning is almost impossible to prove by an autopsy and, therefore, most drownings are eventually ruled to be accidental—especially those involving a young boy who sneaks out for a swim in the middle of the night in dangerous waters subject to riptides."

The bathing suit. That's why Mr. Rock made certain his son brought one along when they went out for candy apples. It will be another costume intended to make us jump to another conclusion for yet another death by suffocation. Just like Katie Landry's death scene, with her dressed up in an S and M leather outfit, was intended to make us see "kinky sex gone bad." Little Richie, found floating facedown in his Speedo somewhere out in the Atlantic, would force us to conclude he was a bad boy who snuck out of his hotel room for a swim when and where he shouldn't have.

"There!" says Ceepak. He points to some bent-over slats and twisted wire in a run of the beach fencing.

We vault over the guardrail, leave the boardwalk for the sand six feet below.

"Footprints," Ceepak whispers.

I see them. Two pairs of feet leading from the boardwalk down to that gap in the fence.

One set of prints is deeper than the other, which, turns into two long trenches tearing through the sand.

Probably Richie, not wanting to go where his father was trying to take him, literally digging in his heels, plowing double furrows with his shoes. On the other side of the bowed fence, I see a big divot—like a stubborn kid's butt might make if his father had to toss him over the fencing because he refused to climb it.

"Richie is offering resistance," says Ceepak softly.

This is good. The kid's buying us some time, maybe enough to make up for that head start they got while we ignored the Great Mandini and busted the massage parlor.

The footprints lead toward the darkness underneath the Steel Pier. The rides up top are all shut down for the night. No flashing lights. No screaming maniacs. The amusement park jutting out into the ocean is a skeletal silhouette of Ferris wheel ribs and the rickety scaffolding propping up roller-coaster tracks.

Ceepak taps my shoulder. Indicates that we should move forward, into the darkness and the very symmetrical array of support columns lined up like cement soldiers underneath the pier. There have to be about a hundred pilings, each one the size of a giant oak tree, straddling the width and breadth of the pier. I count five support pillars across each row, which start at the boardwalk, step out onto the beach, then march eleven hundred feet, almost a quarter mile, down the sand and out into the ocean.

We slip into the shadows, crouching low as we go.

Up ahead, I hear waves crashing against the shore, slapping in a relentless rhythm against the concrete pilings.

Now I hear a different kind of slap. And a scream.

Ceepak hears it, too.

We hunker down, move toward the source of the sound.

Ceepak does a series of hand gestures, up and down, sideways.

I'm supposed to head left. He'll swing right. We'll surround Rock. Take him down.

We move out, keeping low.

The enormous pillars provide excellent cover.

"Walk into the water!" I hear Richard Rock shout over the breaking surf.

"No, Daddy. It's too cold."

Another wet slap.

"Okay!" Richie is crying. "Don't hit me anymore!"

"Where the hell is it?" Rock sounds furious. I still can't see them. I glance to the right. Ceepak is three columns down, parallel to my position. He's hearing this horror show, too. I move faster.

"Where is it? Tell me, Richie."

"Nanny Katie hid it!"

"And what happened to Nanny Katie?"

"She got killed."

"That's right. She got killed because she snooped around in other people's business. I knew she would. Goody-goody kindergarten teacher."

I hear Richie's warbled cries. His father is shaking him.

"Don't make me hurt you, Richie. Where is it?"

"Stop, Daddy!"

"Are you a crybaby?"

"No, Daddy."

"Then stop crying! You told me you had it. That was good. You're a good boy. Where did you put it? Where is it now? Where the fucking hell did you fucking—"

"It's in my bag! It's in my bag!"

"The tiger?"

"Yes! My backpack! It's in my backpack! Nanny Katie put it there, not me!"

I see them. Shadows. Twenty feet ahead. Near the middle piling.

I also see why Richie is all of a sudden spilling his guts.

His father has a knife. The blade is long, maybe a foot. Its sharp edge glints in the moonlight.

The boy shivers and cringes against one of the posts as Rock drops to his knees and roots through the backpack, tossing out books and toys and stuff he isn't interested in.

He finds what he's looking for.

It was a notebook. One of those marble-covered Mead composition jobs.

Rock stands, marches over to where his son quakes in fear. He taps the hardboard cover against his thigh.

"Did you read any of this, Richie?"

"No, sir."

"Richie?"

"I didn't read it."

"Tell the truth and shame the devil."

"A little."

Waves crash. Richie sniffles. I inch closer.

"A little?" says Rock.

"Yes, sir. About Jake. When he was a boy. How you liked him. How you liked him a whole lot. The other boys, too."

Rock sniggers. "Of course I liked Jake Pratt and the other boys. They didn't snoop around in my private things, did they?"

"No, sir."

"Those boys weren't like you and Nanny Katie. We were on to her, see? Me and Jake. We knew she was nosin' around where she shouldn't ought to be because we knew she'd been talking to Jake's momma, listening to *her* lies. We had to get rid of Nanny Katie before she tried to get rid of me. There's no show without me, Richie. No show."

Richie just sniffles.

"Richie, you disappoint me. You really do. Stealing my special notebook? Shame on you, son."

"Britney made me. Honest! Your footlocker was open. We were playing pirates and she said it was our treasure chest."

Rock leans closer. Jabs his son in the ribs with the hard edge of the composition book.

"You went into my room?"

"Just that once."

"Did your sister read what was written in my special notebooks?"

"No, sir."

"You're lying."

"No. I swear. Nanny Katie came into your living room and yelled at me and Britney had already run back to our side of the suite so she wouldn't get in trouble. Britney didn't see nothing, just me and Nanny Katie."

"You gave your nanny my notebook?"

"No, sir. Not right away. I hid it. Hid it under my shirt."

"I see. But later?"

"Yes, sir. I gave it to her."

That would be Monday afternoon. Right before Katie called me. Mrs. Rock came into the room and it was Katie's turn to hide the notebook. She stashed it in the boy's backpack.

Later, when Jake Pratt sent the kids out for ice cream, Katie told Richie to take his book bag.

This is why Katie didn't talk when they tortured her.

She knew what Mr. Rock would do if he found out who had read his precious notebook.

Katie died protecting Richie. A child.

"I'll deal with Britney later," says Rock. "All right. Stop crying, Richie. Don't be a sissy. Tie up your swim trunks. Pull the string snug, there. You need me to do the loop for you, son?"

This is whacked. Now Rock almost sounds like a real dad.

"No, sir. I can tie it."

"Show me, son. Show me what a big boy you are. Tie your trunks, Richie."

The boy props his chin on his chest and goes to work tying up the waistband string. I duckwalk closer.

"You were a good boy tonight, Richie. Tellin' me what you done. But, you should'a told me sooner."

"Yes, sir."

"Hell's bells, boy. We thought your nanny had the notebook. It's why she had to die."

"I'm sorry. I didn't know. . . ."

Richard Rock playfully rumples his son's hair. "That's okay. Next time. Next time. All righty, now. Quit your blubberin'. This is fun. Moonlit swim in the ocean!"

"I don't want to."

"Sure you do."

"No, Daddy!"

Rock forces his son to walk down to where the sand is wet and the foam of the ocean floats across their feet.

Man, I so need my Glock. I could take him down, easy.

Rock places his hand on Richie's back, urges him forward, walks him into the roiling surf. The waterline is up to Richie's knees now; higher when the waves crest.

What the hell is Ceepak waiting for? Why doesn't he do something?

Why don't I?

"The water's cold, Daddy."

"No, it's not! Don't be a big baby, Richie."

"Daddy? I'm scared. Daddy?"

"Hush."

"Daddy?"

Rock moves his hand up to the top of his son's head, palms it like it's a basketball. "Sissy boy, sissy boy," he chants. "Richie Rock's a sissy boy."

A breaker surges in. The water washes up over little Richie's head. Recedes.

"It's cold, Daddy!" He's choking, coughing.

"Hush!"

They keep moving. Further under the pier, deeper into the ocean.

I move forward, too.

No way am I letting this sick pervert drown his son.

They reach the next row of concrete pillars. Surf smacks into the boy's ribs. A sudsy wave swamps up over his head again. He comes out of it hacking and spitting. He's chest deep and getting deeper.

I'm closer now. Squatting in the shallow water. Slogging forward. I can see Rock tense the muscles in his back. He stops, stands right next to a pillar and stares out at the horizon like he's on the beach with his Boogie board waiting to catch the next big wave to roll in.

I see it.

A swell, maybe fifty feet out. Billowing up like a ruffling sheet on a clothesline. When the crest of that incoming wave reaches the pillar, I know exactly what Rock plans to do: he'll dunk his son under the breaker and never let him back up!

"Freeze!" I scream.

Rock whirls around.

I bolt up out of my crouch. Slog through the water.

"What the—"

That's all Rock gets to say before Ceepak springs out from behind the concrete pillar to his left. Guess my partner snuck down that far without me knowing it.

"Grab the boy," Ceepak yells as he tackles Rock. The two of them topple under the incoming wave.

I slosh forward, snatch Richie, hoist him up as high as I can so he doesn't have to suck down any more salt water.

I can see Ceepak and Rock wrestling under the waves. Rock's twelve-inch blade shoots up through the surface.

I have Richie in my arms but leap up as best I can into an awkward sideways kick.

My shoe slams into the hilt and the knife flies out of Rock's fist, skims across the water, sinks.

My momentum trips me up. I slip and flop backward under the surge as it reverses engines and hauls ass back to sea.

I extend my arms and try to keep little Richie's head above the water that's already stinging my eyes, making those fingernail gouges on my cheek burn like I cleaned the wounds with Clorox.

I'm flat on my back, seawater shooting up my nostrils. I scrape along a canyon of seashell shards. The water's only two, maybe three feet deep but the undertow hauls me forward with a rush of seaweed and liquefied sand.

I'm still carrying Richie, keeping his head above the waterline as I slide along underneath it. We're dragged about ten feet down to the next piling. My left foot slams into the concrete. I brace against the pillar, dig my other shoe into the mucky bottom, lever myself up and out of the water.

I gasp for air.

The boy is shivering and sputtering.

"Are you okay?"

Richie nods.

"Hang on."

He hugs me, wraps his shivering arms around my neck, his legs around my chest. He's trembling. His heart racing. Mine, too. We make our way through the swirling lather toward the beach.

Ten feet ahead of us, in water up to his waist, I see Ceepak using both hands to hold Mr. Rock under the water.

"Ceepak!" I scream. "I've got Richie! We're clear."

Mr. Rock's legs thrash hard, stirring up murky sand clouds. A shoe breaks through the surface. Not his head. Ceepak won't let go of his grip.

"Ceepak? I've got Richie!"

My partner acts like he can't hear me.

He forces Mr. Rock's head down even deeper.

He's drowning him.

"Ceepak!"

Mr. Rock stops kicking.

"Goddamnit! Ceepak!"

Ceepak slowly turns. There's a dull look in his eyes, a terrifying emptiness I have never seen there before.

"Let him up!" I'm begging. I know how John Ceepak feels about selfish fathers who would sacrifice a son because the kid cramped their lifestyle.

That's what brought us down to Atlantic City in the first place.

If Ceepak can't kill his own dad for what he did, Mr. Rock makes a handy stand-in.

I play my last card. "It's what he would do!"

Finally, Ceepak hears me. Blinks.

"Let the bastard live!"

A flicker of light returns to Ceepak's eyes.

He yanks Rock's head up out of the ocean by his hair.

He lets the bastard gasp and choke and breathe again.

46

The Great Mandini called 911.

One of the ACPD cops who had responded to the scene of the child prostitution situation at Lucky Lilani's massage parlor was the first one down to our location underneath the Steel Pier.

Richard Rock was led away in handcuffs. Not the kind he's used to, either. There was no hidden escape latch.

The ambulance guys showed up next. Wrapped little Richie up in a wool blanket. Took him to the hospital. I had to tell the kid he did the right thing, holding out as long as he did. I told him Katie would've been proud.

Britney joined her brother at the hospital. DYFS, the state's Division of Youth and Family Services, will be the kids' new nanny for a while. Mrs. Rock and David Zuckerman were arrested, too. Accessories to murder. Conspiracy.

There will be no more performances of "Rock 'n Wow!" at the Xanadu Casino or anywhere else any time soon.

That's a very good thing.

When Dr. McDaniels took a crime-scene unit armed with a search warrant into the Rocks' hotel suite, they uncovered a treasure trove of notebooks similar to the one tucked in little Richie's backpack. Apparently, Rock was obsessive-compulsive when it came to keeping notes on his conquests. Inside the padlocked trunk, the CSI crew found 154 marble-covered Mead composition books. The pages were filled with crisp block handwriting.

Richard Rock's handwriting.

He kept meticulous records. Times. Dates. Who, what, when, where, how. The journals listed the names of 3,994 boys. Detailed descriptions and scores for 18,453 different sex acts. All the graphic details were written down. The entries noted nicknames he gave each of the boys: Slim, Whitey, Curly, Jake the Snake.

Jake Pratt.

The notebook detailing Rock's Beverly Hills romps with his nephew was the one his son had snatched out of the footlocker when he and his sister went into the parents' side of the hotel suite to play pirates.

It's the one Katie Landry eventually saw.

She had her suspicions about her employers when we first met near the candy store because Sherry Amour had already been drunkenly pleading with her about looking after her son, Jake Pratt. "Family," she said to me. "You never know who's telling the truth."

Late Monday afternoon, when Richie showed his nanny the notebook he had snatched out of his father's treasure chest, Katie took a quick look inside its pages. Read what it said about Jake the Snake. That's when she called Julia Pratt, then left me that message.

That's why she said she wanted to talk to me about Jake Pratt.

Why she got killed.

She hid the notebook in Richie's backpack and wouldn't give the kid up, no matter how much they humiliated her with the S and

M costume or tortured her with that bolo tie. When she wouldn't crack for Pratt, he left and Richard Rock came into the room, tried once more to force her to tell him where the notebook was hidden.

She didn't.

He killed her. Dropped a clump of Pratt's pubic hairs on the floor. Came back onstage to take his bows.

We know every step of what Mr. Rock did because he wrote it all down in his most recent notebook. It smelled like coconut oil. It was the one he had been using as a suntan-lotion coaster when we talked to him near the indoor pool.

Rock didn't trust Katie. "We never should've hired her," he wrote. He thought she was a "goody-goody Catholic girl" who "could quickly pose a serious problem to our way of life."

Sunday morning, he jotted down: "My suspicions continue to grow. Miss Landry's been looking at me funny today."

Maybe because the night before Julia Pratt, aka Sherry Amour, had told Katie hard-to-believe horror stories of what had happened to her troubled son out in California.

Later that same morning, Rock visited the massage-parlor boys.

Sunday afternoon, Jake Pratt demanded to see Rock and told him what his mother had said on the elevator ride after the photo shoot, that Katie would be his new nanny, protecting him from Mr. and Mrs. Rock.

Rock became obsessed with "our Katie problem."

"She is a threat that must be dealt with swiftly, before she finds out too much," he wrote in his journal. "We must stop her before she stops us."

Rock spent the rest of Sunday seducing and pretending to fall back in love with Jake Pratt so the young dancer would help him "take care of our mutual nanny problem." He also harvested a "handful of his hair" as an "insurance policy" because "someone will have to take the rap should we decide to kill Katie. Jake is not integral to our lifestyle. In fact, he is something of a liability." Rock stored the pubic hair in a Baggie.

On Monday, Rock went back to the massage parlor for sex with two different underage boys. He returned to room AA-6, discovered that the "J.P. notebook" was missing. He angrily confronted Katie, asked if she had ever been in his room.

Yes. Just that morning.

She didn't rat out the kids who had also been in there playing pirates.

Had she taken anything? he asked.

"Of course not," she told him.

Rock didn't believe her.

"THIS CONFIRMS MY SUSPICIONS," he wrote in thick block letters, all capitals.

In his raging paranoia, Rock became convinced that Katie had to be the one who had his notebook.

He needed to get it back.

Richard Rock decided Katie Landry needed to be tortured into telling the truth.

Then, even after she cracked, she needed to die.

"It is the right decision now," he wrote, "and will be the right decision forever."

Over lunch on Monday, Richard Rock and Jake Pratt finalized their plans. They had to move fast. "No time to waste. This thing could blow up in our faces."

They didn't know Katie hadn't even seen the notebook yet; little Richie still had it.

After the lunch with Pratt, Rock went and had sex with the boy being kept for him up in the Crystal Palace Tower. It's why I saw him getting off the glass elevator the first time I went up to my room.

Rock then met with David Zuckerman, ordered him to invite Lady Jasmine to the Monday evening performance to insure casino security would be focused exclusively on the auditorium while he and Jake "took care of business backstage, got the nanny to confess to what she'd done."

Right before curtain time, Rock also had Zuckerman contact Kenny Krabitz and advise him to stand by to perform additional "janitorial" services. "Can't clean up one threat just to see another one blossom in its place. Jake Pratt needs to be eliminated, too."

Krabitz came to the lobby of the theater, right before showtime Monday night. He and Zuckerman stepped outside, haggled over price, finalized a deal for a hit on Pratt. "We gave Kenny-boy a couple of the trick notebooks, including Lucky Numbers, to make the setup against Jake look even better."

When, after repeatedly torturing her, Rock was convinced that Katie didn't have the missing notebook or know its whereabouts, he killed her and widened the search. Gave Krabitz additional responsibilities.

"We realized we may have taken action against Miss Landry based on faulty information, false assumptions. However, that didn't matter. She would have eventually become a problem. We eliminated the threat before it had a chance to attack us."

Krabitz was charged with finding the notebook "before the police stumbled over it." The ACPD detectives killed in Jake's room were considered collateral damage because, as Mr. Rock wrote, "stuff happens."

Krabitz also found Jake's personal journal with the Katie to-do list. Thought it was gold, he told Rock later. Made sure the police saw it along with the incriminating Pink Pussycat shopping bags.

When the missing notebook still couldn't be found, Krabitz, under orders from Zuckerman, was sent after Julia Pratt and the two dancers.

Mrs. Rock?

She helped out. Rented the room across the street for Jake on Sunday. Kept a close eye on Katie all Monday afternoon, after Mr. Rock learned the nanny had been in the parents' side of the suite. Agreed to take the initial fall, if need be. She knew she would ultimately be set free when the casino cameras showed her "sneaking out" to play the slots during Monday evening's performance of Lucky Numbers. Her sister, Julia, signed all the autographs in the lobby Monday night. In fact, Jessica Rock barely made it back to the theater in time to play the hysterical mother-of-the-missing-children in the hallway for us.

She knew what Richard Rock was up to with all the boys.

She didn't care.

They were rich. Famous. And, as Rock wrote in one of his journals, "I let Jessica have all the young men she wants. Including her current favorite, David."

Zuckerman.

None of the boys listed in the mountains of Mead composition books stacked inside Rock's treasure chest were over the age of twelve. Some were as young as eight.

The dark-haired boy in the pool? Rock nicknamed him "Stromboli." He was from up in Seaside Heights but currently residing in a very nice room in the Crystal Palace Tower.

One passage in a notebook from back in August suggested the whole reason for bringing the show to Atlantic City: Richard Rock had a "hankering" to explore "back east" for "fresh ethnic treats." Italian. Puerto Rican. "Rosy-cheeked Irish lads."

Mr. Krabitz then came to New Jersey a week or two before everybody else involved in giving Richard Rock whatever he wanted. He was the advance man, a talent scout trolling in the housing projects and trailer parks, looking for parents eager to make a fast buck by renting out their sons, sending them on the vacation of a lifetime to Atlantic City.

Three thousand nine hundred and ninety-four boys over twenty years.

None older than twelve.

Some as young as eight.

In other words, can you blame Ceepak for wanting to kill the sick bastard underneath the Steel Pier?

I can't.

But, man, Ceepak sure blames himself.

Early Wednesday morning we're on the first Coast City bus back to Sea Haven.

Ceepak takes the window seat so he can stare out it and silently torture himself. His honor code? It's something he imposes on himself, not others. Now I think I know why. When you've seen as many horror shows as John Ceepak, in war zones all over the world, you probably want to drown bad dudes on a daily basis.

Especially if they remind you of your asshole of a father.

But Ceepak knows acting on his darker impulses would diminish his soul. Debase and degrade him. So he keeps to his code. Keeps himself in line.

"It's okay," I finally say.

He turns from the window. "No, Danny. My behavior was inexcusable. Certain things are set in stone. Who we are, what we'll do, and what we won't."

He's channeling Springsteen again. "I won't tell anybody."

"Really? I intend to tell anyone who asks me about it. Hopefully, by owning it, I will be able to learn from it."

"Hey, that's why pencils have erasers, right?" I'm parroting this corny thing Ceepak always tells me when I screw up. "We all make mistakes."

He nods. Fakes a weak grin.

He's not buying it. I can tell: John Ceepak thinks there isn't a chunk of rubber in the world thick enough to wipe his slate clean. I guess there never is. All you can do is stumble back to your feet and try to find your way home.

Ceepak looks back out the window. New Jersey's pine trees clip by. Tires hum. He remains disappointed in who he almost became, what he nearly did.

It's a good thing his wife is meeting us at the bus terminal. Rita's the only person capable of walking beside Ceepak when he ventures into these shadowy recesses of his soul. He won't let me in there, that's for sure.

She'll help him find his way home. I know it.

And if Richard Rock, the bogus hocus-pocus cowpoke, can actually make John Ceepak believe he is a bad man then he really is the most amazing illusionist in the world.

The truth? John Ceepak is the most decent and honorable man I have ever met.

I mean that.

How do you think I knew to tell Ceepak to let the sick bastard live?

I learned it from him.